COLIN DEREHAM

Nervous Kid

Contents

Ryan's Soundtrack

Ryan is a big fan of Aussie rock in "Nervous Kid." Many songs by great Australian and New Zealand artists are mentioned in the book (along with a British one just for good measure.)

If you're keen to hear how they sound, scan the following QR code for a Spotify playlist of all songs in the order they appear.

Happy listening!

I

Part One - NOW

Sydney, Australia

Prologue

"Sweetie, this call for a quote came in before. Art Deco bachelor pad in Bondi. Some guy called… um…" I can hear Marisa rifling through papers. "Dom. Wants a full bespoke kitchen, period-style. Wow. Must have a few dollars in the bank!"

I smile at her melodious tone. She's an awesome singer, gigging on weekends here and there with her lesbian band. I love Marisa to bits. All new-age wild rock chick with jangly bracelets, crystals, incense and meditation. And a self-proclaimed psychic. I reckon it's just a unique talent for human observation rather than any kind of magic, but I'm not gonna burst her bubble. A human sunflower, a cheerful and open presence—she runs our office like clockwork and has every one of us builders under her thumb.

"I'm driving back east right now, Marisa. I can be there within the hour. Will you give him a call and see whether that suits?"

"It's Friday evening, Ryan. You should be knocking off! Don't you have a life?"

She has a point there. I am kind of boring. I own (well, me and the bank) a tiny, minimally-furnished one-bedroom terrace house in Newtown. It's old, but as a carpenter and builder I'm just the man to fix it up—on those rare occasions when I have the time and energy. The hustle and bustle of King Street is just a few minutes' walk away. Best of all, there's a rear lane access to my minuscule back courtyard so I can park my ute. You might think that's an unnecessary detail, but you've clearly never tried to park in Newtown.

Now I'm done banging on about my house, there's not much more to tell—like I said, I'm boring. I pretty much keep to myself. I go to the bears night down at the Townie some weekends. I even manage to score the occasional sub-par fuck. I have a couple of friends—just enough to temper my hermit-like existence. And I'm perennially single. *Boring.*

Which is why, at five-thirty on a Friday evening, I'm making the forty-five minute journey over to Bondi to see a prospective client. If not for that, I'd probably be at home glued to Netflix and stuffing my face with takeaway.

When I reach my destination it's already well after six. I'd been expecting to trawl the streets of this trendy beachside suburb to score a parking spot, but luck is on my side and I find one on the same block. I take a minute to tidy myself in the mirror, roughly finger-combing the thick locks that hang down to my collar. I'm thirty-nine, but I still get away with the longer hair. I've undercut the sides so it isn't too Fabio. I'm not thinning and my mop has yet to go grey. Plus, I've had long hair all my life. People I know would have a heart attack if I cut it all off.

I glance down at my work clothes, worse-for-wear after a hard day on the job. A big, tattooed, cuddly bear in dirty tradie gear and steel-capped boots might go down well in certain gay circles, but it's hardly a good look to present to a snooty, rich eastern-suburbs client. Oh, well. Tough titties, really. I could have made him wait till next week, now, couldn't I?

The building is one of those Art Deco ones with curved, solid-brick balconies. I buzz the doorbell as I check through my bag, making sure I have everything.

"Hello?" The male voice is confident, commanding, masculine.

"Hi, uh…" *What was his name?* "Dom. I'm here for the kitchen quote."

"Great! Come on up. Third floor."

Inside the lobby, it's like something from an old Woody Allen film. Exquisitely-polished dark wood panelling, carved bannisters, one of those quaint old elevators with the cage closure. I decide to take the stairs. When I reach the apartment door and knock, I spend a moment trying to brush some of the dust off my high-vis shirt and Hard Yakka shorts. The door opens, I look up and do a double-take.

It can't be, can it?

The longer I stare, the more my suspicions are confirmed. How long has it been?

Over twenty years, that's how long, Ryan.

The man before me is the same guy from back then, but he's aged beautifully. Still has the same tanned, olive skin. Still has the same short black hair, though flecked with a small amount of grey these days. Still has the same piercing dark eyes, charming expression, ruggedly-handsome Hispanic looks—now beautifully enhanced by a well-trimmed black beard. His untucked business shirt is open down to the last few buttons, revealing a carpet of fur a lot more substantial than the uni student I last saw decades ago. In a nutshell, he's a whole lot more *man.*

And he recognises me, too.

My mouth falls open. Somehow, I find my voice. *"Dominic?"*

II

Part Two - THEN

Darwin, Australia

Chapter One

That caravan was my favourite place in the world during my childhood. In a way, it was my childhood. I still remember the day dad bought it. I was eight years old and he was hyped-up about taking us all on an adventure. Dad had got a new university lecturing position in a strange, far-off place called Darwin. I didn't know anything about it, except that it was right at the top of Australia.

Me and my brother Nathan were real excited about the caravan. I'd read about them in books at school and all the kids in my class were jealous when I told them about it at show-and-tell. It had a sleeping area down one end, with two single beds that mum and dad pushed together to make a big bed, just like the one they had in our house. Down the other end of the caravan was a booth-style living area made up of two long couches that doubled as beds for Nathan and me, with a long, thin dining table stuck in between them. In the middle of the caravan, there was a tiny kitchen and a bathroom that was about as big as a broom cupboard. "This is for wees *only*," mum snapped, as she pointed at the toilet. She obviously didn't want anyone to stink the place out. Me and Nathan didn't mess with mum. She was a schoolteacher and could be a bossy old cow.

Everything was all real busy after the day dad got the caravan. Mum made me pack up my room and chuck out any old toys and things I didn't use anymore. She packed up Nathan's room for him, which I thought wasn't fair. But then I remembered he was only three. Dad and mum ran around sorting out the rest of the house and putting all the stuff into big boxes. Mum was even more of a snappy cow than usual, so Nathan and me kept right out of her way.

Finally, one cold winter morning mum and dad loaded all our suitcases and food and stuff into the caravan. Men had come to our house the day before and taken all the furniture and boxes away in a great big truck. We weren't allowed to be in the caravan while dad was driving the Landcruiser, so Nathan and I had to travel in the great big four-wheel-drive with him and mum. We sat for hours on end in the back seat, reading our books and playing our Nintendo games, while mum and dad talked and smoked in the front. Sometimes Nathan got grumpy and cried. But I knew better than to complain.

Dad said it was going to take a few days to drive from Sydney to Darwin, but as a special treat we would stop off each night and camp somewhere in the caravan. Nathan and I were even allowed to go outside and play, so long as we didn't go too far. If there was a river, dad would take us down there to skip stones. It was way too cold to swim. And if there was enough sunlight, dad would even play cricket with me. Nathan tried hard, but he couldn't play. He was too little.

* * *

I remember those few days as the happiest of my childhood; a pristine little capsule of the only time things were truly perfect. Sure, we took the caravan out on several trips when we lived in Darwin. Me and Nathan loved the fact it had air conditioning, because Darwin was so bloody hot. I have fond memories of those subsequent trips as well, but we never did quite recapture the magic of that first one.

We settled into life in Darwin. Mum and dad had bought a three-bedroom house in Parap, which wasn't too far from the city centre. Well, nothing was too far in Darwin. Not after living in a sprawling metropolis like Sydney. I went to the nearby primary school and I was able to walk there or ride my bike. Believe it or not, kids did that in those days. They weren't all chauffeured to the front door by 'soccer moms' in brand new SUVs. Eventually, Nathan was old enough to start school and mum went back to teaching.

Dad also enrolled me in boxing classes. It was hard at first. The physical confrontation distressed me and the kids could be really nasty. I'd go home and cry, but dad convinced me to persist. "If you can learn how to do this, Ryan," he said, "then nobody's ever going to hurt you. Bullies won't try to beat you up if they know you can fight back at 'em." And so I kept it up, just like dad said. I knew he was right and I was desperate to please him. I really loved my dad.

Anyway, life was good. Until it all went to shit.

One day, when I was eleven, Nathan and I were pulled out of our classes at school. They didn't tell us what was going on; we were just driven home by one of the teachers' aides and left with mum. She looked like utter shit. She kept crying. Finally she sat us down and explained that dad was gone and he was never coming back. In that annoying, roundabout way that grown-ups sometimes have, she eventually made it clear that, yes, he was in fact dead. A plane crash, she'd said. Dad had been on some shitty little local airline flying to some small remote town for some university study. I didn't really understand. I hadn't been on an aeroplane my entire life. But I swore right then I would never set foot on one.

Fuck, I missed my dad. I cried myself to sleep every night for months. Dad and I had had a special relationship. He was calm and quiet like me. Nathan and mum were the rowdy, temperamental ones. For years, I would dream that dad came back. I'd experience a joy so great I could hardly stand it. I was so happy, I'd be weeping and refusing to let him go. Then, of course, my eyes would open and I'd realise it wasn't true. It got to the point where the sadness never left me. Often, when things became really dark inside my head, I'd go to sleep at night and pray that I wouldn't ever wake up.

And as for my beloved caravan, it sat in our rear carport for years, never to be taken out again.

* * *

"Ryan, I need to talk to you."

I was fourteen and I'd just arrived home from boxing practice to find mum hunched forward on the couch, elbows on her knees. The air conditioner was humming away in the window and she was staring at the TV, though it wasn't even switched on.

I was used to mum's dramatics. As a pretty reserved kid, I just let her carry on and kept my mouth shut. But there was a tone in the air that gave me a bad feeling in my gut. The pain of what happened to us three years previously still hit me as hard as it had when dad had just died. *Fuck, don't tell me something else like that.*

Mum patted the couch next to her, not looking at me. My heart started thumping with fear. I was barely conscious of my movements as I sat down.

"Sweetie, you're a sensible boy. And I know you can handle what I'm about to say." She lit the cigarette she had dangling between her fingers and drew in a deep drag, before launching into her monologue. "You don't know this, but I was a wild girl when I was young."

No shit, mum. As if I couldn't have guessed that.

"After I finished my teaching diploma, I decided I wasn't ready to start my career. I took off to go backpacking around South America. I had a lot of fun, met a lot of wonderful people, and I made a lot of mistakes." She glanced at me sideways, but I remained expressionless. "Anyway, I fell in love with a man in Brazil. And..." She paused for a second. I could see her hands trembling slightly. "And I had a baby."

Now, she turned to look at me, her face twisted with contrition. "I was overwhelmed, Ryan. I became so depressed. So I did something I'm not proud of. I took off back to Australia and left your brother with Joe and his family."

I could see the tears in mum's eyes as she smoked away furiously. I know she was expecting me to be shocked, but it was like I was hearing the plot of a daytime soapie. It didn't seem quite real. Over and above all this, it sounded just *so like mum.*

After studying me for a reaction she wasn't quite getting, she averted her eyes. "I've never forgiven myself. After I settled back in Sydney, I met your dad. We married pretty quickly and... well... then you came along." She ground out her half-finished cigarette and sat up a bit, trying to smile at me. "I kept in touch occasionally. I'd write letters to Joe and sometimes I'd hear back from him."

Fidgeting with her hands, she reached for her Peter Jacksons and lit another one. "There's more. Joe and his son—" she looked at me again, "—your brother, Dominic, moved over here to Perth from Brazil when you were little."

As if answering a question I hadn't actually asked, she blurted, "I never saw them, you have to believe me. I loved your father. I love my boys." I nodded slowly, giving her the faintest of acknowledgement. She looked mildly relieved. "But since your father died, I've thought about them both a lot. And in the last year, Joe and I have talked constantly on the phone."

I suddenly recalled the many times I could hear mum chatting away in her bedroom at night for ages, the content of her conversation obscured by the cyclonic noise of the massive ceiling fan. *So that's what she was up to.* I'd been too busy playing with my dick to give it much thought. As long as I could hear her voice carrying on faintly in the next room, I knew she wouldn't be able to barge in and catch me masturbating in bed.

Mum grabbed my hand, squeezing it. "I'm telling you all this now because Joe's got a job in Darwin and he's just moved up here. You might be seeing a lot of him. And—" her voice halted abruptly and she fixed her gaze on me with pleading intensity, "you're going to meet your brother."

It sounded weird. *Nathan* was my brother. Not some random kid a couple of years older than me. But I wasn't appalled. I was intrigued. Mum's eyes didn't falter as she waited for my verdict. "That's cool, mum. I'm sure they're nice."

* * *

I met Joe Duarte first, shortly afterwards. By that stage, I'd read enough Judy Blume books to know that I was supposed to hate whoever my mum dated after losing our dad. But Joe was great. He told me his real name was José, though people were too dumb to pronounce it right and thought it was 'Josie' when they read it written down. He had an accent, but he spoke English totally fine.

Joe made a big effort with us. He'd take us to eat at Hungry Jack's. He even took us to the movies. He came and cheered me on at my boxing demos and competitions. He was awesome like that. And mum was happy again. It was all good as far as I was concerned.

Then there was Dominic Duarte. I couldn't believe my eyes when I first met him soon after Joe. *He was fucking beautiful.* Even at sixteen, he was a *man.* I mean, I already looked a lot older than fourteen. I was shaping up to have my dad's hairy body. My voice had broken to a full baritone. But Dominic was something else. He had that *air* about him. He was cocky and confident, with the most gorgeous, white-toothed smile. The kind of bastard who could get what he wanted from anyone by charming the pants off them.

Dominic had the same olive skin as his dad. He didn't look like mum or Nathan. He certainly didn't look like me, I took after *my* dad. If I hadn't known differently, I would have thought Joe and Dominic were Spanish, because all those hot Latino boys and men I'd seen on TV had darker, cinnamon skin. But Dominic told me a lot of Brazilians and Argentinians looked more like Spanish people with lighter skin and dark hair. His sun-kissed complexion was beautifully complemented by his piercing, darkest-brown eyes and short, thick black hair. I just couldn't stop looking at him. I was mesmerised from the word go.

Since I was twelve and had worked out that my dick wasn't just for pissing, I'd realised that all I wanted to think about was boys. I would videotape racy foreign movies on SBS on TV, hoping to catch a glimpse of a male arse. Very occasionally, I was even lucky enough to see a flash of penis. Whenever I had a moment of privacy, I would jerk off frantically over these scenes, making liberal use of the pause and rewind buttons.

Most of the time, though, I'd have to settle for wanking in my room in the middle of the night, when mum and Nathan were safely shut in their own bedrooms. My privacy issues would become a lot easier, however, when mum and Joe sat me down just before the start of the next school year.

"Ryan, sweetie," mum said gently, "You know how Joe and Dominic have been coming over here a lot?" She paused, carefully choosing her words. "Well, now that Joe and I are in a serious relationship, we think it would be much easier for everyone if they both moved in with us."

My heart began racing a mile a minute. It was nearly impossible to keep a poker face, but somehow I managed. "Sure. I really like Joe and Dominic," I said. I looked over at Joe, smiling at me, good-natured as ever. Then I looked at mum again. She was still all apprehensive. I could tell there was more to it. She cleared her throat.

"Dominic's going to need a bedroom. It's a big change for him, too, and I think it might be a nice gesture if you gave him yours." She eyed me closely once more. I was still poker-faced, giving nothing away. "So, sweetie… I know how much you used to love the caravan. Would you think about moving into there?" She glanced at Joe, getting his approval over something, then turned back to me. "Joe will be moving his big TV and VCR into our living room. So we think that it's only fair that you can have our old TV and VCR in the caravan, seeing as you're giving up your bedroom."

I was turning cartwheels inside, just about pissing myself with glee, but all I gave mum and Joe was an affable little smile. "Sure, that sounds fair," I told them in a breezy tone.

Mum turned to Joe, her face dripping with relief. I could hardly believe my luck. The weather was stinking hot and the caravan had *air conditioning*. The bedrooms in our house didn't, and their ceiling fans were woefully inadequate in the hotter months. Plus, I got the privacy of my own little oasis *and* my own TV and VCR.

And mum and Joe think I've made a huge sacrifice.

In amongst all my excitement, I nearly forgot the cherry on top of all of this: *Dominic was coming to live with us.* Other than the fact I was hopelessly infatuated with him, he was *fun*. Every time he visited, his enthusiasm sucked me right in. He *included* me, even though I was two years younger than him. And he was a bit of a bad boy, too. At his suggestion, we'd steal cigarettes from mum or Joe and run down to the park to smoke them on the play equipment. Or he'd show up to my house with one of those bicycle drink bottles filled with orange juice and vodka he'd stolen from his dad, and we'd sit in the garden getting pissed long after mum and Joe had gone to bed.

I couldn't wait for him to move in.

* * *

Dominic fast became the centre of my world. He didn't go to my crappy public school, he went to a private Catholic secondary college in the next suburb. I was happy about this. I knew how obsessed I was and I didn't want him to get sick of me. At least we had our own groups of school mates, something to divert our attention away from each other. And I didn't want to feel like a shitty little Year Eight student when he was a cool Year Ten one. So long as our school environments were separate, Dominic and I were on more of a level playing field.

Outside of school hours, there was still plenty of time left over for us to spend together. We'd play Nintendo in the lounge room, have a game of cricket with his mates in the park, catch the bus into the city, go bowling and roller skating in Nightcliff, go swimming and water-sliding at Parap pool. We were like part-time best friends and I loved it that way.

Settling in was hard for Dominic, though. I was used to mum's drama-queen ways. But he'd been thrown in the deep end.

"You know, she's a bit of a crazy bitch," Dominic said one day, a while after they'd moved in. We were perched atop the jungle gym in the park, smoking our pilfered cigarettes. He turned to face me with an evil grin. "No offence."

Fuck, I laughed every time he gave me that wicked look. "Like I care. She's your mum too, remember."

"Yeah, well, she seems more like a stepmum to me. It's like she's trying to assert herself too much and show me who's boss. Gets on my fuckin' tits."

"Did you ever have a stepmum?"

"Nah. It's just been me and dad. He had lots of girlfriends but they never stuck around long. Think he just liked rooting them, nothing more. Typical Latin horn-dog."

"Do you think they root a lot? Mum and your dad?"

Dominic guffawed. "Fuck, yeah! I gotta put my Discman on loud so I don't hear them in the next fuckin' room!"

"Yuk." I didn't want to think about that.

All I wanted to think about was Dominic. His magnetic personality and raw masculinity drove me absolutely nuts. My hands would be stroking my dick at every available opportunity, and I was always dreaming about him when I came. I never once thought about our familial relationship. I was young and I didn't really understand. Things weren't the same with Dominic, not like with me and Nathan. Dominic and I hadn't grown up together or anything. He was my mate, my best friend, and I couldn't help how I felt. My fascination was fierce, my hormones were raging, and my fantasies were my own private business, fuck you very much.

Still, Dominic didn't make it easy on me. He had no inhibitions. He'd quite happily urinate at a public toilet trough right next to me—not all guarded like most boys, but leaning back a little, brazenly splashing piss everywhere, proud of the penis he was holding. Even though my natural instinct was to be shy, I would always try to match his exhibitionistic behaviour. I'd hold my dick with the hand furthest away and angle myself slightly towards him. I *wanted* him to see what I was packing down there. Maybe, *just maybe*, he'd get a subliminal hint.

Deep down, I knew I was living in some kind of bullshit dreamworld. Dominic, by all accounts, was straight. Plus, he was as popular as he was horny. He spent most of year ten, eleven and twelve screwing his way through a host of willing girls. Seems they were as attracted to his plucky confidence and striking Latin looks as I was. Fortunately, they weren't the bring-home-to-meet-the-parents kind of girls. By all accounts, they were every bit as promiscuous as Dominic—so, predictably, nothing serious ever came of it. I was thrilled about this: Dominic was happy he got his dick wet on occasion, and I still got to keep my best friend. There was no pain-in-the-arse girlfriend to make demands on his time.

As for me, nothing changed in those couple of years. I was still a constant wanker and a total virgin. Somehow, my lack of female love interests flew under the radar at school. I was just *the quiet guy*. I wasn't flamboyant. I took all the butch trade subjects. And, if pushed, I was capable of punching a few lights out with years of boxing practice under my belt. I had long, messy hair—that fashionable grunge-singer look of the nineties. Students had little reason to hurl homophobic abuse at me.

By the time I finished Year Ten, I'd had enough of high school. I was really good at subjects like woodwork, metalwork and auto mechanics. I had a practical mind and worked well with my hands. I was not, however, academically inclined. I did not need Year Eleven and Twelve, no bloody way. So, I left school and took up a carpentry and building apprenticeship.

Mum was dead against this move. Joe wasn't too happy either. They kept pointing out Dominic as a shining example. Yeah, he was brilliant. Dominic was a real brain. He'd just aced his Year Twelve exams and he was all set to start a business and law double degree at uni. Dominic was going to go on and do great things.

But I didn't care what those oldies thought. Quitting school and getting a job meant I wasn't still some crappy secondary student while Dominic became a big deal at uni. It was the greatest leveller of all. We were young men moving into our adult lives—me in my blue collar, him in his white one—but we were equal, now.

And I knew where my strengths lay. I loved my apprenticeship. I also loved the fact I made an income, however meagre the wages were. Having money at that age was the best feeling. Plus, I was fucking good at my job.

Chapter Two

On May the sixteenth—my eighteenth birthday—life changed forever. My official entry into adulthood was a low-key affair that night: a couple of my old friends from school, a few of the younger guys from work and TAFE college, and my family in the backyard.

Dominic's twentieth had come and gone back in March. Given the fact I looked way more mature than seventeen, I'd enjoyed an epic bar-crawl with him and his mates. I'd also endured a king-sized hangover: something mum had turned a blind eye to, and something I never wanted to repeat. So, for my own party, I paced myself much more on the alcohol. I still managed to have a decent time on a few beers, though.

When all the guests had left and mum and Joe went to bed, Dominic pulled me aside. "Meet you in the caravan, mate," he said. "I've got a surprise for you."

I was intrigued. I scurried into my little mancave and turned on the aircon. I tidied up the few things I had lying around, then straightened the sheets and settled myself on the bed. It was a strange ensemble—two single beds pushed together and made up as one. The join in the middle meant I always slept to one side. I'd set the TV and VCR up in there, because that was the best spot for playing video games and watching movies—preferably ones with at least a bit of male nudity that I could jack off to. Now, of course, I'd be able to buy some actual gay porn. There was only one big adult shop in Darwin at the time. All I had to do was find the nerve to go in there.

As if he had read my mind, Dominic burst into the caravan, locked the door and chucked a few VHS tapes on the bed.

Porn! Fuck me dead!

Sure, it was straight porn, but I'd still see guys with hard cocks. Guys stroking their hard cocks. Guys bending over, their arse cracks spread open and their balls flapping as they slammed into the women's pussies. Guys *coming.* Guys *shooting huge fountains of creamy white spunk from their big, thick penises.*

My heart was in my throat. "Fuck, Dominic. This is awesome!" I pored over the tapes, looking at all the photos.

"It's your eighteenth birthday, Ryan. You're a man, now. You pick one for us to watch."

Oh, God... oh, God. Oh, my fucking God. He wants to watch PORN with me!

I took a few deep breaths to calm myself. I picked up the last tape and my eyes bugged out.

'Bob & Carol & Ted & Phallus.'

On the cover, there were three naked people, side-on to the camera. First was Bob, a hunky, waxed muscle-man, his nude front pressed against the rear side of Carol, a svelte brunette with a perky boob-job. Said perky boob-job was pressed against the back of a slender, athletic and hairy man, who could only be Ted. And when I looked very closely, I saw that Carol was covertly holding a large vibrator—*and it was pointed right against Ted's arse crack.*

I'd heard about movies like this; I'd seen them in adverts in tittie magazines. They were bisexual pornos, but if you didn't look closely it seemed like two men were rooting a woman and that was it. I reckoned they were made for straight men who secretly liked a bit of dick. Trying to keep my hand steady, I gave Dominic that movie. I could barely look at him. My cheeks must have been beetroot red. But Dominic had a huge, shit-eating grin on his face.

He stuck the movie in the VCR and settled on the other side of my bed to watch. My cock was throbbing so hard I was seriously worried I might come in my pants. The second the movie started, I was transfixed. These two men—their dicks, their *arses*—they were fucking incredible. All the while, I was hyper-aware of Dominic next to me. I could hear his breathing getting heavier. I could feel the heat of his body. I noticed when he adjusted his position and I could have sworn he ended up a little closer to me.

I was barely able to breathe as I watched the story unfold. While Bob and Ted did their best to please Carol, she happily wielded said Phallus into either available male arsehole. My blood pressure skyrocketed, however, when Carol lit a cigarette and reclined back to watch Bob enjoy a detailed romp with Ted. I gasped as they went down and swallowed each other's fine, upstanding erections. I stifled a shriek as Ted drove his cock into Bob's smooth, muscled arse. And I was convinced I was having a heart attack when Bob pulled Ted's butt cheeks apart and buried his face in there. *And then the camera moved right up to them.* In glorious close-up, there was Bob's tongue licking in firm strokes across Ted's gorgeous, puckered little anus.

I was disturbed from my coronary by some movement to the right of me. To my absolute shock, I noticed Dominic sliding his footy shorts and undies right down, then kicking them off altogether. He wrapped his hand around the most beautiful erection I could ever have imagined. I was gobsmacked. It was nice and long and handsome as all get-out. Dominic relaxed his legs apart and I could see his balls, too. Both his dick and balls were a little darker than the skin on the rest of his body. And all around them was a big bush of black pubic hair.

I watched in awe as he began shuffling his long foreskin up and down, revealing a plump, dark knob each time his hand jerked to the base of his penis. How I felt as I watched those first few seconds of his masturbatory technique is something I'll never forget. Before that night, the only erect penis I had ever seen was my own. I'd never even seen one in movies or on TV or in magazines. And this one—this first-ever hard dick I got to look at—belonged to *Dominic*.

I didn't even know that anyone wanked the way Dominic was doing it. I had no idea other guys did it differently to me. I had a long foreskin just like Dominic, but I didn't like it getting in the way when I masturbated, so I'd always pull it right back and hold it there as I slid my other hand up and down over my exposed knob—using whatever kind of lubricating stuff I could get my hands on. Vaseline, olive oil, even margarine—I was pretty resourceful.

Dominic looked over and noticed me staring at him. "You don't mind, do you?" he asked.

I swallowed hard, forcing myself to look him in the eye. It was almost impossible for me to speak. "Um, can I? I mean… um… can I do it, too?"

Dominic chuckled and reached over to my waistband, tugging on the elastic. "Fuck yeah! Get these off."

I slid my shorts and undies right down and kicked them aside like Dominic had done. Sitting back, I delicately palmed my rock-hard dick, but I kept my foreskin exactly where it was, covering right over my knob. I couldn't touch that part of me. I was terrified I'd explode immediately.

"Wow!" Dominic was looking intently at my erection. "Fat dick, mate! It's fuckin' bigger than mine."

"Um… nah, it's not." I could feel my face flushing. In eighteen years, absolutely nobody had ever seen my erection.

"Wait here," he said. Bending forward, he scooted down to climb off the end of the bed. My cock jumped and my heart thundered as I got a full view of his olive-skinned butt cheeks. As he moved, they spread open and flashed a brown arsehole surrounded by lots of black hair.

I thought of the rimming scene we'd just watched. I'd dreamed of tasting a man's arse since I was thirteen, when I'd watch my Physical Education teacher stand at the blackboard in his tight little footy shorts. Back then, Aussie Rules shorts were little more than thick, stretchy hotpants—so tiny they would have put Samantha Fox to shame. Mr. Benson's shorts moulded each of his bouncy, round arse cheeks and chewed right up the most heavenly buttcrack God ever made. I'd just sit there salivating, dying for just one little touch, one delicious lick, with my cock tensed up so hard I could feel the gushes of precome running through it. I didn't even know people actually rimmed arses back then. I thought I was some kind of sick pervert.

God, I want to eat Dominic's arse. Desperately.

Don't be fucking stupid, Ryan. He's straight. He's not gonna let you near his arse.

But he's got a bisexual movie! And he's just taken his cock out and started wanking in front of me!

No, Ryan. He's probably just curious. And you know that straight guys wank together all the time! Remember all those dickheads at school who went on and on about playing Soggy Sao? Creamy Cracker? Last one to shoot his load on it has to eat the damn thing?

Yeah, well why the fuck was I never invited? Why am I still a total fuckin' virg? Everyone else has been rooting each other for years. Jesus Christ, don't you think I've waited long enough?

Dominic came back from the dining section of the caravan, which I used as a study area. He held up a plastic ruler, grinning from ear to ear as he climbed back on the bed. *Then he grabbed my fucking dick.* I couldn't stop a small moan escaping me.

"Oh, fuck, Ryan! Did you just come?"

I looked down with alarm. I was hornier than I'd ever been in my life, but I was pretty sure I hadn't felt an orgasm. I saw Dominic staring at the long river of precome running down my shaft. "Um, no. That's just pre-jizz, mate. Don't you get it, too?"

Dominic's face was a mass of fascination. His hand was still wrapped around my stiff cock, absent-mindedly squeezing it from time-to-time and driving me fucking insane. "Nah, mate. My dick doesn't get juice like this. That's fuckin' awesome. Must feel great when you wank."

I chuckled to hide my embarrassment. "I certainly do it often enough."

He turned his attention back to the task at hand, holding the ruler against my erection. "Let's see…" He moved it around my shaft—front, back and side. "Nearly six and a half inches." He looked up at me with a wry expression. I noticed he didn't let go of my dick. "Yours is still bigger, mate."

"Bullshit." I wasn't going to leave it at that. I wasn't going to miss out on my chance. Snatching the ruler, I pushed Dominic backwards onto the bed. I watched in slow motion: as my hand moved towards that majestic penis, as my fingers made contact, as my grip closed around his girth. That first touch was pure heaven.

I'm finally holding another man's cock. And not just any man, but the one I've been obsessing over for four bloody years! My fuckin' br—Shut the FUCK UP, Ryan!

Dominic's shaft was firm and warm; like kid leather to touch. Suppressing the urge to moan again, I quickly placed the ruler against it the same way he'd done to mine. God, he was so hard. His cock flexed again and again in my hand. "Sorry, mate," he said. "I can't help it, I'm so fuckin' horny."

I looked up at him and grinned. *Never apologise,* I wanted to say. *By my calculations, I've pulled my dick well over a thousand times thinking about you.* But I didn't dare. I just focused back on the task at hand. I leaned in further, pretending I needed a better look. It wasn't part of the deal—the only reason I was even *allowed* to hold his penis was to measure it—but I couldn't resist slowly working that beautiful foreskin further and further down as I repositioned the ruler. It goes without saying I did this many more times than I needed to, though Dominic never said a word. His dick just continued to jump every time I moved my hand.

By this stage I was practically passing out with lust. Not just from the sight of his fully-emerged knob, not just from the fact he was clearly letting me get away with far too much touching, but—over and above all—from the wonderful musky scent of his entire crotch. I couldn't quite understand why, but it was making me feel aggressive. Animalistic. I wanted to fucking devour him.

I really needed to get a grip. I took a deep breath in through my nose to steady myself, but it only made things worse as that masculine smell stormed right through my senses. *Fuck, Ryan! Behave! Don't screw this up!* I had to bring my focus back once again to the ruler. "More than eight inches, ya smarmy cunt!" With an air of smug satisfaction, I tightened my grip on his penis and it flexed again for me.

"Yeah, but yours is *way* thicker, mate. Pity we can't measure *that* with a bloody ruler." Dominic wasn't wrong. My dick had a formidable girth. But I wasn't going to say anything. That long, slender prick of his was perfect. I never wanted him to feel like it was anything less than magnificent.

Dominic started to say something else, but I wasn't paying attention. I was in some kind of trance, mesmerised by the sight of his shiny red knob. It was so close to my face. Something inside me snapped. In one lightning-fast move, I'd clamped my mouth right over that succulent bell-end.

"Fuck!" Dominic cried out, his body jolting in shock. But nothing was going to stop me now. I was bobbing my head up and down, rolling my tongue around, revelling in the wonderful flavour.

It's a dick. In my fuckin' mouth. It's Dominic's dick. And I'm sucking on the juicy fucker!

Dominic started to groan. Encouraged by his reaction, I slid more inches into my mouth and sucked even faster. I didn't really know what I was doing, but my hunger for this amazing prick was insatiable. I'd read about blow jobs in gay magazines like 'Outrage' and 'Campaign.' All that research escaped me right now. I just had to consume Dominic. I slid my hand between his legs and began to stroke his balls. God, I loved the soft fur on them.

"Holy shit, Ryan, that's incredible," Dominic whined. I was lying kind of sideways and he reached down, grabbing at my penis. "Get this fat bastard up here and let me taste it," he panted.

WHAT THE FUCK? He wants to suck MY DICK, TOO?

I scurried into a sixty-nine straight away. Dominic didn't waste a second, pulling back my long hood, jamming my wet knob into his mouth and sucking hard. He got to work rubbing his tongue firmly against every surface, licking up the rivulets of precome that leaked incessantly from my slit. I practically bellowed, even though my mouth was crammed full with Dominic's sumptuous prick. I had NEVER imagined it could feel this good to have my dick stuffed in another man's gob.

As if this wasn't enough, I felt Dominic's hand slide right over my hairy buttocks, letting his fingers come to rest just inside my arse crack. The shock nearly sent me through the roof.

His dick started flexing even more rapidly. He began a constant stream of muffled moans, sucking more furiously on my knob. I began to feel that sweet, sweet pain inside my groin—that sure-fire signal I was going to come at any moment.

Right then, Dominic let out a strained nasal holler. His body seized up and the hand that had been cradling my butt cheek jammed straight inside my cleft, multiple fingers prodding hard against my arsehole. "*Nnnnnnnngh!*" I screamed, my mouth so chock-a-block with Latino cock that I sounded like a thrash metal singer.

While I belted out my ecstatic vocals, Dominic's long dick grew bigger and firmer against my tongue and warm, creamy spunk torpedoed into my mouth. Over and over it spurted. I didn't even need to think, I gulped it down with relish. I'd tasted my own jizz many times before, but Dominic's was out of this world. Sweet. Savoury. Absolutely fucking delicious.

Coming down from the high of swallowing my first ever load, I realised that my cock, taint and arsehole were tensed in rapturous agony. Right through Dominic's orgasm, he'd been diligently slurping away on my dick, his fingers round the back still jabbing at my tight arse-pucker, keeping me teetering on the edge of glory. I was so moved by his dedication that I hurtled right over that edge and my whole body went rigid. I howled as my cock exploded in a painful frenzy of spasms, shot after shot of sperm firing into Dominic's mouth.

To my surprise, Dominic guzzled down every drop of it. Of course, there'd been no question that I'd swallow *his* load. I'd waited *years* for that kind of opportunity. But the fact he drank my come almost brought a tear to my eye, especially when I looked down at him and found him grinning back up at me, his hand still wedged in my hairy butt, his fingertips still wiggling against my arsehole. "Fuck, Ryan. That was fuckin' *awesome.*"

I didn't want Dominic's hand to leave my arse. But I had an urgent need to be closer to him. I wasn't quite sure what it was, but it was pointless trying to resist. I slithered around, repositioning myself on the bed so we were lying face-to-face. "You blew my fuckin' mind, Dominic."

"And your cock, too," he smirked.

I stared into his eyes, finding myself leaning in even closer. I didn't know if it was OK, but, *fuck me*, I had to kiss him. As soon as my lips touched his, he pulled me tight against his body and slid his tongue into my mouth. I could taste our combined come and it made our kiss all the more erotic; sharing the riches we had just gained from pleasuring each other. Dominic's mouth was warm and soft and his tongue was on a constant exploratory mission. He made tiny little grunting sounds as he kissed and it touched my heart so deeply I wanted to cry.

Our lips parted and we moved our heads back slightly so we could look at each other. My hand was clasped around Dominic's back. I could feel the ridges of his shoulder blades through his t-shirt. I slid my palm downwards, tracing the slight line of sinewy muscle either side of his spine. I kept lowering my hand, till it went over the bottom hem of his shirt and landed on his finely-furred arse cheeks. It was fucking mind-blowing, that first touch. Warm, small mounds of muscle, with a thicket of hair in the crack between them. My fingers stroked up and down this furry crevice, dying to slip inside it, yet not quite brave enough to make that move. But, blow me down with a feather, Dominic seemed to *like* where my hand was. He even gave a little moan and smiled at me.

His eyes became serious for a moment. "Ryan, are you like… full-on gay?"

"Um, yeah. Totally." *Well, duh. Your come's still coating my tongue, mate.*

"You won't tell anyone about what we just did, will you?"

I laughed incredulously. "Fuck, no! I don't want people finding out about this. Especially with us being—" I cut myself off, letting the words hang. No further explanation was needed there. "It's *you*, Dominic. You're my mate, and that's all I care about." I looked at him for a second, gathering my thoughts while I scrambled to change tactics. "Anyway, I'm not ready to come out. Not for ages. And I'm never, ever gonna say anything, not to anyone. It's our secret, OK?"

The look of relief on his face was palpable. But a moment later his eyes became serious again. "You know, mate… I really like girls. I'm not gay like you. I'm straight." Even though his declaration was resolute, he still seemed nervous, as if there was something he couldn't quite bring himself to say. I didn't prompt him. I just laid there quietly, willing him to open up to me. When he started to speak again, his voice was small and vulnerable. "Actually… um… that's not true. I… I think I might be bi. I mean… *fuck*." He screwed his eyes up. "You saw the movie I bought. I never did anything with a guy before, but I've kinda been curious."

I could feel his body trembling with the magnitude of admitting something he'd never voiced before—something he maybe never even had accepted prior to tonight. It was a shock to see Dominic this way—the guy who had been nothing but cocky and confident since the day I'd met him four years previously. He took a deep breath, then paused as his eyes searched my face. I could see his mind tick over; I could sense his urge to tell me even more. "I definitely wanna do this again with you, mate. *Lots* of fuckin' times."

I could hardly believe what I was hearing. My face lit up like a Christmas tree. "Wow! Shit, yeah! I'd love to. And I know you like girls. I don't care if you fuck them. I just don't want anything to change between us, you know? Doing this kind of stuff with you is like the icing on the cake." I hoped to God I was getting my message across. I couldn't bear it if he thought I was gonna become some sort of crazed stalker.

"You're bloody awesome, Ryan, you know that?" He leaned in for another kiss and I fucking melted, I really did. My hand was still gently stroking his arse, my fingers tracing his furry crack. He shifted position a bit, slinging his leg over my hips. As he moved, his taut little buttocks opened wide and my fingers slipped straight inside, brushing through the soft hair and skimming over his puckered anus. His body jerked in surprise and I quickly slid my hand out.

"Shit, sorry, Dominic. I was just touching you. I promise I wasn't trying to stick my finger up your arsehole or anything."

He laughed and pulled my hand back to his buttcrack. "It's OK. You caught me unawares, that's all. Keep touching me. It feels nice."

"Certainly felt nice when you did it to me before. Felt like I was gonna shoot straight off the bat."

"Did it, really?" Dominic's eyebrows shot up in a mixture of intrigue and amusement.

"Fuckin' oath, mate. Never blew so hard in my life. Stick 'em up there anytime."

I lay there with my brother, staring into his eyes, listening to him breathe, while I ran my fingers through his hairy cleft and caressed his beautiful hole. It was the perfect ending to the best night of my life. When Dominic's eyes started to get a bit droopy, he yawned and gave me a final kiss on the lips. "I'd better go inside and go to bed, Ryan. Don't want mum or my dad to get suspicious."

I was sad to see him leave, but we both knew he had to. When I eventually turned out the lights and got back into bed, I lay on my side and brought my fingers to my face. To my absolute delight, I could smell the faint, smooth musk of Dominic's arse. My God, it was incredible. I fell asleep like this, tantalised by Dominic's most intimate scent, and I dreamt of happiness.

Chapter Three

The following couple of days were torture. I wanted to launch myself at Dominic every time I saw him. I wanted to rip his clothes off, I wanted to ravage his cock, I wanted to taste every inch of his body. And fuck, I wanted to kiss him again. Long, slow, languorous kisses while we lay together in each other's arms. But it wasn't gonna happen till we could steal some more private time together without raising eyebrows. Meanwhile, Dominic was his usual jovial self and we carried on like the best friends we had been for ages. Every now and then he'd give me a surreptitious little wink and my heart would pound with anticipation.

Once again, my caravan proved to be the gift that kept on giving. The week after my birthday and that life-changing night with Dominic, the two of us were summoned to the lounge room by my mother and Joe. My initial instinct was to panic.

Did they find out what Dominic and I did the other night?

No. That was impossible. Not unless they'd woken up, gone out the back and pressed their ears to the caravan.

"Dominic," Joe started, "I've taken a redundancy from the accounting firm and I'm going to start my own business. I have my clients lined up already."

It was my mother's turn to speak now, and she aimed her tentative words in my direction. "Joe's going to start off working from home, so he's going to need an office space."

Shit. You want me to leave my caravan, now? No bloody way. I'll move out.

Next, mum looked at Dominic. "We're going to be short on space. Nathan's still a kid and I don't think he's going to want to share a room. I don't think you or Ryan would be happy with that, either." Mum looked between me and Dominic. "You boys get along so well. Would you consider sharing the caravan? I know it's a huge ask, but there's plenty of space in there."

Dominic didn't miss a beat. "Sure. Ryan's my best mate. Of course I don't mind sharing."

I looked at him. He was wearing his most charming smile. My heart was turning somersaults. *Could this really be happening?*

I realised mum was looking at me for a response. "Yeah, sure. I think we'll have an awesome time." *Fuck. I hope I didn't sound too keen.*

Thankfully, mum and Joe were oblivious, despite the fact my pulse was going a mile a minute. "We're really grateful to you boys for helping us out," Joe said. I could have said the same thing back to him.

When mum and Joe had left the room, Dominic leaned in to whisper in my ear, his hand reaching into my lap and squeezing my throbbing dick. "We are gonna have *so* much fuckin' fun, Ryan."

* * *

Dominic and I didn't waste a second. Under the guise of helping mum and Joe out, we lugged all of Dominic's stuff to the carport and dumped it next to the caravan. He went back to do a final clean-up in his old bedroom while I sorted out our new sleeping arrangements. There was no way I was gonna agree to Dominic sleeping on the couches in the caravan's dining area. They weren't as comfy as a proper bed. Plus, we both needed that space for studying. The looming end of semester meant TAFE college exams for me and a mountain of uni assignments for Dominic.

Instead, I separated the two single beds in the sleeping area and made them up individually, placing the bedside table in between them. Personally, I would have preferred Dominic and I to share the big bed together, but that was a fantasy that was never gonna happen. In any case, with Dominic sleeping in the bed across from me, he was still close enough for us to act on impulse, to talk dirty with each other, to tumble into either bed together and make each other feel good. Even if he was just having a wank, I'd still have a front row seat.

Once we'd loaded all Dominic's stuff into the caravan, set up our study area and found a home for all his random things, he pushed me up against the wall and brought his face close to mine. I shivered as his warm breath moved over my lips. My pulse was sky-high again, my heart thudding in my chest. "Just wait till bedtime tonight," he growled. He reached his hand down, rubbing it over my balls and rock-hard cock.

I moaned, grabbing onto his penis as well, thrilled to feel it flexing at my touch. "I *can't* fucking wait, Dominic."

He leaned in and gave me a soft kiss, swishing his tongue inside my mouth. His lips brushed against mine in the aftermath, his voice a low rumble vibrating against me. "Well, you're gonna have to. Now let's go and have a smoke before I rip your clothes off right now."

* * *

"Dominic?" I asked tentatively that night, as we were lounging on our respective beds playing FIFA on Nintendo.

"Yeah?" he said, not looking at me, still concentrating on the screen.

"Do you think anyone might eventually suspect we're kind of… um… messing around?" Dominic paused the game and looked over at me.

Fuck, how awkward. Why the hell did I bring this up?

I rushed to explain myself. "We're just gonna have to be really careful. Um… assuming, you know… that you wanna keep doing stuff with me for a while." Fuck, I was squirming.

Dominic grinned at me. God, I loved that cocky smile. My heart sang every time I saw it. "Don't worry, Ryan. Nobody will ever know. And stop all that bullshit. You know I wanna keep messing around."

I growled quietly, physically grabbing onto my bed to restrain myself from launching across the room at him. It wasn't late enough yet and I hadn't checked the house to see if people were in bed. I always locked the caravan door at night, but I wanted to be extra cautious.

Dominic restarted the game and continued to beat the shit out of me. I didn't mind one bit. Hearing the joy in his voice was worth any humiliating defeat. "YEEEESSSS!" he shouted as he won by a mile. He jumped up, ran over to me and pulled his shorts down. "You can kiss my fuckin' arse, mate!" I barely knew what was going on before he planted his buns on my face and ground around, his hairy crack rubbing against my nose.

I couldn't believe what was happening. It was meant to be an insult, but I was smothered in the most glorious scent I'd ever encountered in my life. It was so mind-fuckingly wonderful I was getting dizzy. Finally, it dawned on me. Year Nine science. This is what pheromones were: like a smell so intensely pleasurable it did weird, awesome things to your brain. I grabbed onto Dominic's hips and licked hard. The taste was every bit as incredible as the scent.

"What the hell?" Dominic yelped, reflexively trying to get up. But if he thought I was gonna let go, he had another thing coming. Dominic was the same height as me at about five-ten, but he was a slim guy, like his dad. I, on the other hand, was broad and stocky, just like *my* dad. Dominic was no match for me—he wasn't going anywhere. I jammed my tongue into his arsehole, licking hard against his sphincter, poking it in and out of that mouthwatering little pucker.

Dominic quickly gave up the fight, and from the panting and whining coming out of him I could tell he'd just realised how great it felt. His body began to jiggle, his arse vibrating against my face as he took hold of his dick and jerked it fast. "Holy shit, Ryan… fuck, mate… ugh… fuckin' amazing!"

God, I wanted to know what it felt like to have this done to my arse. I'd experimented with fingers. I'd slid penis-sized carrots up my arsehole. I'd even found a brand of lube in the chemist that came in a suspiciously penis-shaped bottle. Fuck, it felt good with that thing shoved inside me. But as hard as these objects made me come when I used them, I was desperate for a real tongue, or—even better—a real cock.

"We gotta stop, Ryan." Dominic was breathless as he slid his beautiful bum off my face. "I don't wanna come so soon." He moved down to lie on top of me, planting a huge kiss on my lips. He pried them apart with his tongue, swishing it inside my mouth, gaining momentum as he went, grunting over and over. He couldn't get enough. He would have been tasting himself. He would have been tasting the exquisite arsehole I'd just been gorging myself on. That thought was enough to make me moan hard against his lips. He moved back to grin at me. "You dirty fuckin' bastard. I never knew my arse could feel that good. But don't go thinking you're gonna stick your fat cock up there." His hand snaked down between us as he spoke, clutching my aching dick.

Here was my golden opportunity. "You could always stick your cock up *my* arse."

Dominic's eyes nearly popped out of his skull. "Fuck! Really? You'd let me do that?"

"I'd fuckin' love it."

"Have you ever been fucked up the arse before?"

A laugh of disbelief erupted from me. "Mate, you're my first. I never did anything with anyone before you."

His eyebrows shot up in wonderment. "You mean you were a virgin? Jesus. You *never* had a root before?"

"Nah. Fuckin' sad, eh?" I was turning crimson. My face was burning. I felt like the only eighteen-year-old in the world who'd never got any. "I still am, technically. A virgin, I mean. Hope you're gonna change that in a minute, eh."

A sudden frown clouded his face. For one awful moment I thought he was put off by my inexperience. Like I was so undesirable nobody had ever wanted to touch me. "How do you know it's not gonna hurt like hell?"

My instant relief at his question turned to embarrassment once more. *Oh, fuck. Do I have to admit this?* "I've… um… stuck things up there before."

"Shit, really? Like what?"

I reached down beside me, opening a drawer in the bedside table. Retrieving a toiletry bag from the back, I unzipped it and showed him the phallic bottle of lube. It was a slender cylindrical shape, with a rounded top and a flip-open lid at the bottom. "Like this."

"Wow… that fits in your arsehole? Does it hurt?"

I shook my head. "It's fuckin' fantastic."

I flicked open the bottle, squeezed lube onto my hand and reached down to grab Dominic's hard cock. It jumped in my fist, his erectile muscles in overdrive as I rubbed the lube over it. "I want you to fuck me, Dominic. I fuckin' need it so much."

"Should I use a condom?"

I shrugged. "I'm a virgin, remember? Did you use condoms with all those girls you fucked?"

He looked at me like I was mad. "Shit, yeah. I didn't want them to get pregnant."

"Well I'm not gonna get pregnant. And you've had safe sex. We don't need a fuckin' condom."

"Far out… I've never done it without one!" I could see the glee in his eyes. "Fuck, this is gonna be epic!" He pulled his shirt over his head, then reached down and helped me get mine off. There he was, in all his bare-chested glory. His body was youthful and slender. You'd even say it was skinny, but he couldn't have been more beautiful to me.

Pulling him close, I buried my face in his chest, breathing in his masculine smell, rubbing myself through the glorious fur that decorated it. Every hair caressed my nose and cheeks and lips. My mind was exploding with this new sensation. I could hardly believe the pleasure I was getting from something so simple. I bombarded him with kisses, reaching around and sliding my finger into his arse crack to stroke his moist little hole.

Dominic moaned long and low, his hand caressing the back of my head. "Hey, mate," he said softly. "You're gettin' me too horny doing all this stuff to my arse. My cock's aching to fuck you and I can't wait any longer."

Oh, God. I'd almost forgotten about the best part.

As we clambered to get out of our shorts and undies, Dominic frowned. "What should I do?" he asked. "No chick ever let me fuck her arse before. Believe me, I've tried." He paused a second to ponder. "I can't just shove my dick straight in like with a cunt. Arseholes are much tighter."

"Put your fingers in first, Dominic. Get two in there and kind of stretch them apart like scissors. That's what I do to myself, anyway." I was nervous. I wondered whether he'd feel weird about having his fingers in my arsehole. But I needn't have worried. He immediately slicked his hand with lube. In a split second he had shuffled down the bed between my legs. He put his hands under my knees and pushed them up high, taking a long look at my furry buttocks and arsehole spread out in front of him.

A lusty groan erupted from his chest. "Jesus, Ryan, you have a great big hairy arse. You're a fucking *man*." I found myself wishing he'd bend down and give me a good rimming. But instead, he slid a finger straight into my pucker. I whimpered instantly. I guess I must have sounded like I was crying, because Dominic stopped in his tracks. "Did that hurt?"

"No," I panted. "I'm lovin' it. Gimme more." I felt a second finger shove inside with the first. He'd been a little rough and it burned a bit, but Dominic did what I'd asked and slowly stretched the fingers apart several times, making my ring give in and relax.

"Should I fuck your hole with my fingers for a while?" Dominic was looking up at me with a mixture of concern and excitement.

All I could do was nod while I whimpered. He slowly started to piston his fingers in, his knuckles bumping over my elastic sphincter. Further and further he fronched me, changing his angle here and there, till the pads of his fingers brushed right over my magic g-spot. My whimpers became whines and my hands strayed to my dick. Holding my foreskin right back, I started tentatively rubbing my knob. "I… um… I think it's time for the real thing now, Dominic."

"Fuck, Ryan," Dominic growled, grabbing his cock and jerking his hand back and forth on it. He aimed his knob at my hole and rammed hard. Straight in he went, and *fuck* it hurt. I cried out, tears in my eyes.

Dominic looked startled. "Shit, mate! I thought you'd be all set after I fingered you. Do you wanna stop?"

"No," I managed to choke out. "Just stay still for a sec." The burning in my arse was so intense I was scared I might piss myself. Like, literally wet the fucking bed. Which was stupid, because my dick was still so hard. I tried not to squirm, desperate to ride out the agony. I breathed slow and deep. I imagined myself opening up wide and becoming all loose. To my great relief, the pain died off, my hole relaxed into a sore stretch and my bladder no longer felt like it might burst. "Keep going now, mate," I croaked.

He pushed in his last couple of inches. I felt his pubes hit my taint and his balls flop against my tailbone. It was beginning to feel amazing. His cock was definitely better than my makeshift lube-bottle dildo. It was hot and fleshy inside me, not cold and plastic. And it was attached to the most wonderful man in the fucking world. The constant, grinding pressure on my prostate was so exquisite it seemed like my orgasm was just around the corner. I grabbed hold of my dick and began to rub, bumping my fingers over the rim of my knob, stroking over my frenulum.

Dominic looked down at me masturbating. "Can I start fucking you now?" he asked.

"God, yes," I panted. "Please, mate. Please fuck me."

Dominic began to pump slowly. "Man, this is so much tighter than a cunt! It's like your arsehole is wanking my cock hard."

"It's fucking awesome, Dominic." He took that as his cue and began to speed up a bit. I was jerking myself firmly now. I couldn't believe how incredible it all felt. It was like I was in the early stages of coming, but the pause button was on, hovering in the most delicious part. "Oh, God! Fuck me hard! Pound me with that fucking dick, mate!" I was practically yelling now.

"Holy shit! Really? No chick ever asked me to do that!" He started slamming his cock in with brute force.

Tears were running down my cheeks and I was whining non-stop. "It feels so fuckin' good, mate! God... you know what? I think I'm gonna blow! Oh, Jesus... FUCK! I'm coming, man! AAAARGH!" I wailed as my arsehole pushed outwards, trying to expel Dominic's penis as he continued thrusting into me. My cock was more tense than it had ever been. The pressure was fucking insane—I felt like I was gonna be blown to smithereens. It climbed to an excruciating peak before my dick began to pulse, squirting thick missiles of spunk right up to my chin and chest.

"So fuckin' hot, Ryan. Fuck, that's so, so fuckin' hot! FUUUCK!" Dominic rammed into me one more time, jerking and wobbling as his cock unloaded deep inside my rectum. He was gasping. His whole body was wracked with violent shudders. Finally, he collapsed on top of me. "Je-e-e-esus!" he laughed. "I never want to use a fucking condom again." He kissed me on the cheek, pressing his face against the side of mine, breathing into my ear. "Your arse is now full of my spoof."

"Feels like it belongs there, mate." I wrapped my arms around his chest and squeezed tightly. "I can't believe how great that was. Thank you, Dominic. You're the fucking bomb!"

He rolled us round onto our sides, smiling at me. "Can we do that, like, ten times a day from now on?"

"I think I wouldn't be able to walk, my arse would be way too sore." I grinned back at him. "But *once* a day would be great." I wasn't so sure about that, either. My anus felt pretty raw. But I doubted I'd last very long before I'd be craving a repeat performance.

"Well, the more often, the better, Ryan. That was by far the best fuck I ever had."

"You rocked my world, mate. I don't reckon anyone's ever lost their virginity with such a monumental fuck. I'm really lucky it was with you." I wondered if that sounded too sappy. But I was way too high on endorphins to care.

"Me, too, mate," said Dominic, and leaned forward to kiss me. It was soft and tender. Our noses blew warm air on our faces. When our lips parted, he brushed his fingers across my cheek. "It's getting late. Let's go for a piss and a smoke before bed, eh?"

He helped me up and we went outside and stood near the bushes, urinating together. Watering the garden had been my nighttime habit for years. The dodgy little bathroom in the caravan was only used for storage these days, and I couldn't be bothered going all the way into the house. Having Dominic join me in this little pissing ritual added a whole new dimension to the experience. I loved the sound of his stream hitting the bushes and pelting down onto the grass, cascading in tandem with mine. I loved how the sexual collided with the non-sexual; seeing him standing there holding his long dick, looking so hot, yet so innocently going about the call of nature.

After we finished, we sat in the lawn chairs, quietly smoking. In the dark, Dominic gently took my hand, holding it until we'd had our last puffs and stubbed out our cigarettes. The silent way he'd reached out to me, the simple intimacy of that connection, the tacit lifeline between us—it moved me in a way I'd never thought possible. I'd remember this for the rest of my life.

Chapter Four

Over the coming months, Dominic and I honed our lovemaking, discovering more and more about each other, about our bodies, about what pleased us the most. It was uncharted territory for both of us. By his own admission, Dominic's sexual exploits with girls were mostly limited to plain fucking—a diddle on the clit, a condom on the cock, and off they'd go. Other than that, he'd just been given a few reluctant head jobs—something he constantly mentioned when I blew his mind with my rampant cock-sucking enthusiasm, well-studied technique and sharp attention to his bodily needs.

I was so proud that it was me who could give him the most pleasure. A part of me was insecure about the fact he was mostly into girls. I worried he may just be settling for sex with me whilst willing females were thin on the ground. To his credit, though, he never, ever got with a girl again once we started fooling around. I would have known, because we were together every night and going at it like rabbits.

Another way I managed to please him like no other was with my deep enjoyment of rimming his arse. He didn't seem that keen to be fucked, but by golly, he loved my tongue down there every bit as much as I loved giving it to him. And eventually, he discovered why I liked it so much.

Late one night, I was naked on the bed, innocently studying a textbook, propped up on my elbows as I lay on my stomach. I heard a growling sound, then a pair of lips started kissing up the rear of my thighs, over the crease of my buttocks, then all around each big, muscular mound. Closer to my crack Dominic advanced, kissing, gingerly sniffing, sussing out new territory, indulging a curiosity he seemingly could no longer resist. Slowly, slowly, he began to pull my buttocks apart. I could feel his apprehension, but he was still kissing, still sniffing, working his way further inside. By the time his nose touched my arsehole, he was inhaling deeply. His lips brushed my pucker, placing a kiss where no man's mouth had ever been before. "Fuck, Ryan. I can't believe it! I was worried it might be horrible but it's so fuckin' nice! Your pheromones are messing with my head, mate!"

The warm wetness of his tongue made contact with my hole and we both groaned at the same time. I was shocked at how fast he accelerated. Within seconds, he was rubbing his face around, licking with force all over my arsehole, pressing his tongue just inside my ring, snarling like a dog. My cock was throbbing hard as I ground my hips slightly. I reached underneath myself and freed my knob of its foreskin, drawing it down so the friction against the sheets could tantalise my frenulum. The added intensity had me moaning non-stop, but I desperately needed more. I slid my hand back down and began to stroke myself. I was in awe. This was beyond my comprehension—not in a million years could I have imagined having my arse eaten would feel so good. I don't know whether it was the pleasure of his tongue roaming over my twitching hole, or the thrill of it nudging inside my sphincter, or the fact he was loving it so much it had driven him completely feral—all I knew was I wanted as much of this as possible.

Just as I got to the point where I thought I'd speed up my masturbation and come into the bedsheets, Dominic resurfaced from my furry arse crack, turned me over and lunged at my lips. I knew where his face had just been. I knew the high it had just given him, and I kissed and licked at him with all the hunger I could muster.

I have to admit I felt as much relief as I did elation. I'd begun to worry about his lack of reciprocation when it came to eating arse. It wasn't because I needed Dominic to please me—by God, he sent me to Planet Orgasm every night. I just felt dirty—as if I was some filthy pig committing an act of gross indecency, an act which he let me commit because it made him feel so great, but something he would never be able to stomach doing himself. That night, though, hearing him moan as he tongued my hole, feeling his genuine, unbridled enthusiasm as he lost control, knowing he was as ecstatic as I was—that was the greatest gift of all.

* * *

Our next major sexual discovery didn't come until December that year. Throughout the second semester, Dominic and I had grown closer. I was working long hours and he was slogging his way through his fourth term at uni, but what was an intimate friendship with nightly, mind-blowing sex evolved into something much more significant. Dominic still had his fun, cocky nature and his dirty, horny side, but he became even more tender and loving towards me. We'd lay there cuddling for hours, he'd kiss me at every available opportunity, he'd look into my eyes with an honesty and fondness so potent it'd knock the wind out of my sails. I loved this side of him. Every gentle stroke, every soft word, every warm hug he gave me was precious.

We'd never really discussed the future. I was eighteen, he was twenty and we had our whole lives ahead of us. Once he'd finished his exams in November, Dominic had been at a loose end. So, I'd put the feelers out and got him some casual labouring work with our company. Hard slog, but good exercise and money in the pocket to boot.

One night, he came into the caravan after a long day at work. He was fresh from the shower and he pulled his towel from his waist, gratuitously drying his penis and testicles in front of my face, then turning around, pulling his cheeks wide open and slowly rubbing the towel over his anus. I didn't need any further encouragement.

Ripping the towel away from him, I buried my tongue directly in that succulent little hole, stretching it open with my thumbs so I could probe it deep inside. In front of me, Dominic bent forward, moaning as his hand shuffled frantically on his dick. Spurred on by his obvious enjoyment, I worked hard, squeezing my tongue up his hole as far as I could, expanding it thickly so it pushed against his sphincter.

To date, this sort of oral love was the only sexual contact I'd had with Dominic's arse. I'd been respectful of his boundaries. But he was masturbating with verve now. He was whining non-stop. I couldn't resist; I pushed a finger deep inside him, butting straight against his prostate.

"Oh, fuck! What was that?" he panted.

"Your g-spot, mate." I was strumming over it now, wildly excited by the noises Dominic was making.

"Jesus, it feels so fuckin' nice!"

Game on, mate.

I slid a second finger inside and his entire body shivered. "Oh, God. Is this what it feels like for you when I fuck your arse, Ryan?"

I moved up his body, all the while pumping my fingers in and out of that hot little quoit. I was over the fucking moon he was letting me do this. "It feels even better than fingers, Dominic." He turned to look over his shoulder at me, his face one big question mark. I knew it was time. "Let me fuck you, mate. I wanna show you how bloody amazing it is. I'll be really gentle, I promise."

He didn't reply; he just slid his arsehole off my fingers and lay on his back against the mattress. "OK. I wanna do it. Please, mate, take it easy, though."

I grinned at him, lifted his legs up and looked down at his pretty hole. It was moist, pliable and oh, so inviting. But I knew we'd still need to use a ton of lube. I grabbed the bottle from the drawer, squeezed a generous amount over his pucker, then coated my cock. Holding my foreskin back with my left hand, I slid the fingers on my right hand up his hole again. His ring tightened around them, but I slowly stretched them apart. This was the first time I'd ever fucked anyone, so my only frame of reference was what I'd experienced with my own arse—what I'd done to cope with Dominic's prick.

"Relax your arsehole, Dominic. Don't try to fight what my fingers are doing." My instructions seemed to work and I felt him slacken immediately. In and out I worked my digits, getting his rubbery sphincter as loose as possible. When I thought he was ready, I rose up and pointed the end of my dick against his pucker. "Now, push out against my knob."

Dominic's face was twisted in a mixture of panic and confusion. "What do you mean?"

"You know… like you were gonna… um… go to the dunny."

The panic on Dominic's face intensified. "But what if I shit the bed?"

"Do you need to go?"

"No."

"Then you'll be fine. Trust me, this will make it so much more comfortable. Once you get through the pain you'll feel more fucking incredible than you ever have before."

Dominic screwed his face up as he started to bear down. This was my cue. My cock was flexing so hard I thought I'd come just from the anticipation. I slowly pushed it in, centimetre by centimetre. Dominic opened his mouth and made little crying sounds. I grabbed his dick. It was still rock-hard and I started moving my fist up and down, jerking his foreskin the way I'd seen him do countless times by now. With a firm push, my cock seemed to bust through and surged right up his rectum.

Oh, fuck. That was way too fast.

His eyes shot wide open and he let out a strangled grunt. "Fuck, mate. It hurts so much!"

"Let it sit for a moment. Relax your hole. Concentrate on what I'm doing to your dick and your arse will feel better really soon, I promise."

He nodded, screwing his eyes shut and breathing deeply. I continued to stroke his penis, working my fist back and forth, bumping my fingers over the ridge of his knob through his rolling foreskin. Eventually, a smile formed over Dominic's face. "Startin' to feel really good now."

Oh, Lord, I knew that sensation only too well. In small, carefully-timed increments, I began to move my cock in and out of his arse. Dominic's whimpers kicked in again. The faster I moved, the louder he got. I sped my hand up on his penis. This was going to be a spectacular fuck. Now that I was getting the friction going, my dick began to thank me. I'd never felt anything like this before. God, the heat of his rectum was heavenly, the way it wrapped its fiery wetness all round my shaft. Too much more of this and I might shoot my load.

"Fuck, mate, I'm gonna blow!" yelped Dominic, a look of tortured bliss all over him. We'd only just started, but I was elated he loved it so much. One tense, long wail came from him and I pounded that horny mancunt as hard as I could, jerking his dick as it thickened and began to squirt out long ropes of come. I watched intently, thrusting conscientiously, waiting till the ropes turned to dribbles, till the pulsing in his penis slowed down. Then I gently, gradually pulled out of his arsehole. I really wanted to bust my nut inside him. I wanted to feel the moist warmth of his back passage against my dick as I planted my seed. But it was his first time and that cute little bum needed a good rest.

Instead, I scooted up the bed, straddled his head and plonked my hairy arsehole over his nose. I was wanking hard and I was going to shoot any second. His tongue pushed upwards, searching my sphincter. When it barged inside, I tensed up. He'd hit the switch and the throb went from my anus to my prostate to my cock. I hovered in this ecstatic phase, the momentum building to a fever pitch, before the semen blasted from my aching knob. "Fuuuuuck!" I screamed, as it projected in huge arcs all over my pillow. I didn't care. I was beyond euphoric.

Suddenly, a young voice sounded from outside the caravan. "Hey guys, what's going on?"

My eyes went wide as saucers. I shuffled off Dominic's face and was met by a look of sheer terror. "STOP PUNCHING ME, YOU CUNT!" I yelled at Dominic, jumping up and ushering him off the bed. "What's up, Nathan?" I called out, as Dominic and I scrambled to put on our shorts.

"Can I come in?" Nathan's voice was at the door now. I glanced back at Dominic, who had quickly assumed a casual position on his bed, lounging back and switching on the TV with its clunky old remote.

I scuttled over to the door, my heart rate still pounding, but slightly less panicked after my apparent save. Unlocking it, I was greeted by my kid brother, who sprung up the last step, sauntering right past me into the caravan. "What were you guys doing?" he asked in his innocent, high-pitched voice.

"Fighting," I replied.

"Yeah, and I was winning." Dominic lay there with a smug grin on his face. His lazy demeanour was a stark contrast to the horrified man I'd seen just seconds ago.

"Watch it, dickhead. I'll deck you for fuckin' real." I pushed past

Nathan and flopped onto my bed. Plonking my face on my pillow, I was met with sticky wetness. *Fuck! My come!* Nathan's eyes were looking in my direction as I nonchalantly flipped it over, plumping it up all innocent-like, then settling down on it with a fake yawn.

"Can I watch TV with you guys? Mum and Joe are having some kind of argument in their room and I can't sleep."

Poor kid. I felt bad for him, stuck up there in the house with only two adults to keep him company. "OK. But only for a little while. Mum'll kill you if she finds you out here this late."

One hour and a whole repeat of 'Melrose Place' later, Nathan's eyes were closed. I shook his shoulder as he laid next to me, squished on the edge of my single mattress. "Bedtime, mate. I'm sure mum and Joe will be asleep now."

Still half out of it, Nathan rose with a childish groan. I saw him out, locked the door behind him and turned to look at Dominic. "We gotta start being quieter."

He was cool as a cucumber, his arms behind his head, the bushy black hair in his armpits flanking either side of his Cheshire Cat grin. With total disregard for my stern statement, he spoke in a carefree tone. "You know, it was kinda nice with that big, hairy arse of yours on my face, Ryan."

Fucker. I should have been annoyed at his lack of concern, but I was too thrilled at hearing how much he liked that part of my body. "Well, it was kinda nice with my cock in that warm, tight hole, Dominic."

He groaned, covering his eyes in embarrassment. "Mate, I never thought I could come that fucking hard. Guess I'm a *real* poofter now, eh?"

God, how I wished that were true. "I don't think so. Straight guys stuff things up their arseholes all the time. You know how often I've read in 'Australian Women's Forum' about wives who strap on dildos to fuck their husbands?"

Dominic reached his hand out to me, beckoning me to join him on his bed. His face glowed with a warm smile as I made my way forward, intertwining my fingers with his and landing with a soft thud on his mattress. My face found its way directly into his armpit and I sniffed deeply. "Fuck, I love how you smell, mate."

He let out a soft chuckle, reaching his arm down to rake his fingers through my hair in gentle strokes. "It's all yours, Ryan."

Is it? Do you really mean that?

Dominic's fingers came to a standstill, the pads of them resting on my head as I relaxed completely, surrounded by his potent musk. I was in a state of complete and utter bliss. I couldn't want for anything more than this.

After some time, he shuffled around to face me. For several long seconds, he lay there gazing into my eyes. The fondness flowed from him in powerful waves that crashed straight through my heart. "You know," he started tentatively, "when my arse is all better after that pounding you gave it, I might want you to fuck me again."

"Of course. Anytime, Dominic. You know that."

He reached round and moved his hand into my furry cleft, rubbing his finger on my anus. "But you're still gonna be copping it most of the time, you dirty fucker."

His cheeky grin triggered a powerful rush through me. I wanted to use the L-word. But I'd hold off for now.

Chapter Five

Nathan's little visit to our caravan had not been prompted by an isolated event. Whilst Dominic and I had been ensconced in our own little day-to-day nirvana out there, things weren't quite so rosy in the main house. Self-employment had been hard for Joe and he was moping around the house a lot, looking miserable. I didn't quite know what had gone wrong for him and neither did Dominic when I probed him for answers. I wondered why Joe didn't just get another proper job. I mean, he was an accountant and drove a nice car. Surely there was work for people like that.

My dad had been a lot like me: a quiet, laid-back burly bloke. Mum, however, was a slender beauty. She had boobs, a pretty face and a flirtatious personality. And she had always been a bit of a social butterfly. So, while Joe was stewing at home, mum was doing the opposite. Predictably, her regular nights out started causing all kinds of friction with Joe. And poor Nathan was stuck up there in the middle of it all.

"Joe's really fuckin' pissed off, eh. He reckons she must be doing it with some other guy." Nathan had joined Dominic and me down the back while we had a smoke, seeking refuge from the arguments that were now happening on a daily basis. I felt really bad for Nathan. He was a good kid and he shouldn't have been exposed to all of that. I couldn't help thinking it was just the tip of the iceberg. A sick feeling began growing in the pit of my stomach.

A few nights after that earth-shattering experience fucking Dominic's arse, there was a major argument inside the house. Screams and stuff smashing. Dominic and I were sitting in the garden smoking as usual, and Nathan darted out of the back door, looking shaken. "They've fuckin' lost it," he said. "I can't go back in there."

I glanced over at Dominic, who gave a small nod. "Just stay with us on the couch tonight, OK?"

I set Nathan up with cushions and a blanket down the other end of the caravan. There was no way Dominic and I would be able to fool around with him there, but Dominic did give me a soft kiss and a brief hug just before we got into our respective beds. "Let's make up for it tomorrow night, eh?" he whispered in my ear.

Famous last words.

After a long, hard day at work, I got home with Dominic the next evening and headed straight for the shower, then went to the caravan to dry off and jack up the aircon. I lay down naked on my bed, fondling my penis, thinking about what I was gonna do with my sexy man later on. Dominic emerged sometime afterwards with wet hair, wrapped in a towel, his face ashen.

"What's wrong, mate?" I said.

His expression alarmed me. He didn't answer right away, just pulled off his towel and started drying himself with it. As much as I loved seeing him rub it over his balls, arse and cock, I was too distressed by how upset he looked to appreciate the floor show. He sat down on the edge of his bed, knees spread with his elbows on them, resting his forehead in his hands.

"I gotta leave," he said.

My heart started galloping. "What do you mean?"

"Dad found out mum's having an affair. He fuckin' hates her. He wants us to go back to Perth as soon as we can."

"What? Perth? Why?! What the fuck?" My head was swimming. Panic was rising up to throat level. I thought I might choke.

"He reckons he can get a job easy there. We can stay with his friends while he finds a place. It's really cheap in Perth, eh. I can go to uni down there. I killed it in all my subjects this year. I'll definitely get into Curtin or Murdoch or UWA." Dominic finally looked up at me with red-rimmed eyes. His brow was wrinkled with fear and worry. "I can't afford to stay here and study now, mate. I've got no choice."

I was gonna scream. I was gonna lose it. A fucking inferno was building rapidly inside me, but all I could do was stare. "When?"

He swallowed. "This weekend."

That was it. "No. NO. NO FUCKIN' WAY!" I shot to my feet and turned on him, shaking with rage, my voice seething. "Can't even be done that quick. Whatcha gonna do with the car and all the furniture and stuff? That shit's gotta be booked WEEKS in advance!"

Dominic was like a deer in the headlights, his eyes wide with fright. He'd never seen me like this. *I'd* never seen me like this. He took a couple of shaky breaths and started talking, his tone of voice pleading with me. "Nah, it's all backloading from Darwin. Dad's got it all worked out. Booked the removalists, the plane tickets, everything."

"FUCK! So it's all been pre-arranged? Done and dusted? Well isn't that FUCKIN' MARVELLOUS!" I was rabid. Losing my shit entirely. My face would have been beetroot red.

"Sorry, Ryan. I really am. Nothin' I can do." He reached out and touched my arm, but I yanked it away. "Mate, be realistic. This thing with you and me could never go anywhere, could it?" His voice was thick. "We gotta call it off, Ryan." I could hear his voice breaking and he stopped for a few seconds. His eyes shone with tears as he made one last-ditch effort. "We had an awesome time though, didn't we?"

The finality of it all knifed me hard in the guts. That was the last straw. Sobs exploded from me as I fell apart at the seams "No. No, no, no, no…*fuckin'* no…" I crumpled in a heap onto the bed as the howls came hurtling forth at alarming speed. I was bawling hard; a mass of agony and snot and guttural wails.

I've fucking lost everything. Everything I ever fucking cared about is gone.

"Fuck, Ryan! Stop it! Don't be such a fuckin' sook!" Dominic's words were harsh, but I could hear the pain in his voice, the hitching of his breath. "Please stop," he said as he began to sob, too. "Please, mate. Don't cry like that. It fuckin' hurts too much." His body slumped over mine and he crawled onto the bed, holding me tight.

We lay there and wept together, numb with shock, unable to process the kind of pain that was tearing us into pieces. We cried and cried and fucking cried until we were shattered. With my arms around Dominic's naked body, pulling him against me, I imagined never letting go. I dreamed of us staying like that forever, suspended naked together, two souls joined as one.

* * *

I remember very little about the next few days. I went about life as if I was in a bad dream, all my senses dulled by a loss I couldn't even bear to confront. I remember helping Dominic pack up his stuff in the caravan, helping him chuck out everything he wasn't taking. I didn't go near the house. *They* could fucking deal with all of that shit.

On our last night, we made love one final time. Dominic looked down at me as he thrust into my arse and I wept. "I'm sorry, I'm sorry, I'm so sorry," he kept saying, tears streaming down his face. We came together: him deep inside me; me rubbing out my load as I felt him filling me, completing me. It was a perfectly-timed conclusion.

All night we clung together in that little bed, touching each other, wiping the tears from each other's eyes. At some stage sleep came to us, because I awoke and it was daylight. Dominic's eyes opened slowly as I touched his face. "I love you, Dominic," I said.

"I love you too, Ryan."

I don't know how I held it together as I walked outside with him and Joe, helping them with their luggage. Mum gave Dominic a hug at the door, but opted to stay inside. Joe grabbed me, patting me on the back just before he got into the front of the taxi. "I'm gonna miss you, son," he said. "I'm really sorry things ended like this."

Poor Joe. He was so kind. I wished things had turned out differently, too. All I could do was nod and try to smile.

The last person left was Dominic. He pulled me into his arms and pressed the side of his face against mine, a small sob escaping him. "Look after yourself, man. I love you."

"I love you too, Dominic. I always will." I drew in a sharp breath, stifling a cry, stopping my emotions dead in their tracks. Dominic broke the embrace, fished around in his pocket and gave me a small photo. I recognised it instantly, it was from my birthday party. In the background, there was mum, leaning over Dominic and me, beaming. Dominic's arm was around my shoulders, squeezing me tight against him. The joy emanating from both of us was a cruel and painful reminder—that was the beginning. Now, it was the end. Looking back up at Dominic, I saw the sadness in his eyes. No-one would ever know the kind of heartbreak we were enduring. It was our burden to suffer in secret.

A large part of me died that morning as I walked out into the middle of the street, my eyes fixed on Dominic's as he looked at me through the back window of the cab, never breaking contact till it turned a corner and they were gone forever.

* * *

After that day, I withdrew. I went about my business, moved through the machinations of daily life, but I didn't engage. Mum clearly thought I blamed her for everything and I guess it was true in a way. Logic told me there was more to it, but my youthful mind could only see her selfish behaviour as the catalyst for all this destruction. For a while she tried to make it up to me, but eventually she gave in. After a few years she'd upped sticks and moved to Adelaide, taking Nathan with her. But in the meantime, we co-existed at an unspoken distance. Our relationship had reached a stalemate from which we never really recovered.

The numbness I'd felt after losing Dominic quickly descended into a full-scale depression. I went to my GP, a kindly man I'd gone to for years, and I cried. I hadn't slept properly in ages. I ate sporadically and badly, my appetite was absent most of the time.

The doctor tried me on two different kinds of antidepressant, one after the other. I hated them both. They made me jittery. They gave me terrible dreams. They made my jaw clench and my teeth grind in my sleep. Worst of all, I couldn't come when I masturbated. It was like the only pleasure I had left had been taken away from me. I went back to the doctor in absolute despair.

Third time proved lucky when he put me on a drug called Mirtaza-pine. Food tasted good again. At night, I was knocked out and I slept right through. And I was hornier than I had been since before Dominic left. Sure, it was hard to get up in the mornings at first, I was so groggy. But I adjusted and it wasn't so bad. Sure, I ate lots of carbs and put on a few pounds. But I had a physical job so I had no option but to exercise all day. And being a little bearish was better than being miserable.

The thing that got me through all of this turmoil, the thing I waited with bated breath for day after day, was my occasional contact with Dominic. He had a dodgy pre-paid mobile phone, but the calls were so expensive we just made do with our landlines. It was always awesome to hear from him and he was friendly as ever, but it was like we'd gone back to how we'd been before we ever had sex. I was just an old mate, now. I was no longer a lover. *His* lover. Physical distance had separated us, but emotional distance is what sunk the boot in good and proper.

As months flew by, the calls became less frequent. Dominic was having a great time at uni in Perth. He had a fantastic bunch of friends. He and his dad were renting a cool house in an inner suburb. Everything seemed to be on the up-and-up. I was truly happy for him, but this new life of his was pushing me further and further into the background and fuck, it hurt.

I didn't have a computer or internet access back then, loads of people didn't. Even if I had known how to use email, it would have meant driving to an internet café in the city, which seemed silly. Instead, I wrote Dominic letters, pouring my heart out to him, telling him how much I missed him. Occasionally, he would write back—a brief, scrawled note—until one day, even they stopped.

After many months of silence, I tried to call. First, I dialled Dominic's mobile. I wasn't that surprised when it came up as disconnected. Then I gave the landline a go. That was disconnected, too. I began to feel sick. They'd moved and he hadn't even told me. I was fucking gutted, but through my tears I clung to one last hope. I sat down and wrote him the nicest letter I could, praying that they were having their mail forwarded.

The day that letter came back to me, marked 'Return to Sender,' I knew we'd come to the end of the road.

As far as Dominic was concerned, I was dead to him.

III

Part Three - NOW

Sydney, Australia

Chapter Six

His face goes white as a sheet. "Jesus… *Ryan?*"

I drop my bag on the floor, rushing forward and pulling him into my arms. "Oh, God, Dominic." Anger and hurt are decades in the past. The only feeling coursing through my veins right now is indescribable relief. I clutch the back of his head, our faces aligned side-by-side, my other arm wrapped tight around his back. The warmth of his body, the strong, masculine scent of his day-long exertion, the feel of his arms as they clasp tightly around my thorax, the urgency of his hands as they dig into my shoulder blades—I'm forced to stifle the cries that threaten to break forth. "I thought I'd never see you again." My voice is a turbulent whisper.

I can feel Dominic pressing his nose against me, breathing deeply, reacquainting himself with an aroma he may have stored somewhere in the furthest recesses of his memory. He doesn't seem to mind that I've just spent a hard day at work in summer heat. In fact, I feel him grabbing me even harder; I hear the faintest of growls rumble deep within his chest. Pulling back out, he places his hands on my upper arms, surveying the man in front of him. "Christ, you're built like a tank, now, Ryan. You've gone from a solid bugger of a teen to a sexy big bear."

"Are you referring to my gut?" I'm still trembling from the shock, but I give him my most good-natured smile.

"No! I'm referring to these guns." He strokes up and down my deltoids and biceps. "And these *huge* pecs!" He slides his hands inwards and kneads each chesty bulge. My scalp tingles. It's bizarre having him touch me like this again. Intense. Cock-stiffeningly wonderful.

"Um, they're not *all* muscle. I'm a porker, mate."

Dominic growls, giving my pecs a squeeze. "Well, I have a thing for muscly fatties."

A defiant chortle instantly blasts from my throat. "We're onto the insults already?"

Dominic's evil smirk is charming as fuck. The past is rushing back to me at breakneck speed. "I'd never insult you, mate. I love what I love, and I don't apologise."

Those words are loaded. But they evoke so many pleasant feelings; things I lost long ago.

He moves his hands down from my chest and runs them over my rounded belly. "And this big tummy's so fuckin' *woofy*."

OK, so he's convinced me now. I'm starting to blush. His flattering appraisal comes hot on the heels of my initial shock and it feels otherworldly, like one of those ecstatic dreams you get once in a blue moon. "I'm a tradie. Any burliness I have is thanks to the hard labour of my blue-collar job. Any padding is thanks to beer and pizza."

"Well, at least you get some decent exercise. I certainly don't do any."

"Yeah, but you're a skinny bastard, Dominic. You'll never put on weight."

He shakes his head with a small chuckle. "Nah, mate. I have a dad bod now."

"Bullshit."

"I do! Look at it!" His well-groomed black beard splits into a wide, white-toothed grin, and he quickly undoes the last few buttons on his shirt, pulling it open to display a slim torso covered in a black carpet even more dense than mine. "See?"

"Yeah. Fuckin' skinny, just like I said."

Dominic grabs my hands, pushing them against his waist. "Look at this! *Dad bod.*"

"What? These tiny little love handles? They're fuckin' adorable." The scant layer of body fat over Dominic's trim waist makes him all the more appealing. I can't help myself. I rub my hands up and down, roaming them all over the thick black fur on his chest and stomach. My heart is thumping in my ribcage, but I match his grin with one of my own. "You're perfect. *Minha lontra peluda.*" *My hairy otter.*

"Mmmm, Your Portuguese is very sexy."

"It's all courtesy of trawling Brazilian porn sites, mate." My dick flexes in my tight shorts. Dominic's gaze flicks down my body at the same time I remember my fetish for going commando. My eyes move south in the same direction as his. We both survey the outline of my dick, pointing downwards and to the left, leaving a grotesquely visible bulge.

"You should put that on Instagram, you'd get a ton of followers," he chirps, meeting my gaze with one eyebrow raised. "And no, I'm not perfect. You should see my arse."

Of course, I can't, since we're facing each other, but just the mention of his posterior has me wishing I could turn him round and whip his duds down. "I'm sure your backside is as beautiful as ever, mate."

"Ha! I have no arse," he scoffs. "See for yourself." And with that, he does a 180 and presents me with a little bum so finger lickin' good it makes me drool.

I have no idea what to say. I'm agape. "It's stunning, Dominic," I blurt.

"No. I have *no arse.* Go on, cop a feel," he calls over his shoulder.

Fuck me! He's given me the green light. I can hardly believe my luck. I've forgotten why I'm actually here and I don't care. I slide my hands over the small buttocks. I don't even bother to stifle the moan that rattles up from my chest.

"See what I mean, mate?"

I laugh out loud. "It's a perfect little otter arse." My palms traverse the surface of his thin microfibre slacks. I can't resist digging my fingers in, massaging the squishy cheeks and pulling them apart as I go. Before I can restrain myself, my thumbs have moved inside his arse crack. Up and down his cleft I rub them till I find his hole. Possessed by an unstoppable urge, I press against the tight pucker, rubbing just inside the edge of his sphincter.

"Oh, God," Dominic sighs. "I've missed this more than you could ever know."

I'm not quite sure of the scope of his statement, but right now I don't care to analyse it. "It's purely selfish, Dominic. I'm trying to get as much of your scent on your undies as I can, then I'm gonna steal them when you're not looking."

I can't believe I just said that. Thundering back to reality, I remove my hands from the equation, dangling them awkwardly by my sides.

Dominic swivels back to face me, cocky grin firmly in place. "I'm thrilled you enjoy my body so much, Ryan."

"I love it, and I never want to hear you say anything bad about it again." *Fuck.* The words are just slipping right out of my mouth. I catch Dominic's eye and my face begins to burn.

"But you said I was a fuckin' scrawny bastard one minute ago," Dominic shoots back, the deep espresso of his eyes twinkling as the light dances over them.

I may be embarrassed, but my mouth still has a mind of its own. "Well… maybe I like wrapping my big arms round a warm, skinny fella."

"Oh, mate," he says quietly. His brow creases and he holds out his arms. "Come here." I sink into him again, pulling him tight against me, purring as I savour the heat of his flesh once more. A potent surge of energy floods my body. I feel like a big brute as I cover this lithe, furry stud in protective manliness. He's absolutely divine. And he smells *so good*. That pungent, masculine aroma evokes memories so strong it rattles me to the core. My scalp comes alive with a rush of tingles that it sends straight down my spine, right into my arse, making my anus clench with delight. Dominic's breath caresses my neck. I can feel myself evanescing.

Just as I start to move away, fearing I've gone too far, Dominic draws me even closer. "Please, gimme a bit longer," he whispers in my ear. So I stay there with him, revelling in the warmth, the security, the sheer joy of our reunion. I haven't felt like this in so long I've forgotten how powerful a hug can be.

"OK. We'd better stop now," he says at last, pulling away. He grabs his crotch, pushing his penis into a new position. "Sorry, as you can see it's making things a little, um… hard."

I laugh politely, but what I really want is to free that big long dick from its confinement. My own cock will have saturated my shorts by now; I've felt every gush of precome pulsing through it since the second Dominic and I first touched. I straighten my back, vigorously shaking my head, giving it a firm reminder that this visit is meant to be a professional one. But, *fuck me…* the lines are blurred beyond recognition.

Dominic smiles fondly, taking in the whole sight of me once more. I desperately need this to go on longer, but we both seem to realise that it's time. "Come through," he says, as he turns to lead the way. "I'll give you the grand tour."

I grab my bag and follow him down the hall to the lounge area, which has polished dark wood floors and matching picture rails. The decorative plaster ceilings are in pristine condition. Dominic notices me looking around at the distinct lack of furniture. "This was an investment property, but since my tenants moved out I've started spending weekends here," he says. "During the week I live down in Cronulla with the wife and kid."

Reality hits me like a ton of bricks and an alarm blares inside my head. I'd just *assumed* he was… I mean, Marisa told me this place was a bachelor pad. I do remember vague mentions of Dominic getting married and having a son *years* ago, but other than that, Mum and Nathan rarely mentioned him during our sparse phone calls.

And what the fuck was that groping session we just had all about?

Seeing my uncensored reaction, Dominic chuckles and pats my arm. "Poor choice of words. Anna and I separated a year ago when I finally came out and told her I was gay. We got along fine after the split, so I wasn't in a rush to leave. Oscar's only eight and I've kind of been reluctant to go for his sake."

Gay? As I process this three-sentence rundown of Dominic's adult life, I spot the huge window and beautiful leadlight-panelled door at the end of the lounge room. It's through this that Dominic leads me out to the large, curved balcony. I can see the brilliant blue of the ocean here and there, in between the rooftops of other buildings. "I'll be moving in here full-time once I've finished renovating, though." He grins as he points to a big wooden hot tub in the corner. "See, I've already had my spa put in."

Leading me back through the living room, and down the hall, he ushers me into a bedroom with a queen-sized plush bed, gorgeous vintage dark wooden side tables and the same picture rails as the lounge.

"Gotta have some mod cons, eh?" Dominic says, noticing me admiring a huge TV mounted on the wall opposite the bed. It isn't the TV that pleases me, *per se*. It's the fleeting image of curling up naked in that bed with Dominic, spending a cosy Saturday night watching movies.

Get a hold of yourself, Ryan.

The bathroom is next, a perfect time capsule featuring period chequered floors, a claw-foot bath and one of those grand old toilets with a high-level cistern. "You know, Dominic," I say, inspecting the ornate chain flush, "there's nothing quite so underrated as having a good shit on a nice, comfy old dunny." I pick up the copy of *The Sydney Morning Herald* sitting on an antique table next to the toilet, crossword half-completed. "But it looks like I'm preaching to the choir, eh?"

The charming blush that spreads across Dominic's olive complexion is something I can't remember ever seeing. "You caught me out, there."

I wander back into the hall, Dominic trailing behind me. "So, this is a one-bedroom place?"

"Yeah. Swingin' digs for the unmarried Roaring Twenties fella. Though there's a small sunroom." He leads me towards a door off the side of the lounge room, opening it to reveal an enclosed balcony. "This is my little study. I'm gonna have to get a foldaway bed for Oscar when he comes to stay. It'll be a squeeze in here, but better than him having to sleep out in the lounge room."

"What a beautiful jarrah desk," I muse, running my hand over the sleek surface of his grand-looking workstation.

"It is, isn't it? I had it shipped over from Perth." That's hardly surprising, given jarrah only grows in the southern part of Western Australia. I notice the ugly metal filing cabinet plonked alongside the desk. It sticks out like dog's balls next to all that resplendent timber. Dominic pats me on the shoulder. "Anyway, come back through and I'll show you the kitchen."

Once I see it, the reason for my visit becomes clear. The whole thing is an awful nineties monstrosity, a cookie-cutter nightmare of apricot laminate completely unworthy of such an elegant apartment. "Jesus, how the hell did they ever get away with installing this?"

"I know," says Dominic. "It was fine when I was renting the place out, but I want it redone in original Art Deco style."

I spin around the modest room, mentally sizing it up. "You realise it's a bespoke job, don't you? All those curved counters and cupboards, they'll be handmade. So it ain't gonna be cheap."

Dominic flashes me his best cocky grin. "Yeah, but I'm a lawyer. And not the interesting kind you see on TV. A boring corporate one who gets paid the big bucks."

He's standing so close to me now. If I lean forward just the tiniest bit, I'll be able to taste those lips. Before I'm tempted any further, I turn and take another look around. "Well, it'll certainly help the resale value when it's done. Do you cook much?"

Dominic looks at me with a dour expression. "Gee. He's a funny man, isn't he? I do a mean barbecue, but that's the extent of it."

I can't help but smirk. He's such a *man*, but, *fuck me*, it makes him even hotter. "Well, seeing as you're not living here, I can rip the whole debacle out first, then get the designer through. It's not a huge space, but she'll probably still need a couple of weeks. Then it'll take a few more to get it all built and installed." I dig into the flap of my bag. "Let me grab my stuff and I'll take some measurements."

"Nah, Ryan. Come on, join me for a beer, first. Please? There's so much I wanna ask you." He's already fetching two Coronas from the fridge. Popping the tops, he hands me one without waiting for a response. He slaps the ugly peach countertop. "Dump your bag here and follow me." As I trail behind him out to the balcony, I fix my eyes on that hot little bum, watching the square buttocks flex with each step, a sexy dance he doesn't even know he's performing. Once we've settled our arses into a couple of upmarket outdoor chairs, he holds up his beer to click with mine.

We sit in silence for a few moments. Dominic fiddles with his bottle. After our easy banter before, he doesn't seem to know quite what to say. I don't either, frankly. There are so many fucking elephants out here I can hardly breathe. He takes a huge swig of his beer and clears his throat. "So, Sydney, eh? How's it been working out for you?"

Well, it's a start, at least. "Alright. Work's fine. Great team. Bought a house in Newtown that I'll do up one of these days."

Dominic chuckles. "Yeah, they say that doctors always have the sickest kids. I guess builders spend so much time working on other people's places, they don't ever get around to fixing their own."

How true that is.

I don't know where to go from here. Things are bugging me now and I don't want to open a can of worms. Anything I say is going to drag up shit I'm not sure I want to deal with. *Fuck it.* "I heard you moved here a couple of years ago." *Yes, a couple of years in the same damn city as me.*

Dominic's staring into the distance. Uneasiness hangs thick in the air. "Yeah, Anna got a lecturing job down at Wollongong Uni and wanted to move back here to be near her family. So, we packed everything up and flew four thousand k's over here. Head hunters found me a job, no worries. I work up in the city centre, so we bought an apartment at the mid-way point in Cronulla. Made the daily commute the same for both of us."

Dominic's dodging the topic and I'm kind of relieved. I'm not surprised I never bumped into him, living and working in a completely different part of this sprawling city. That, and my insular existence. Regardless, it still kills me that he never once tried to make contact when he was living so close.

"Dad's over here in Sydney now, too. He wasn't coping anymore." Dominic glances at me. "Dementia. I got him into a nice nursing home in Sutherland down near us. He's happy as a pig in shit there, but he's regressing. He keeps lapsing back into speaking Portuguese all the time."

"Oh. I didn't know anything about that."

Dominic seems to be reading my thoughts. Adopting a brighter tone, he tries to steer the conversation in a new direction. "I heard Nathan turned out to be a bit of a hit with the ladies. Nice kid, but I always thought you were the better-looking brother." An evil glint forms in Dominic's eye. "Maybe he's hung like a horse."

Once again, I'm glad for the reprieve. I force a laugh. "Ha! No. He's no bigger than me in that department."

"How do you know what his boner looks like? Don't tell me you fucked that brother, too!"

My laugh turns into a guffaw and I almost choke on my beer. "Fuck off! As if!" I literally shudder at the thought. "If you *really* wanna know, I walked in on Nathan naked and wanking to porn in the lounge room when he was about seventeen. He covered his crotch with his hand and he was all, 'What the fuck are you doing here?' and I was like, 'Don't worry, mate, I wank all the time,' and he was like, 'Fuck, man, I don't need to know that,' and I was like, 'Dude, I can still see your knob. We have no secrets now.'"

I watch as Dominic cackles away, wiping the tears from his eyes. That joyous laugh. *God, I remember it like it was yesterday. How I've missed it.* He eventually calms down, letting out a long sigh. "How's he and his family going over in Adelaide?"

"Yeah, um, they're good. I phone them sometimes. Probably a bit more often since last summer. You know..." My voice dies off. We're moving into dangerous territory.

Dominic shifts in his chair, turning to face me. The sadness in his eyes cuts right through me. I'd hug him, if the emotional gap between us right now wasn't so wide. "I'm sorry I didn't make it to the funeral back then, mate. I was stuck overseas for work and I couldn't get back into the country with all the Covid restrictions."

I'm not going to expand on what he's saying. I'm liable to blurt out something I'll regret. Things seem so tenuous. I'm not sure I even have the perspective to voice what I need to, anyway. "Yeah, it was sad losing mum. But she was much closer to Nathan. I hadn't had much contact with her for years." I drain my bottle and reach into my pocket for my leather tobacco pouch. "You mind?"

Dominic smiles. "Not at all. So long as you roll me one." Once I've skilfully completed two pristine durries, I hand one to Dominic and flick my Zippo to light it for him. He drags tentatively, blowing plumes of smoke out as I light my own. "Fuck, I haven't had one of these in years. Anna and I quit when she got pregnant with Oscar."

"Well, I never quit. I'm a tradie. It's practically compulsory to have a fag dangling out the corner of ya mouth, mate." I take another couple of deep drags, calming my nerves, satisfying the addiction that's been niggling at the back of my mind for the last couple of hours.

"I can't believe how fast mum went, Ryan. I know pancreatic cancer's a bitch, but I thought she'd have at least a few months left."

"Yeah, so did I. They said they could operate because it was in the neck of her pancreas. She didn't survive the whipple surgery very long, though. The hospital called me to say she'd really gone downhill. I had to fly over to Adelaide. It's the one and only time I've ever been on a plane, and it'll be the last."

"Really? You've never flown *anywhere*?"

"No. No fuckin' way. Not after what happened to my dad. Before my flight, I went to my GP and begged him for some Xanax. I took two of them and it was still a nightmare. I was freaked out the whole fuckin' journey. I thought I was gonna have a heart attack, especially when we hit some turbulence."

"You know, flying's way safer than driving, Ryan."

Bless him. His heart's in the right place. But he may as well tell me that smoking's bad for me, for all the help it's doing. "Thanks, but you can save your breath there, mate. I didn't even fly back from Adelaide after she died, I took the train. There was no fucking chance of getting me back on a plane. Ever." I gaze at Dominic for a moment, wondering if I should venture into yet another delicate topic. Taking a big breath, I bite the bullet. "You know, mum knew."

"Knew what?"

"About us. Just before she died, she told me she could see what was going on between you and me. She knew we were in love. She said of all people, she understood that love sprung up in the most unexpected places and she'd never forgiven herself for tearing the two of us apart." Long-buried feelings are bubbling to the surface with rapid intensity. My chest tightens. "I'd basically shut her out for decades. I wish I'd made more of an effort. But by then it was all too fuckin' late."

Dominic's brow is now twisted in pain. I can see his eyes brimming over. It's a stab in the heart, but a cruel surge rips through me and I spew it all out. "You know, Dominic, I was terrified of seeing you up there at the funeral. I don't know if I was relieved or disappointed when you didn't show." I'm beginning to tremble. With rage, with grief, I don't fucking know. "Two fuckin' years, mate. *Two fuckin' years* you've been just down the road and you never once reached out to me?"

I've kicked him hard enough. Dominic buries his face in his hands and begins to cry. "I'm sorry, mate, I'm so fuckin' sorry." I can see him trying to suppress it and it's making his shoulders shake violently. I can't bear to see him in this kind of pain. Fuck my anger, fuck my resentment, fuck me and my big fucking mouth. Why the hell didn't I keep it shut?

Before I know it, I've chucked my smoke aside and dropped to my knees in front of him, holding him as fucking tight as I can. "Please, mate," he sobs. "Please. You've gotta understand why I stayed away."

I move one hand up, stroking the back of his hair, doing my best to try and calm him. He's so distraught, the scope of his anguish seems to go way beyond our altercation. It hurts so fucking bad knowing I was the who tipped him over the edge. "It's OK, Dominic. I know. I didn't mean to be such a cunt. Really."

Dominic makes a supreme effort to halt his emotional outpouring, drawing a few wobbly breaths. Sliding his hands around my body, he lifts his head, pressing his cheek against mine. The intimacy is overpowering. I feel like we're joined together in the most significant way possible. His beard is soft against the side of my face. His potent scent infiltrates my consciousness. I'm not even fully aware of it, but somehow I'm suddenly kissing his neck, his cheek. He moans softly, moving his face around, his lips brushing against mine.

We're jolted out of our embrace by the rude sound of the intercom buzzing. Dominic jerks his head back and glances at his watch. "Shit. Is that the time?" He jumps up, wiping his eyes, then scurries inside. I follow him with my gaze as he strides through the lounge room, listening to his footsteps grow confident as they make their way down the corridor. "Hey… just getting changed. I'll leave the door open," I hear him say in a chirpy tone.

I rise to my feet, sure that this is my cue to leave. I'll do the measurements another day. That is, if Dominic actually wants me to after all that's just happened.

"I'm so sorry," says Dominic, coming back into the lounge room moments later as I enter from the balcony. "I've gotta go out to dinner." He's now topless, wearing a sexy pair of tight-fitting jeans. He looks like one of those thin, hairy seventies male models, save for the fact his pants aren't flared at the ankles. Handing me my bag, he shoots me an apologetic smile. "You didn't even get to do what you came here for."

"Not to worry. After all these years, I think we earned ourselves a catch-up." *Catch-up. Yeah, Good one, Ryan, you dickhead.* I do my level best to smile. "Tell you what, if you're still interested, I can drop by tomorrow to get it all measured. I promise I won't show up too early."

Dominic looks incredulous. Hurt, even. "Still interested? Jesus, Ryan." He closes the short distance between us, drawing me into another tight hug. "Mate, you're not getting away from me now."

With a pat on the back, he breaks our brief embrace and looks at me. I can see the redness in his eyes, the residual pain. What I wouldn't give to make it go away. I gaze back at him fondly, admiring his handsome face, the lines around his eyes from half a lifetime of smiles. "Well, I'll take any excuse to see you again, Dominic."

That's perfect, Ryan. Hit and run. Make your escape now and let him stew on that thought.

It's not necessary, though. Our moment is cut short by the arrival of a tall man in a tight button-up shirt that shows off his sculpted muscles. He's on the phone, sniping away to some hapless person on the other end of the line. For such a masculine-looking fellow I'm surprised to hear handbags falling out of his mouth as he speaks.

He loiters in the doorway to the lounge room, winding up his bitch session. Sliding his phone into his pocket, he sashays up to Dominic and plants a long smooch right on his lips. "Hey, baby," he purrs. He draws his head back in mild distaste. "You've been crying. And you've been *smoking.*"

Dominic glances my way, a picture of embarrassment.

Oh, Jesus. You've got to be kidding me. A fucking boyfriend?

My fantasy bubble bursts immediately. The fleeting visions of me, Dominic and his little son playing happy families goes right down that antique toilet of his, chain flush and all.

You stupid git, Ryan.

"Hey, Peter, I want you to meet Ryan," says Dominic, a little too brightly. "Can you believe I haven't seen him in more than twenty years? He's gonna be doing my kitchen."

I'm about to extend my hand, but all I get from Peter is a glance down at my scruffy tradie clothes and a dismissive grunt before he struts off to sit down. "Are you ready to go, Dominic?" he snaps.

"I'll walk you to the door, Ryan," says Dominic, ignoring Peter.

"Nah, it's fine, mate." I give him a friendly pat on the shoulder and my best we're-just-buddies smile. "I'll see you tomorrow, eh?" I'll honour my promise. But no more hugs, no more flirting. No more touching those toothsome, prime-beef little buttocks. *Just mates.*

What a crying fuckin' shame.

When I reach my ute, I fish inside my bag for my keys. My hand lands on some kind of foreign article. It's fabric, and I pull it out to discover a small black pair of briefs. Holding them to my nose, I breathe in deeply. The unmistakable scent of that Brazilian stud storms through my sinuses. Suddenly, my world seems so much better.

Chapter Seven

The next morning I fluff around like a teenage girl trying to decide what to wear. In the end, I settle on a white Levis-logo t-shirt that shows off my bearish contours and a pair of Hard Yakka dark denim work shorts. They're short shorts indeed. Very eighties, highly unfashionable outside a worksite, but they make my big bear arse and tree-trunk legs look hot as fuck. If I can't have Dominic, at least I can taunt him with my assets.

He greets me at his front door with an open smile and a warm hug. It's so fucking hard to stop myself from kissing him, holding him for way too long, sinking deep into his embrace. "Jesus, Ryan," he says, staring down at my lower half. "Are you wearing those shorts to torture me?"

Thank you. That was exactly the reception I was hoping for.

"I had to pay you back after that little gift you left in my bag." I offer him a wry grin as he looks back up at me with raised eyebrows.

"Did you enjoy it?"

"Twice, Dominic."

With a lusty growl, he pats me on the shoulder, turns on his heel and leads me down the hall to the kitchen. He loiters in there with me, seemingly reluctant to leave. I'm pretty sure he wants to have an intimate chat, but I can see Peter through the servery window, sitting back on the lounge with his shirt off reading the paper. His body is lean and highly-toned from countless hours in the gym, and his torso is waxed within an inch of its life. *Hmm.* Dominic clearly liked my burly, hairy bearishness, so I guess he must have eclectic taste in men.

Dominic follows my eyes out the servery window to his paramour. "I guess I'll leave you to it, then," he says, disappointment written all over his face. I don't like disappointing him. I'm trying to think of a way to alleviate this when he cuts through my train of thought. "Maybe you'll join me for a drink out on the balcony when you're finished?"

I'm relieved we've found a compromise. I need this contact with him. "Sure. I'd love to." I flash him my most sincere smile, then he takes off so I can get to work measuring, photographing and making notes. I know more than enough about Art Deco kitchens to have a fair idea of what the designer might recommend. And seeing as funds aren't an issue for Dominic, I'll be able to source some expensive retro appliances which will complement the period cabinetry. There's no way I'm going to slog my guts out hand-making every benchtop and cupboard, then ruin the whole aesthetic with a horrible modern stainless steel fridge and oven. Fuck that for a joke.

The next I see of Dominic, he's sauntered into the kitchen wearing the tiniest little Bobo Bear Speedo.

You bloody little tart. Who's the torturer now?

His sexy, slim body is even more tasty than I could have imagined now he's all but naked. It's like the lissome slenderness of youth never left him, but the fur continued to spread like wildfire. The generous carpet of luscious black hair he'd shown me yesterday extends in a fine pattern over his shoulder blades, then trails sparsely down his back. My mouth is literally watering as I take it all in. And his arse! Oh, God—his *arse*. It's like two little lamb rump roasts inside those tight Lycra togs. Just the thought of what I could do with it has me salivating.

He catches me staring and smiles. I don't fucking care enough to feel embarrassed. He's beautiful and I'll look as long as I bloody well want. None of that my-eyes-are-up-here bullshit. *Yeah, mate. But your cock and balls and arse are down there and I really think they deserve my attention, too, don't you?*

"Can I get you a drink, Ryan?" he asks, opening the bar fridge and bending right over, making sure his arse cheeks spread open in the most gratuitous way possible. If only that fabric wasn't obscuring the view.

Yeah, I'll take whatever is furthest back on the bottom shelf. "Sure, thanks mate. Maybe just a Coke or something, though. Probably not quite beer o'clock yet."

Seems like I've made the right choice when he bends over even lower, emerging with a red can. The good kind; not the shit with no sugar. "There you go. I'm off for a quick dip in the spa." He eyes me up and down as he leaves. "Come out and join me if you like."

I smile to myself once he's taken off.

Fuck, Ryan. No more flirting, remember? You're the one who's gonna get hurt, not him.

Yeah, but it's so fun and he's so fucking gorgeous.

No! Just... fuckin' no, OK?

It doesn't take me long to finish what I'm doing once I get stuck into it. And it doesn't take long for Dominic to come swanning back into the kitchen, towel in hand. Once again, he bends right over, rustling round in the fridge, before standing back up, plopping two Coronas on the counter and slicing a lemon up to stuff in the bottlenecks. I can't help noticing how the Bobo Bear bathers are now wedged right up in his little arse crack. Fuck, I need to stop gawking, but he's making this so difficult for me.

"It's after twelve now, Ryan. Time for a beer outside." He plants one of the bottles in my hands. "And I'm not taking no for an answer."

I trail behind him back out through the lounge room, keeping my eyes up, studiously avoiding the sexy arse that's trying to talk to me. I can see Peter's gaze following me as I pass by, his face all but scowling. I shoot him a broad smile and nod slightly, which I'm sure pisses him off even more.

The weather is blisteringly hot outside. "Take off your shirt, Ryan." It's not an invitation, it's a cheeky order, as illustrated by Dominic's evil little grin. Who am I to argue? That Levi's tee is off in a jiffy.

"So… Oscar must miss having his dad around on weekends, eh?" I say as we sit down in the sun chairs.

"Nah. Anna's folks are in Wollongong and she usually takes him down there to spend time with them. He's too busy having fun with his grandparents and cousins. You know what those Italians are like—big families, nonna fussing over everyone." We both sit quietly for a while, enjoying the wafting sea breezes that give us respite from the fierce sun. "You'd love Oscar, he's such a great kid. I know every parent says that, but he's quiet and low-maintenance. A lot like his mother." He glances over at me. "A bit like you, too, for that matter. I can't wait for you to meet him."

My heart jumps at the prospect of such a significant future event. But I have to remind myself that Dominic's invitation is a friendly one. That's all I'm going to let it be. "I'd really love that, Dominic."

We're rudely interrupted by the appearance of Peter in a tiny pair of trunks. He fairly prances out, a show pony flaunting his wares—his buff, waxed, coconut-oil-slicked wares—in an effort to show up the big, hairy kodiak who dares to talk to his man. He bypasses me and leans into Dominic, kissing him on the lips. "You gonna jump in with me, baby?" he simpers.

Dominic seems to lack enthusiasm as he stands and turns to me. "You really should join us, Ryan. It's a three-seater." His smile is so hopeful, so charming, it breaks my heart to turn him down. But it isn't a good idea.

"Thanks, mate. I'd love to, but can I take a raincheck for today? I really should get going." I down the last of my beer and hop to my feet, giving Dominic a bro-hug. I'm hoping that will let me off the hook and he won't feel tempted to show me out. I need to escape fast before I do something I'll regret. "I'll be in touch early in the week and send you some more design ideas. Feel free to shoot me any you have, too."

With that, I grab my discarded t-shirt and prepare to beat a hasty retreat. I can see Dominic is disheartened by my departure and it upsets me more than I want to admit. But *he's* the one with a boyfriend. *That awful boyfriend.*

* * *

I drop in again the following Friday evening. I could have just emailed Dominic all the stuff I wanted to show him, but I convince myself it's better to do it in person. Fuck, who am I kidding. I'd make up any excuse to be around him. I've been pining all week, constantly thinking about him, picturing the disappointment on his face at my last visit and dreaming up scenarios in which I'd been able to stay and make him happy.

One other pretext for my visit is to help him move stuff out to the living room, seeing as I'll be starting to dismantle the kitchen tomorrow. Yes, that's right, I've wangled it so I'll be working there on Saturday while he's around. Fucking sue me, OK?

After we've lugged the fridge out, Dominic excuses himself to shower and change—presumably another date with the boyfriend. Right on cue, the intercom sounds. "Ryan, can you get that, mate? It'll be Peter," Dominic's calling through the open bathroom door, shower running in the background. I do as I'm told, but I just press the button and don't say anything. For a moment, I consider answering it sounding all breathless and mid-coital. But I behave myself.

After opening the front door a crack, I return to the kitchen, grabbing the microwave and hauling it out to the lounge room to plonk on the table we've set up as a makeshift cooking space. I may as well help as much as possible while I'm here.

Peter slinks in behind me without a word. I don't see him, I can just smell the overpowering aftershave he's doused himself in. I return to the kitchen, packing things into boxes. Some minutes later, I hear a queeny, nasal voice.

"First you're here last weekend, now this one. Don't you have a home to go to?" *Oh. So now he speaks.* His snipey tone makes me bristle.

I rise up from the cupboard I'm clearing out and turn to face him. There he is, lording it over me in his designer clothes, while I stand there in my scuzzy tradie gear. "Apparently not." Screw him, he doesn't deserve my politeness.

"Going a bit above and beyond the call of duty for Dominic, aren't you?" And there it is. He may as well just come out and accuse me of trying to steal his man.

"He's my brother and I love him dearly. Nothing is too good for Dominic as far as I'm concerned."

Peter's face is like thunder. It's hard not to smirk.

Go fuck yourself, you bitchy queen. Don't cock your leg and piss on me.

A split second later, Dominic comes in, doing up the cuffs on a white shirt with beautiful, intricate detail all over it.

"I'm going to the little boy's room," says Peter. "Then maybe you'll be ready to leave, babe?"

He doesn't wait for a reply, just stalks off down the hall. Dominic's eyes follow him. The second Peter is at a safe distance, Dominic turns and grabs me, drawing me into an intense hug. Long past the time he should be letting go, he's still clutching me tight, nuzzling me, breathing in deep against me, making no bones about the fact he's sniffing my scent. We can hear the gushing sound of Peter pissing directly into the toilet water. As soon as the flush sounds, Dominic plants a long kiss against my neck. "I love you, too, Ryan," he whispers.

All the way home I'm floating on a cloud. Yeah, I know. He loves me as a mate. He loves me as a brother. But maybe there's more to it. There's definitely no way Dominic can be anywhere near in love with that arrogant wanker. I'll just stick around, treat Dominic like a friend and wait for their inevitable split. I don't need to be the scarlet woman, Peter is digging his own grave.

Chapter Eight

The next morning I make sure to show up at a reasonable hour. I'm pleased to see that the rubbish skip has been delivered on time and I know I'll have to get cracking if I'm gonna fill it. Dominic is on the phone as he opens the door. He gives me a smile and a quick hug, before disappearing back down into his little sunroom study.

I make a start straight away, emptying everything out of the kitchen and dismantling what I can. Up and down I carry armloads of stuff to the skip, working up a sweat in the hot summer weather. At one stage, Dominic sticks his head in the doorway and lets me know he's going out to run some errands.

Now that I know he won't be disturbed, it's time for the fun stuff—I get to smash the shit out of that ugly nineties fit-out. It's tough-going, swinging that sledgehammer. Hard slog in the stifling heat. I've been stupid enough to wear a nylon Ford racing polo, because it shows off my shoulders and pecs and belly. Predictably, said polo is now saturated with sweat. Peeling it off, I revel in the fresh breeze that wafts through the open kitchen window.

I still need to cool down a bit more, though, so I venture into the bathroom and splash my face and upper body with water. Standing back, I admire myself in the mirror. I'm now wearing nothing but my work boots and the tiniest pair of King Gee short shorts I own. And

I own a *lot*. They're my trademark, OK? Plus, I look fucking hot in them. Prime bear candy. I want to drive Dominic to distraction.

As I stroke my nipples and feel my penis hardening, my focus hones in on the mirror itself. I notice it's a concealed cabinet. Of course I'm going to snoop inside. As soon as I open the door, I spot it—the telltale bottle of PrEP. *Oh, God.* Instantly, the fantasies become more potent. Dominic and I flipping back and forth, sinking our bare cocks into each other's warm, steamy…

Fuck, Ryan. No. You will not fuck an attached man behind their partner's back, no matter how much of a prick the partner is.

My cock is now standing to full attention, straining in my little shorts.

Maybe I could have a quick wank? That'll solve the problem.

No! What if Dominic comes back? He'll hear you, dickhead. Or he'll think you're taking a massive dump in here and that's just as bad.

Cold water. That'll make it go back down. I undo my fly and my penis springs out. Pointing it over the edge of the basin, I pull my foreskin back and splash myself several times with frigid water from the tap. But it's not long before my hand clasps around my knob and begins to rub.

Jesus, fuck, Ryan!

Tucking myself back into my shorts, I try to shake my horny thoughts out of my head by returning to the kitchen to continue demolishing. It seems to do the trick. I'm making really good progress; I'm quite proud of myself. Amazing what you can achieve when you're this sexually frustrated.

At some stage, I hear the front door open. I assume Dominic has made his first stop the bedroom when he doesn't alert me to his presence. Just as I'm squatting down removing the bottom shelf under the sink, I hear a wolf whistle. "Gee, Ryan, when did you become so goddamn hairy?"

"I always was." I'm on a roll with this shelf. I've nearly loosened it, so I don't stand up to face Dominic.

"Sure, but not like this."

"I had my shirt off last weekend, remember?" I say.

"Yeah, I know you did, but I only saw the front of you. Now I can see you're covered on both sides."

"Well, I don't wax, I don't shave, I don't clipper. I hate that."

Dominic sniggers. "Yeah, I can see that from the thick forest down in your arse crack."

I stand bolt upright and turn around, my face aflame as I hike up my wayward shorts. "Sorry, didn't mean to give you an eyeful of workman's bum."

Dominic is perched in the doorway wearing another slutty little pair of budgie smugglers, this time lemon yellow and showing off his meaty bulge with aplomb. He takes a step forward, moving right in front of me. "Never, ever apologise about showing me something so incredibly hot." He eye-fucks me slowly, taking in my pecs, the swell of my belly, my tiny shorts, my thick, hairy legs. "Speaking of hot, you must be roasting. And I can see from your little display before that you've got no undies on, you harlot. So whip off those King Gees and come have a skinny dip in the spa with me."

I chuckle nervously. My cock is now well on the way back to stiffyville, but I have to nip this in the bud. "Um, mate… I'd love to, truly I would, but it's a bad idea. I couldn't promise I'd keep my hands to myself and I really don't want to be messing with someone else's boyfriend. It's just not my thing."

Dominic looks confused at first, then like he's swallowed paint stripper. "Who, Peter?" he scoffs. "He's not my boyfriend! He's just a fuckbuddy. And not even a good one." A palpable sense of relief floods my face and Dominic notices, giving me a warm smile. "I called it all off at dinner last night. There's no way I was gonna keep screwing him now you've come back into my life."

Into his life? Really? Sure, he's been flirting with me. It's a safe bet he wants to fuck. But there's more to it?

I gulp. "Does that mean you're actually interested in me?"

"Holy shit, Ryan! I haven't thought of anything else since you appeared on my doorstep last Friday! Peter knew something was up when I wouldn't fuck him that night. But how could I?" He searches my face for a moment. "And don't feel bad for Peter, OK? He's an arrogant arsehole."

"Well, you said it, not me." I can't help the smug grin that creeps over my face.

"And above all that, he's a dud root. I mean, sure—he's got a huge cock, but what fuckin' use is it to anyone? I may be a top, but my arse still needs a bit of attention. Oh *no*, he wouldn't ever go near it—not with his tongue, not even with a fuckin' finger. He just laid there with his legs in the air like I should be the one doing all the work. Can't stand total bottoms. They're so greedy and entitled."

I snarl at the mere mention of this. "Who in their right mind could resist your gorgeous arse?"

Dominic's eyebrow raises, highlighting the evil glint in his eye. "You don't have to resist at all, Ryan." He smirks at my obvious blush before remembering he was mid-rant. "Anyway, Peter told me he wouldn't even consider doing anything to my arse unless I manscaped and waxed. He couldn't stand my hairy bush and balls and arse crack. I told him to fuck off. I love my fur. I don't want some bikini line and boi-pussy. I'm a man, for fuck's sake. Far as I'm concerned, they can take me as I am or bugger off." Dominic's little tirade has sent me into fits of suppressed sniggers. His big white grin makes another appearance and he leans in a little closer to me.

My voice drops half an octave. "I always loved your hairy bush and balls and arse crack, *lontra*."

He moves in even closer, his furry torso now mingling with mine. The heat radiates between us, humidifying the microscopic gap separating my body from his. But something else is happening, too. I'm now completely surrounded by his natural masculine fragrance. That pungent, blissful aroma of a day spent in hot weather. Of a day that *Dominic* spent in hot weather. I start to tremble. "I can smell you, Dominic."

"Is that your way of telling me I need a shower?"

"NO!" I jump a little, rattled by the force of my reply. "I mean, no. It's like… it's like I'm fourteen all over again. Trying to sit really close to you on the couch while we played Nintendo so I could smell your scent. Breathing in deep as I squeezed past you in the kitchen or the hallway." I pause, wondering about my next admission. *Fuck it.* "Stealing your dirty underwear and wanking as I sniffed them deep and long and hard."

"Even back then, eh?" Dominic moves his face alongside mine, his beard grazing my cheek, and murmurs into my ear. "I had no idea you were such a kinky little shit." He bends down, plants his nose against one of my armpits and inhales across my chest to the other. "*You* smell so good, Ryan. Look what you've done to me." He leans back a little, grabbing his package and showing me the long, hard outline underneath his yellow lycra togs. "Now, are you gonna join me in the spa or what?"

"No, Dominic." I'm breathing heavily now. "I don't want you to wash any of this glorious manstink off you. I want to take you to bed and drown in it. I want to run my nose over every inch of you and sniff so hard I pass out."

"Jesus, you are one filthy cunt." He grabs my hand and tugs hard, pulling me down the hall to his bedroom like it's a dire emergency. And, fuck me, after twenty-plus years it fucking well is.

Dominic is easy to undress. One sharp tug of my hand on his bathers and his penis springs free, pointing high and proud like a knackwurst.

Oh, God, I remember that so well.

I could dive straight onto that juicy fuckstick, but Dominic is busy fiddling with the fly of my King Gees—wrenching the button undone, yanking the zip down and sending them to the floor with a flourish. Groaning at the sight of my schlong, he grasps it with one hand as he bends down and undoes the safety zip on my boots with the other. In order to expedite things, I fair stomp the fuckers off my feet and kick them aside, gathering Dominic in my arms and flinging the both of us onto his plush bed.

God, it's paradise sinking into the obscenely expensive mattress, wrapped around the gorgeous, slim body of the sexiest man alive. It's hot in the room, the only respite being the gentle sea breezes flowing periodically through the curtains, but I still relish the tactile warmth of Dominic's body pressed against mine. And Dominic can't get enough of me, either. His hands work me over as we grind our mouths and erections together, rubbing his palms up and down my back and over my arse. "Fuck, Ryan, this fur! God… you're like a fuckin' grizzly!" He rubs the globes of my big, burly buttocks, delving his fingers into the hairy crevice between them. "I can't believe how fucking wonderful you feel, mate. Jesus, I don't think I'm ever gonna stop touching you!"

"Then please don't," I say softly, my emotions overloaded by his unbridled enthusiasm, his unrestrained appreciation.

"God, how I've missed you, Ryan." The sheer relief at hearing him say this has me choked up. I never cry. But damn, I feel like it.

Fortunately, we're distracted when Dominic's phone starts ringing right then. "Ignore it," he says, pulling my mouth towards him again and latching on tight, his tongue barging inside to forage once more.

Whoever is calling is annoyingly persistent. Twice they ring and it goes through to voicemail. "Fuck 'em… they can… leave a… message," Dominic mutters between wet, full-lipped kisses. When the caller attempts a third time, he breaks our embrace and shoots me an apologetic look. "I'm so sorry, mate."

He turns onto his stomach, reaching right over to the bedside table to grab his phone. "I've gotta take this," he calls over his shoulder.

I'm only half-listening, because his arse is now on full display. I'm gobsmacked at how stunning it is. Fur explodes from his crack, spreading like wildfire across each little buttock. The skin on these hirsute buns is considerably lighter than the rest of him; testament to many hours spent in the sun wearing his tarty little Speedos.

Suddenly, I find myself more ravenous than I've been in years. I grab one buttock in each hand, squishing my fingers into the flesh. I'm panting, breathless at their sheer beauty. I begin to plant small kisses over them, half an ear open on Dominic's conversation. It sounds like a family issue; Oscar's name is coming up often. I don't care, really—I'm having way too good a time to stop.

The faint, musky smell of Dominic's arse intensifies as I pull his buttocks open. I stifle a cry as the pheromones storm my olfactory receptors, screaming at my amygdala and releasing memories buried long, long ago. That scent. That special, heavenly Dominic scent. God, how I remember it now.

He relaxes his glutes and the cute little cheeks become malleable as I squeeze and massage them. Staring at the special place inside, I lose my breath as I'm finally reacquainted with his taut brown arsehole and its full black beard. And these days, that black beard is twice as substantial as I remember. Nestled in between his two adorable buns, it's a veritable love-garden. I lower my face, burying my nose in heaven. His potent manscent hits me for six. I'm high as a fucking kite, almost passing out with lust. Up and down I brush my snout, running it firmly over his puckered anus, moaning as I lick hard, savouring my first taste of it in twenty years.

Dominic reaches behind and softly taps me on the head, wiggling his little hole against my tongue at the same time. I get his message loud and clear: *I love it, but keep the fucking noise down!*

Fine. I'll limit my vocal appreciation to the heavy breathing I just can't seem to control.

But what I also can't control is the way my oral exploration is speeding up—licking the length of his succulent shallow cleft, sucking on his beautiful butthole, flicking my tongue against his tight ring, spearing it straight through to taste him deep inside. I go wild; salivating, swallowing, scoffing, eating his fine little arse like it's a gourmet banquet.

I'm just about to add my fingers into the mix when Dominic hangs up, groaning at the top of his voice. "You fucking sadist," he huffs. "I'm flat-out trying to be a good parent while I'm being given the most incredible rimjob of my entire life."

"I waited more than two decades for another taste of this heavenly arse, Dominic. You stuck it right in my face and you expected me to resist?"

He growls and turns over onto his back, plonking his sweaty scrotum against my face. I don't waste any time, licking every nook and cranny, running my tongue up the little ravines where his thighs meet his crotch. Dominic threads his fingers through my hair, grasping my scalp and giving constant little moans.

I lift my face up to find him grinning down at me. My attention suddenly zooms in on the long, rock-hard penis lying against his abdomen. I grab it and pull it upwards, giving it a squeeze. "And as for this cock… I've been in love with it since I was fourteen years old." I want to slide the whole thing in my mouth, to suck on it wildly, to feel it thicken and pulse against my tongue, to taste the rush of sapid sperm that would inevitably shoot down my throat and be swallowed with gratitude. My penis throbs against the bed with these thoughts, but I decide to draw out the pleasure of rediscovery a bit longer. Slowly, I roll back Dominic's foreskin, exposing his shiny maroon bell-end. I run the tip of my tongue along the underside of his penis and tickle it against his frenulum.

"Fuuuuck," Dominic whimpers. He raises his head again, looking at me quizzically, like something has just occurred to him. "Since you were fourteen? We never had sex till you were eighteen."

I've been busy teasing his knob with my tongue, giving it feather-light licks, savouring the salty taste, enjoying the piquant musk. But now I stop and look up at him. "You're forgetting stuff. Remember that time not long after you moved in with Joe? We were playing cricket in the park with your mates and it started to get dark, so they went home?"

A grin of recognition works its way across Dominic's handsome mug. "Oh, yeah. How could I forget that."

"I was busy packing up the kit and you came and stood right next to me. Next thing I knew, you'd lifted up the leg of your footy shorts, hoiked out this long, uncut dick and started pissing all over the grass. I was so fucking mesmerised I couldn't take my eyes off it the whole time, not till you'd shaken off the last drops and tucked your dick inside again."

Dominic sniggers at my recollection, scrunching his fingers in my hair, combing through the long, thick strands. "I knew you were staring at me. For some reason, I really wanted you to see my cock. I think it must have been an awakening, 'cause at that stage I'd never really let myself fantasise about other guys." He ponders a moment. "But that wasn't the only time, was it? We stood next to each other at urinals more than once. I remember, because I couldn't take my eyes off your long fuckin' foreskin. I'd never seen one like mine. Every time I saw guys' dicks when they pissed, they were either cut, or if they weren't, the end of their knob was poking out."

My face is on fire, turning scarlet at the thought of Dominic observing my private peeing habits so closely. Yet at the same time I'm shocked to discover he'd been that interested in me so many years before we'd had sex. "Trust me, I was just as fascinated with yours, mate." I squeeze Dominic's hard member in my fist. "You see, this is why I've had a watersports fetish ever since I was fourteen. All my early experiences with your dick involved pissing."

"Watersports? Damn Ryan, I love how fuckin' kinky you are."

Shit. How did I get so bloody comfortable that I'm revealing my deep, dark fantasies? "Um, it's a fetish in theory only. I haven't done it, but I wank to porn clips of it all the time."

"Well, maybe someday we can chug down half a slab of beer and turn that latent fetish of yours into a real one, eh?"

My dick flexes hard as I suddenly realise the true gravity of his suggestion. "Does this mean I get more dates with you in the future?"

Dominic grabs my shoulders, pulling on them. "Get the fuck up here." I shuffle up to face level and he wraps his arms around me. "What the hell do you reckon, eh?" He grunts as he kisses me hard, thrusting his tongue into my mouth and licking around my lips. Leaning back a bit, his eyes twinkle with an evil glee. "Mmmmm… you taste like my cock and balls and arse." He launches in for another helping, another comprehensive lick around my lips and moustache. "I fuckin' love it. But now I need a good go at yours."

I start to purr as his mouth drifts over my beard and down my neck, blessing it with soft, moist kisses. He's so damn considerate, not biting or sucking, careful not to leave any kind of embarrassing hickey. Making his way over my hairy chest, he kisses down to my stomach, eventually meeting my penis. It's ready and raring to go, stiff as a rod, the wrinkled, leaking end of my foreskin resting against the swell of my belly. Dominic runs his nose all around it, sniffing long and hard. "Fuuuuuuuck," he growls, before sticking out his tongue and lapping at it like a hungry cat. He raises his head up to look at me, licking his lips.

"Geez, I remember you and your copious precome. Fuckin' delicious," he purrs, ducking his head back down for more.

I'm dying for him to take my cock in his mouth. But Dominic has other ideas, slathering his nose over my scrotum. "Oh, mate!" he chuckles. "Your sweaty balls are to die for." I feel his tongue gingerly tracing over them, making me squirm as electric shocks shoot up my spine.

"Jesus, Dominic, you'll drive me batshit crazy doing that!"

He lets out another guttural growl as he lifts my left leg and swings it over, making me turn onto my stomach. Bending it at the knee, he pushes it upwards along the mattress so my arse is spread open. Then he pauses for a second. "Fuck, that's beautiful," he gasps, before sinking inside and breathing in deep. I felt the chilly rush as the air sucks into his nostrils, then the vibration as he groans against my arsehole. "My God, you are *all man*, Ryan."

Pulling my left arse cheek aside, he plasters his tongue over my hole and treats it to the same loving attention that I gave his. My moans come thick and fast. His rimming is so fucking exquisite that I whine in protest when he withdraws abruptly. Dominic doesn't respond; I just hear him spit, then a moist hand delves underneath to grab hold of my penis. I cry out as I'm suddenly hit with a double whammy: his fist sliding firmly up and down over my knob, while his tongue darts in and out of my eager hole. "Jesus Christ, Dominic… you're a fucking god!" I begin thrusting my arse at his face, desperate for as many inches of his tongue as he can fit inside me.

Just when I think he's about to go too far and send me over the edge, he vacates my anus and scuttles up the bed behind me, pressing his erection against my arse crack. Reaching up, he turns my head to the side and pushes his tongue into my mouth. "Now we can taste both of our arses," he growls, his lips moving against mine as he speaks.

"So fucking hot," I whimper. I'm beside myself, absolutely overwhelmed.

"Fuck me dead, you are one sexy big bear, Ryan."

"You're the sexy one, *lontra*."

He moves his lips to my ear and growls again. "We're both sexy, then. We're made for each other."

My breath catches. My heart is pounding like a fucking drum. "You keep saying shit like that, Dominic, and you'll never get rid of me. I bloody mean it."

Dominic's voice is soft, his hot breath surrounding my earlobe. "That's exactly what I'm aiming for, Ryan." His penis flexes hard and he moves his hips, aligning his knob with my arsehole. He pushes lightly, nudging the spit-moistened pucker. "How about I prove it to you by slipping my dick in here, eh?"

I moan and laugh at the same time, scooting out from underneath him and pinning him face-down on the bed with my hefty body. "You can fuck my greedy hole whenever you like, mate. But it's my turn first." I gently jab my wet, oozing knob at his taut ring. "I'm sure you could do with a nice, gentle rogering after that fucking starfish Peter."

Dominic giggles, wiggling his quoit against my dick. "After the way you treated my arse before..." he stops for a moment. "You've got me thinking about stuff I never do."

I kiss his slender shoulders. "I'll do whatever you want, mate. I'll go as slow as you want. The main thing for me is that you love what I'm doing."

Dominic moans as I slide my unsheathed knob against his hole. "I gotta be honest. I've been curious about trying this again. I even started on PrEP."

"I know," I whisper, kissing around his ear. "I found your pills in the bathroom cabinet."

"You been snooping through my stuff, have you?" Dominic turns his head and shoots me an incredulous little smirk.

"Yeah, and I'm glad I did. Because now I know we're both on PrEP, I can bareback this hot little cunt of yours." As I speak, my hand finds its way to his anus. The puckered aperture is well-slicked from my comprehensive rimjob and the precome I've just leaked all over it. I slowly push a finger through the tight, rubbery sphincter and Dominic groans.

"Oh fuck, mate, you don't know how good that feels."

"I reckon I do."

Inside, in the depths of Dominic's most intimate place, it's warm and deliciously moist. I start with a gentle thrust, working my finger in and out of him, wiping his own wetness all around, getting the general area nice and prepped. I'm so intently focused on what I'm doing, I've hardly noticed Dominic whimpering away. It's a sweet, heartbreaking little sound, almost like soft crying.

"Please don't stop," he begs. I realise I've stilled my hand as I listened to him. I'm usually pretty good at multi-tasking, but everything about Dominic is bombarding my senses. The searing pleasure of being close to this man again is deafening, mind-blowing, earth-shattering. To compensate for my lapse, I gradually insert a second finger, getting rapturous cries as his anus expands and embraces it.

While I gently move around inside Dominic, I take a moment to rub my erection a few times. It's so bloody hard that I'm almost in pain. "Oh, fuck," whines Dominic, as I start stretching my fingers apart.

"Are you OK, mate?" I whisper. "You gotta tell me if it hurts."

"Nah, it's fuckin' awesome, Ryan. You're so patient. I'm sorry I'm not very good at this."

"This is a special event, *lontra*. You don't know how fuckin' excited I am that you're letting me do this."

Dominic turns his head, his brow creased with potent affection. "Nobody ever gave me so much, Ryan. I just can't believe it… ohhhh, *fuck*. Can you try your cock? I reckon I'm ready."

Swapping my fingers for my dick in Dominic's arsehole is a long, slow process, but I'm beyond thrilled. My memories of the one time I've been inside him come rushing back with full force, every bit as vivid as they were in my teens. I listen closely to the sounds he makes, my mind wavering between intense concern and searing arousal. Millimetre by millimetre, my knob advances through his sphincter into the sizzling heat of his rectum.

Dominic starts to sob quietly. I'm instantly overcome with worry. I can't hurt him, it's too fucking distressing. "God, Ryan. You're fucking sending me to heaven," he whimpers between sniffles.

I lean forward, kissing his cheek. "You make me so happy, Dominic." Emotion is raging through me. We couldn't be closer than we are right now. I'm able to relish Dominic's body in the most personal way, with complete and utter freedom. And there are no fucking words, none.

"Oh fuck, mate," Dominic whines. "Your dick is bloody perfect." His moans are loud, frequent and totally unrestrained as I slowly slide in and out of him. We're on our sides by now; Dominic's back is pressed into my chest as he cries out. His thin physique is exquisite. I've survived my years in Sydney on a steady diet of bears: stocky, muscled, chubby men; men similar to me. Casual sex with these bears always made me feel safe. But being wrapped around a lanky otter is an otherworldly sensation. I can engulf him with my much bigger body. I can smother him in ardent, masculine love.

Buoyed by the sheer power coursing through me, I begin to pump into him a little more firmly. My hand finds its way to his penis. I slowly start stroking my fist up and down, rolling his foreskin, bumping my fingers over his knob with every motion. "Fuck, you'd better stop, Ryan, or I'll come."

"That's the goal, mate."

Dominic isn't listening, though. He wriggles his arse off my cock, turns around and tackles me to the bed in a pillow-biting position.

Laying his chest across my back, he moves his lips close to my ear and growls. "Now it's my fuckin' turn at your beautiful mancunt." His finger is already down at my anus, working its way inside. "God, you've got a nice, hungry hole."

"Mate, I'm so fucking turned on I'll take you with one hard shove."

He reaches over to his bedside table again, grabbing a pump bottle of lube and squirting it into my arse crack. As he begins working two fingers up my hole, he lubes his other hand and reaches under me, firmly grasping my knob and rubbing it in a twisting motion. It's fucking insane. Pleasure overload. My sphincter clenches around his fingers and my erectile muscles tense so hard I swear my dick will explode. I can sense that delicious feeling in my balls and taint, warning me that the end is rapidly approaching.

I reach down and grab Dominic's wrist. "Jesus, mate! Talk about making someone come too soon!"

He laughs and removes his hands from my cock and arse, then slaps my buttock. "Get up on all fours. I wanna see you staked out and desperate for my dick."

I oblige straight away, clambering into position and wantonly sticking my big hairy butt out. "Please, mate, fuck me now. I fuckin' need you so badly."

I don't care that I've only had a cursory fingering. My hole is flexible and very experienced. I'm absolutely *aching* for his dick.

Dominic does exactly as he's been asked, ramming his truncheon of a prick straight inside. Fuck, it's some kind of heaven. The deliciously pleasurable pain has me crying out.

"Is that good, baby?" Dominic's leaning down over me, his voice close to my ear.

"Yes, yes, fucking yes! It hurts so fucking good!"

He gives a lusty roar and begins to thrust. I start moaning like a porn star. No, fuck that, I'm not just moaning, I'm wailing. I can barely cope with how wonderful it all feels. Encouraged by my ecstatic vocals, Dominic ups the ante, slamming into me with such force that my skull starts butting against the padded leather bedhead. I climb my hands up it till I'm braced against it in an almost upright position, my spine bent so my arse sticks right out like a desperate, filthy slut. Dominic hikes me up, wrapping his hands around my chest. "Fuck, you're such a big bear," he growls, pile-driving into my fuckhole with even more venom. His warm breath strafes my neck in large pants, setting my nerves on fire. He steals kisses here and there, grunting with every vicious thrust of his hips. "My beautiful man," he mutters in my ear.

I can't stand it any longer. I yank my foreskin back, wrap my left hand round my knob and start going for gold. My face slumps sideways against the bedhead as I immerse myself in the utter ecstasy attacking me from behind. Dominic is pounding me into a fast and ferocious orgasm and I'm not gonna stop it. "Fuck, man, you're gonna make me come... oh, Jesus fucking Christ! Fuck me deep! God, I love you *so much*, Dominic! AAAAARGH!" Sublime agony rips through my arse and cock as the pressure rises to an excruciating peak, sending sperm barrelling out of my dick to paint the bedhead in long, exquisitely painful spurts.

Dominic continues driving into me, his rhythm becoming all shaky and his voice wavering as he groans. With one almighty slam, he bellows at the top of his lungs. Clasping my hips against his crotch, his body goes into spasms. I can feel his cock purging right up inside me, breeding me deep, marking his territory in the most significant way he can.

With his arms around my chest, he guides me down so we collapse onto the bed sideways. Dominic is still panting hard, his breath rushing against my ear. He swallows finally, his respiratory rate coming back to normal. With a little chuckle, he playfully nuzzles my neck. "You told me you loved me, you know. For real."

"I always have, mate." I know I should be cringing with embarrassment, but I don't give a flying fuck. I turn my head towards him, catching his eyes in my periphery. "Maybe it's just fuck-speak. Orgasm talk." I falter in my words, wondering whether to lay myself on the line. "Or maybe there's a chance we might find it the second time around."

Chapter Nine

Dominic ushers me to turn over, pulling me close as we face each other. "Wild fucking horses, Ryan, OK? I've finally got you back in my life. Do you really think I'm gonna let you go anywhere?"

My head is swimming. I haven't had a tender moment with a man in nearly seven years, let alone a relationship. I've forgotten the rules and I've gone and admitted too much. The fault lines in my hard-worn protective shell are starting to rumble and my instinct for self-protection is going haywire. I lie back, bringing Dominic's head to my chest, and stroke his short, thick hair. At least in that position he won't see the turmoil working its way over my face. But there's no pulling the wool over Dominic's eyes.

"You OK, Ryan?"

"Um, yeah. I'm good."

"What are you thinking about?"

I scramble to summon a vague topic. "I guess… the lost years."

"You mean our lost years?"

"Yeah. Those." I choose my words carefully. "I mean, when you went to Perth, I was fuckin' devastated. I missed you every second of every day. I used to live for your phone calls and letters, but then they died off after a while. Eventually your phone numbers were disconnected. The day my final letter to you was returned unopened was just as soul-destroying as the day I stood on that street in Darwin and watched you drive away."

"I'm so sorry, Ryan." Dominic's voice is small, almost a whisper. "Believe me, I was devastated too. I thought about you all the time and it hurt so fuckin' much. After losing you, I kind of forced myself right back into the closet. Had a string of girlfriends throughout uni. I never slept with another guy for years. Eventually, I met Anna and we got married. And you know the rest."

Well, I don't *know the rest, actually.* "Remember you told me how you came out as gay to Anna last year? When did you realise that for yourself?"

He considers this for a moment. I can practically hear his brain ticking over. "I think my sexual orientation was on a gradual slide up the Kinsey scale. I loved Anna and I never cheated on her. Right at the beginning I admitted to her that I'd had same-sex experiences in the past, but I played it down as kind of youthful bisexual experimentation. You know, something that could be quelled with a little anonymous man-on-man action.

"Once I was in a monogamous marriage it just grew into this monster gnawing at me from the inside. Anna knew something was going on. Our sex life went from regular to perfunctory to non-existent. Finally, I broke down and told her I couldn't resist being who I really was anymore. Said there was no way I was going to be unfaithful to her, so separating was our only option. Sure, it was a difficult situation, but Anna wasn't the least bit shocked. She told me she'd known for ages."

Having a sudden thought, Dominic whips his head up to look me in the eye. "But you weren't an experiment, Ryan. You were the exception—my brother, my best friend and my first love."

His candour is incredibly touching. I stare down into his dark eyes, lifting his chin and planting a soft kiss on his lips. "You were my first love, too. My absolute fucking everything for my entire teenage years, *lontra."*

I settle back and close my eyes, holding this wonderful man, his humid breath against my chest slowly lulling me to sleep.

"Tell me about you," Dominic pipes up, snapping me out of my reverie.

Oh God, I don't want to. I have grave fears about opening up this part of my life to scrutiny. I mean, what Dominic's asking is only fair. He's bared his soul to me, admitted some very difficult things. But in a way they were necessary. They needed to be said in order to explain why the taste of his most private places is still on my lips, why his sperm is still firmly entrenched in my arse. Why an erstwhile married-and-supposedly-straight man has just enjoyed my dick thrusting up his taut little anus.

On the other hand, dredging up *my* past will serve only to cause me agonising pain, and Dominic extreme discomfort.

"How long were you with that guy, Ryan? Mum mentioned him in a couple of her letters."

What the fuck? "So, you two were like penpals or something? With My Little Pony stationery and Care Bears stickers?" I'm trying to sound all light and funny, but this revelation bothers me.

Dominic takes it in his stride. "Nah. She'd send me birthday and Christmas cards and I'd send ones to her. That kind of thing. She'd just stick a short note in there." I glance sideways, to see Dominic's dark eyes staring intently at me. "She was my mum, too, mate. But... yeah. It never really seemed like that. She was pretty much a step-parent I'd had a contentious relationship with as a teenager."

I feel a little stupid over my knee-jerk reaction. Seeing as Dominic's been so gracious, I decide I'll indulge his probing boyfriend questions. But I'm just gonna give brusque answers. "We were together for twelve years."

Dominic turns over to face me. "Wow. What was his name again?

Ewan or something?"

I never say it out loud. Ever. I almost choke on the word. "Owen."

Dominic gives me his huge, white-toothed smile. This isn't the cocky, charming version, though, this one radiates tenderness and warmth. "I know it's hard, mate. Maybe one day you'll feel comfortable enough with me to talk about him."

How the fuck can I say no, now?

I draw in a huge lungful of air and brace myself. "Soon after I got my building qualification, a young sparky started to come and work with us on jobsites. Owen was my age and he'd just finished his electrical apprenticeship. He was very, very cute, a slightly-built little bloke, always smiling and chirpy. But there were a bunch of other young guys at work and they were such fucking arseholes to him. He'd do his best to be friendly with them and they'd just pay out on him. You know, give him shit, treat him like he was some kind of parasite.

"They'd call him a faggot and a poofter constantly, even though he wasn't out or even the least bit camp. But he'd never react. As nasty as they were, he'd always come back smiling. He was just one of those really sunny people, but he was desperate to fit in and these other guys could smell it.

"One of the guys, this fucker named Costa, had actually gone to school with him. He'd delight in telling us what a 'fuckin' reject' Owen was back then, how he had no friends, all that sort of shit. He laughed when he recalled how they all knew his dad used to beat up him and his mother. He even laughed as he told us how in Year Ten he and his mates taunted and bashed Owen so badly that he broke down and cried and was begging them to stop. Apparently, Owen never came back to school after that day."

I'm shaking with anger. Tears of rage threaten to spill forth, but I know they won't. I lost the ability to cry years ago. "Honestly, Dominic, he was such a smarmy piece of shit, this Costa fucker. I was itching to punch him. I could have cried the way those pricks bullied Owen. I thought he was so sweet, so fucking lovely. Fuck, I wanted him. But I didn't even know if he was gay. He was such an ocker, masculine little bloke, nothing was a dead giveaway. I was still in the closet and terrified of putting a foot wrong. I'd give him a smile, I'd be polite, but I never really reached out to him. And I was so spineless I never confronted those arseholes when they abused him. I just stayed on the periphery, kept to myself and refused to engage. I fuckin' hated myself for that.

"Anyway, one night a few months later, we were all having after-work drinks at a bar on the esplanade. I don't even remember exactly what happened—those guys were being their usual fuckwit selves—when Costa and another guy got stuck into Owen. 'You fuckin' sad cunt! Why the fuck do you try and hang around with us?' 'Who the fuck asked you to come tonight?' 'Can't you see nobody wants you here?' 'Nobody likes you, you fuckin' reject!'

"After that tirade Owen had finally had enough. Even he couldn't laugh this one off, but he still didn't get angry. He just stood up and kind of walked out of the beer garden and over the road towards the beach. I was fucking livid, and this time I *did* punch Costa. Hit him in his ugly face so fucking hard he fell off his chair."

* * *

I ran out after Owen, trying to catch up with him. I could see him way ahead on the beach in the dark, stumbling forward. "Stop, Owen!" I called out. "Don't listen to those fucking arseholes!"

But Owen kept running. "Please, mate, please just let me go."

I could hear his voice hitching, see his chest heaving. I understood: for him, having me see him cry was the final humiliation. I just couldn't let it rest, though. I needed to console him; I needed him to know there was at least one person in this fucked-up world who could show him some compassion.

He wasn't hard to catch, he was far too distraught to run properly. I pulled him round and hugged him tight. I pressed his head against my shoulder as he wept and my heart broke at the fucking injustice of it all.

As I began to stroke the back of his head, his sobs slowed down to an occasional sniffle. "I can't stand to see the way those fuckers treat you, Owen," I mumbled in his ear.

"Please don't pity me," he whispered.

"I don't pity you, mate. I fuckin' envy you. You're always so upbeat, so positive. I love the quirky stuff you say, I love your enthusiasm, and, fuck, I love your smile. You make my day, Owen. I'm always so happy when you're around."

I could feel Owen's sniffles had changed and I realised he was actually smelling my skin, sucking in deep lungfuls of my musk. My pulse raced. He must be gay, mustn't he?

"You're the only one of those guys who's ever treated me like a human being," he said. "Why are you so nice to me?"

I moved my head out so I was facing him. My heart was thumping hard now. I didn't know whether I had the guts to take the forbidden step. But my mouth had its own agenda and forged on regardless. "Because I like you, Owen. I mean... really, really like you."

His face contorted in pain, in confusion. "Don't mock me, mate. That's so cruel."

A horrible feeling twisted in my guts. I must have got it wrong. I'd just outed myself and the little bloke wasn't even interested. "Fuck. I'm so sorry. I really meant what I said. I thought you were gay, too." I started to panic. "Please don't say anything to the guys at work. I'm begging you."

"No, Ryan—you're right, I'm gay. I just can't believe you'd be interested in me."

My brow furrowed as a tsunami of emotion hit me. Before I could think, I pulled Owen's mouth to mine and kissed him long and hard. Our lips opened to each other, welcoming our tongues, which rubbed together with the kind of wild abandon that only two young, inexperienced and uninhibited souls could ignite. I clasped Owen's body against mine and held the back of his head as we delved deeper and deeper.

Two and a half years, it had been. Two and a half years since Dominic. Two and a half years without the touch and tenderness of a man—save for the odd seedy blowjob at a beat. My body had never felt such profound relief as it did right then, with Owen in my arms, kissing me as if his life depended on it.

I took him home with me that night. Beneath his shirt, his thin build was wiry and firm to the touch. The kind of small body an electrician finds handy—to squeeze under floors, to crawl through tiny roof cavities. Beneath his shorts was a surprisingly large, uncut cock and a deliciously cute little arse. Best of all, Owen responded in kind to everything I did to him. Every inch of his flesh I tasted, he tasted mine back. All the loving attention my mouth gave to his arse and cock, he paid back to my arse and cock twofold. And we fucked each other, over and over again. Multiple semen-projecting orgasms left us exhausted and we collapsed together, my arms wrapped tight around his slender little torso. He was mine, and I was his. I knew this was it.

Mum caught us in the morning as we emerged from the caravan. We held hands and stood tall. "Mum, this is my boyfriend, Owen." That was it. With those six words, I'd come out. I looked sideways at Owen and saw his face shining back at me, a tear forming in the corner of his eye.

* * *

I pause a moment, smiling fondly at the memory. Of course, Dominic has received only the bare bones of this private part of my life. He doesn't need to know the finer details. "After that first night together, it was all on. Owen and I spent every moment we could with each other. I fucking loved that little man so much. I moved into his crappy rental flat, then later, when we had enough deposit, we bought a tiny apartment in Gardens Hill with a nice view. It was small, but we loved it. It was our home, all ours. We'd built a wonderful life together."

* * *

It really was bliss with Owen. Of course, like in any relationship, things weren't always smooth sailing. On rare occasions we'd disagree. Owen was the type to get hurt rather than angry, but he was so affable, so willing to please, that I had to be mindful of this. It killed me to know I might have hurt him. No argument was worth that.

When the periods of severe sadness that had plagued me after losing my dad and losing Dominic made an occasional return, Owen would quietly support me. He never pushed; he was always there with a sunny smile and a gentle arm. I could sink into Owen and know that, as bad as things were, the sadness would come to an end and he'd be right by my side, waiting for me.

Owen acted like he was lucky to have me. But there's no doubt in my mind that I was the lucky one.

* * *

I suddenly feel sick to my stomach. I really don't think I can continue. I've never spoken this next part out loud to anyone, not even once. My voice starts to waver slightly, but I know I have to finish the story. "Twelve years, we had, Dominic. Twelve incredible years. Then one night, we were at a gay club in Darwin. I was tired and went home at about two. Owen was going to come with me, but his friends begged him to stay out a bit longer. I'd been asleep a while when the phone rang. It was one of Owen's friends and she was frantic, crying non-stop. Apparently they'd left the club and Owen had been king-hit from behind by some gutless cunt of a gay-basher. No provocation, the poor little bloke never even saw it coming. I don't even remember driving to the hospital. I just remember standing out in the hallway screaming when I found out I was too late and he'd already died."

I'm shaking. Starting to hyperventilate.

But I don't cry. I just fucking don't. These walls were put up seven years ago with good reason. "He was the nicest person, Dominic. And he'd been treated like shit all his life—" My voice halts as I stumble out of bed in a blind panic. I bolt out of the room, desperate to escape, but I'm stark naked. I make a beeline for the balcony, slamming the door behind me and collapsing into one of the chairs, bent forward all foetal with my arms over my head. It's all I can do to try and calm myself down.

Mercifully, a good five minutes passes before I hear the door open and a hand is gently placed on my shoulder. "It wasn't *all* his life, mate. He had twelve perfect years with the most caring, compassionate man I've ever known."

Dominic's right. Owen was loved. He was cherished. He was the most beautiful soul that ever lived. On a clear night, I still look up at the stars and imagine one of them is him, watching down over me, making sure I'm OK.

"I'm so sorry I made you relive all of that, Ryan."

I raise my head to look at Dominic, doing my best to smile. "You didn't. I chose to tell you." A burden has been lifted. A heavy sigh escapes me. "So, that's what brought me to Sydney. There was no point staying in that fuckin' city after Owen died. I couldn't bear being in our home. I sold it as quick as I could and pretty much fled down here."

Dominic reaches up and strokes my hair, a sad smile on his face. "It led you back to me, Ryan. For that, I'm truly thankful."

* * *

I leave my story there. I don't tell Dominic about the numbness, the unbearable depression, the three days spent near-catatonic on a Greyhound bus to Sydney.

I certainly don't mention the night I took every pill I had in the house, crawled into bed and said my final goodbyes to the world. I didn't leave a note. I hadn't spoken to mum or Nathan in ages. I had nobody, and nobody would give a shit whether I was around or not. I'd lost everything when I lost Owen, and I was going to be with him again. I still remember it so clearly: I remember as the drowsiness crept in and overtook my body, I remember the indescribable peace that I felt, I remember that final thought of happiness as I sank into my pillow and allowed myself to die.

The ugliness of reality slapped me fair in the fucking face when I woke up sometime the next day. I was sick as a dog. I truly believed it might kill me just like I'd wanted. I called work and made my excuses. I sounded like shit, so it wasn't hard to convince them. Several days passed before I could bring myself to get out of bed again.

I picked myself up, dusted myself off and blindly got on with my life.

111

I never told a soul, and I never, ever will.

*　*　*

Gently taking my hand, Dominic leads me back to the bedroom and turns on the aircon. "Let's cool this place down so I can snuggle with you, Ryan."

While we wait for the temperature to drop, Dominic lays by my side and runs his fingers through the fur on my body. Smoothing his hand over my belly and down to my hip, he begins to trace the small tattoo there. "RU OK?" he says. "Isn't that the logo for that suicide prevention charity?"

"Yeah, it is." I never forget that tattoo's there, but nobody ever sees it. I had it positioned so even briefs cover it. And on the occasions when I have casual sex, the guys are too focused on all the other ink covering my chest and arms, anyway. I ponder whether to expand on Dominic's line of questioning. *What the hell. I have no reason to feel apprehensive. I treasure that thing.* "It also stands for Ryan Underwood and Owen Kendrick. I got it done a while after... you know."

Dominic's still looking at the tattoo, caressing it with his fingertips. It's an endearing sight and it makes me adore him just that little bit more.

"I love the smiling face because it symbolises the happiness Owen brought me. But I left out the question mark in the logo, because there was no question that I loved him more than life itself." I turn my head and look into Dominic's eyes, concerned all of this might be making him feel uncomfortable. All I see, however, is kindness and understanding. "It really helped me heal, Dominic. I could touch it and always feel like he was a part of me."

Dominic leans down and kisses the tattoo, his lips brushing over it in gentle reverence. "It's a beautiful tribute, Ryan. Owen was fortunate he had such a wonderful man."

With the aircon kicking in, Dominic pulls the blankets back and we slip underneath them, cuddling close. I draw him tight against me and he gives a tiny purr. The warm glow of tender affection infiltrates me from head to toe. I close my eyes and surrender myself to peace.

* * *

I don't know what I'm dreaming about, but it's calm and euphoric. I'm intensely stimulated. Blissful sensations are travelling from my chest downwards. I feel like my crotch is going to burst. Slowly coming to, I see handsome black manly hair, I see the side of a beard, I see Dominic feeding gently on my right nipple. As his mouth sucks, his tongue is tickling the very tip. I don't even notice the moans coming out of me at first. But they're constant. My erectile muscles tense so tight I feel a stream of precome surge through my cock. Automatically, my hands are on it, both in their usual position, foreskin stretched right back, fist sliding up and down in a firm motion. I don't know how long this has been happening, but I'm so far up the orgasm pathway already, I'm going to arrive embarrassingly fast. I want to slow down but it feels way too good.

As my pants turn into cries, Dominic's thumb moves to my left nipple and brushes over it in rapid movements. He's gaining momentum, closely responding to me, his rhythm pulsing in perfect sync with the tension-and-release pattern invading my entire being. The delicious agony is amplifying at an alarming rate. I feel sore down there, aching in the best possible way. Every erogenous zone I have seizes up as I bellow. Wild, animalistic howls punctuate every jerk of my hips, every convulsion of my prostate, every catapulting shot from my cock. I can hardly believe the kind of power that has just shaken me to the bone.

I'm still in a daze. It's like I haven't even woken up properly. Dominic has breached the line between sleep and consciousness and I have to remind myself I'm not still dreaming. This happened. This was real.

"Where the hell did you learn to do that, Dominic?" I manage to choke out, amidst gasps of air.

He gives a quiet chuckle. shuffling up into the crook of my arm. "I just listened to the noises you were making and I knew I was on the right track. Fuck, just the sound of you nearly made me come."

I slide my hand over the furry mounds of his little buttocks, resting my fingers against his shallow arsecrack. I feel his hand bumping rapidly against my thigh as he pleasures himself.

Dominic begins to gasp. I push my hand down a bit further and my middle finger reaches for his arsehole. Fuck, I love this part of him. I have to touch him here. It's the most intimate thing I can think of, the closest way I can connect to his body. He whines as I begin to massage it in firm movements. "You've found *my* spot," he gasps.

I'm in rapture at this confirmation. He used to love it way back then, but it's sending him into a whole new level of crazy right now. I press a little into his sphincter, just a fraction of an inch, moving the pad of my finger around. "Ah… ah… ah! God, just like that. Oh, fuck. Please, keep doing it."

"I could do this all day, baby," I whisper.

"You can touch me there absolutely anytime and I'll fuckin' melt. Oh, God, you're gonna make me come!"

Dominic's hole pulsates against my finger. His arm speeds up. His face is right next to mine. His brow is knitted tight, his mouth is slightly open, and he looks like he's going to weep. He stares right into me as he lets out a strangled wail. The beating of his fist against my leg ceases abruptly, his hips thrust forward, and I feel the liquid warmth travel up my hip as he shudders.

"Jesus, Dominic. I'm amazed you're not a raging bottom. I don't think I've ever touched such a responsive arsehole."

An endearing blush overtakes him. I love this look so much. It's a charming vulnerability, a brief peek into a special side of him I need to know more of. "It's not about getting fucked up my arse, mate. It's the outside part that drives me wild. Play with my ring like you just did and I'll be yours forever."

I reach up to his cheek and stroke it. There's a small patch of come there. I think it's mine. "In that case, *lontra*, I'll never stop."

His eyes twinkle as the twilight filters through the sheer curtains behind him. "Please don't go."

My heart swells. I can barely handle how absolutely, desperately, urgently I need to be here. "I was about to beg you to let me stay."

He leans forward, closing the small gap between us, his warm breath against my moustache. "I do, too, you know."

"You do what?"

"I love you, Ryan. I know it's just the beginning. But I've been connected to you for nearly twenty-six years and I don't care what the fuckin' rules are."

I pull his head into my neck, clutching him tight. I can't even speak. We lie there for a long time like this. I meditate on the rise and fall of his chest, the radiant heat of his flesh aligned with mine, the all-encompassing energy of our emotional proximity.

"Hey, big bear?"

"Yeah?"

"I'm fuckin' starving." Peeling himself away from me, I feel the cool air infiltrate my skin where his body has separated from mine. "But we're not going anywhere. And you're staying naked. So, tell me what you want me to order."

"You get one guess, Dominic."

His mouth curves up in a wry smile. "Pizza."

"Bingo."

"What do you like on it?"

I raise my eyebrows, waving a hand up and down my hefty body. "Look at me. What do you reckon?"

Dominic laughs. "Meatlovers."

"You're getting good at this."

He hops off the bed. "I'm gonna start the shower, you're gonna get in while I order, then I'm gonna join you. No arguments." He holds a hand out, grabbing mine and hoiking me to my feet. He's beaming at me.

I grab his naked body and pull him close. "You're not allowed to put any clothes on either, OK?"

* * *

"The best thing about pizza is we can eat it in bed," Dominic chirps, as he plonks a towel on the mattress, followed by two huge pizza boxes. His cheeky little arse disappears from the room and he returns swiftly, dick swinging, brandishing a two-litre bottle of Coke. "Your favourite vintage. Now, dig in." Walking around the bed, he grabs the TV remote and switches it on as he settles next to me. "I'm gonna play you one of my favourite movies. You fine with subtitles?"

I chortle through a gobful of pepperoni. "Mate, I spent my entire teens wanking furiously to European movies on SBS. Best place for a closeted nineties kid to see hot male arse and uncut dick."

"Well, you're gonna love this."

'Do Começo ao Fim' is an experience I'll never forget. Two Brazilian half-brothers have loved each other from the second the younger one was born. I've never seen anything so powerful, so closely representing the long-buried feelings I'm rediscovering with the Brazilian beside me, the one shovelling huge mouthfuls of deep-pan into his cakehole.

Once we've had more than our fill of comfort food, Dominic holds my hand, squeezing it at opportune moments, tacitly highlighting parts during the film that hit so close to home I shiver. I know we've only just reconnected. There's no guarantee where this will go, despite having loved each other so much as teenagers. But the sweet affection he's showing me, the constant touching, the reverent kisses—I can't help but get my hopes up. Will things always be this good between us?

Chapter Ten

At work the following morning, I receive a text.

»I'm floating on air, Ryan. I can't wait till Friday. Oh... and get used to spending your weekends with me. Your lontra needs you, big bear.

And this is exactly how it plays out. Within a couple of weeks, the designs for Dominic's new masterpiece kitchen are done. I'm able to get to work straight away, sourcing materials and appliances, slaving in the workshop, spending the majority of my time on this one job. It's a huge privilege being able to create something so special—not just because I have a seemingly unlimited budget to make it as accurate as possible, but because I'm doing it for the most wonderful man on the planet. I know I sound like a lovestruck sixteen-year-old, but I think I've earned the right to be a little starry-eyed at this point in time.

I also return to my Monday-to-Friday routine. I don't need to have an excuse to visit Dominic on the weekends. Our standing date runs from Friday night to Sunday evening, every week. He says he's happy to come out my way, but I prefer the change of scenery. His apartment is awesome, the weather's hot, and the beach is just a stone's throw away.

We have a blast: going out to dinner; hanging out in the hot tub; curling up on the couch; doing the Bondi to Bronte beach walk; lying in bed together taking in a movie. We even share similar tastes when it comes to cinema: foreign dramas, gay indie flicks and the odd comedy. If Dominic wants to watch anything outside those genres, he never lets on. He's generous to a fault. This also extends to the bedroom department. We literally fuck in every part of the house. My arse hasn't been pounded so good in ages, and despite his self-proclaimed status as a top, Dominic is growing more and more fond of the attention I pay to *his* arse.

* * *

In mid-February, three weeks before Dominic's forty-second birthday, I start working on the idea I've had for the perfect gift. I know it's too early in the piece for a traditionally-romantic gesture. Instead, I scrounge some jarrah leftover from a previous job and get to work. Slogging away at home in the evenings, and making liberal use of the equipment I have at my workplace, I craft Dominic the most beautiful jarrah filing cabinet my twenty-three years' professional experience can muster.

Dominic's birthday falls on a Thursday, but he'll be down in Cronulla with Oscar and Anna. So we've decided to celebrate together the following evening. With everything being so busy, I'm glad for the extra night because I'm not quite finished working on his present.

Now, Dominic's kitchen is all but done and I've never been so proud of my work. I literally puff up like a peacock when I see it. And I'm even more chuffed about the surprise I have in store for him.

As I'm putting the finishing touches to said surprise on Thursday evening, biding my time till I know Dominic's free for a birthday call, he pips me at the post. Quickly wiping my hands free of the varnish that I've been getting high on, I fish my phone out of my pocket and see it's him.

"*Lontra*," I croon into the mouthpiece. "Should I be singing you a birthday song?"

"Of course. Why else would I be calling?" Dominic's voice is smiley. I can always hear the joy in his tone and it makes me swoon every time without fail.

Instead of hashing out that dreadful Happy Birthday dirge, I launch into a kooky rendition of Altered Images' identically-titled song. My impression of Clare Grogan's whacked-out, new-wave simpering has Dominic in stitches.

"Stop!" he laughs. "I'm gonna piss myself!"

"Don't start turning me on with watersports innuendo. You've got my dick hard already, *lontra*. I'm gonna have to rub one out now, you know."

"Save it, big bear. I want every drop of that spunk purged in my presence."

"Fuck, Dominic. You're gonna drive me mad, I swear."

"I can't wait to see you, mate. And I'm gonna empty those hairy balls of yours for sure. But… um… we're gonna have to be quiet while I do it." Dominic pauses for a moment, leaving me to wonder what the hell he's on about. "Anna's boyfriend has surprised her with a dirty weekend in the Hunter Valley. Oscar was gonna stay with his nonna, but that seems silly. I really want him to meet you, big bear. So… he'll be spending the weekend at Bondi with me."

I'm intrigued, but I'm nervous. *What if he hates me? What if he's a spoilt brat?*

Shut the fuck up, Ryan. He's your nephew and you have to make an effort. "I can't wait, Dominic. He's part of you and that automatically makes him fuckin' awesome."

* * *

The following evening at eight, I'm wheeling my heavily-laden trolley up the path to Dominic's apartment building. In front of me, I spot one of his ground-floor neighbours struggling with her shopping. "Let me help you with those, Joyce." I park my trolley and walk up to take several bags from the elderly lady.

"Oh, hello Ryan, that's sweet of you. You still building away up there?"

"No, thankfully. No more noise to disturb you. I'm just doing the last few bits and pieces."

"Oh, you don't disturb me, dear. It's lovely having a nice, helpful young man around."

Young. Well, pushing forty. Joyce unlocks the door and I prop it open with the wooden wedge lying just inside. After exchanging pleasantries and carrying her shopping into her apartment, I return to my trolley and lug it up to the third floor in the elevator.

"Big bear!" Dominic beams when he opens the door, wrapping me in a huge hug. "I missed you." His face is buried against my neck as he squeezes me tight, sniffing in my scent.

"I missed you even more, *lontra*." I move back and plant a soft kiss on Dominic's lips, prompting him to clasp the back of my head and delve his tongue right into my mouth. Our passionate frenchie goes from one to a hundred in a split second, but Dominic quickly backs off with a chuckle.

"If we carry on like this I'll end up fucking you right here in the hallway. Come in, I gotta introduce you to Oscar."

Dominic hasn't even noticed my trolley, which I've parked against the wall outside next to his front door. Seeing him walking down the hallway already, I decide to leave the whole thing where it is for the moment and follow him through to the lounge.

"Oscar, I'd like you to meet Ryan."

A little dark-haired kid is on the lounge reading a book. He glances up, a picture of innocence. "Hello, Uncle Ryan."

Nup. No fucking way. I crouch down in front of him and smile. "We're not gonna use that 'uncle' word, are we? It makes me sound really old."

Oscar looks me up and down. "But you *are* old," he states, matter-of-factly. "Just like my dad."

I have to stifle a laugh. "You're right. I s'pose I am."

"Mum always makes me call *her* boyfriend Uncle Dennis."

"Well, you're good to do what your mum says. But I'm just Ryan, alright?" I give him a big smile and the corners of his lips turn up slightly.

"OK, Ryan."

I have no idea what to say to kids at the best of times. I'm stumped. I spot his book. "Whatcha reading there?"

"It's my homework," he groans. "It's really boring. I hate all these dragons and weird made-up things."

I glance at the colourful cover. Some dreadful children's fantasy book with a dumb, contrived name. Chuckling to myself, I realise this kid and I have more in common than I thought. "Well, Oscar, I'm gonna leave you to your homework. I have to go and show your dad something."

I stand up and spot Dominic hovering behind us. He almost seems anxious. "Cute kid," I mutter to him as I walk past, beckoning him to follow me down the hall and outside into the corridor.

"Happy birthday, *lontra*." I'm bursting with pride as I show him my trolley, huge box strapped in place. I would have wrapped his gift properly, but that seemed stupid. Plus, I ran out of time. "I'll lead the way." Hoisting the trolley backward on its wheels, I power past

Dominic up the hall, through the lounge room and into the study. He saunters in behind me, a quizzical look on his face. "This fuckin' thing," I announce, sinking a boot into the shitty old metal filing cabinet, "is getting chucked. No arguments." Bending down, I unstrap the box and shimmy the trolley away. "Go on, open it. Just rip it."

Dominic follows my orders, tearing the cardboard away to reveal my perfectly-varnished work. I know my shit, and it matches his desk to a T. He turns to me, agape. "Did you *make* this?"

"Yep. Every night for weeks."

"Jesus." He turns back to my masterpiece, opening the drawers, running his fingers over the finish. "I just can't…" He stands up and launches himself at me, lips mashing against mine, his tongue barging its way inside and flailing around. Hot breath rushes between us, urgent torrents escaping our mouths with every rapid tilt of our heads. "If my son wasn't out there," he pants in between kisses, "I'd be making you blow like a fucking volcano right now."

We finish our frenzy with a soft-lipped coda. "Well, he's gotta go to bed sometime, *lontra.*"

As I venture back out to the lounge with Dominic, I notice Oscar now has the TV switched on to some old rerun of 'Will and Grace.' "Just one or two episodes, mate, then bedtime," says Dominic, adopting an impressive parental tone. He settles onto the couch next to Oscar, who immediately cuddles up to his dad. It's so adorable. I plonk myself down on the other side of Dominic. I'm not quite sure of the etiquette here. I don't want to disturb their bonding time, but it would be a bit weird with me sitting over on an armchair by myself. Dominic quells my doubts straight away, reaching for my hand and discreetly holding it throughout the entire two episodes he'd promised Oscar.

"Righto, monkey," Dominic says. "Time to make a move."

Oscar groans, his voice full of the sounds of sleepy kid.

"Come on, up and at 'em. Shower, teeth, *bed.*"

With great reluctance, Oscar eases himself off the couch and stomps off to the bathroom. I jump up, too, heading for the study. "I'll just get all that stuff out of the way."

The room is tight with its long, thin dimensions. I manoeuvre my trolley back into the living room and chuck the cardboard out alongside it. With a bit of deft manipulation, I manage to free Oscar's fold-up bed and shimmy the new filing cabinet into the space where it had been stored. I look at Dominic's hideous metal monstrosity. Tomorrow, while I've still got my trolley here, that piece of crap is getting dumped.

Emerging from the study, I notice the cardboard is gone, along with Dominic. So, I duck back in and unfold Oscar's bed. Scanning the room, I spot a set of stripy kid's sheets and a pillow, so I get to work and make the bed up. It's a bit of a squeeze in the skinny space, me and my big body flung over the mattress, trying to tuck the damn sheets in. But I want it to look nice. Standing back to admire my handiwork, I take in the room's limited floor space. Something *has* to be done here.

"Oh, mate, you didn't have to do that!" A warm voice sounds behind me, and an equally warm body advances to press against my back. Hands wrap around my chest, gentle lips kiss behind my ears, warm breath caresses my neck and fingers begin to stroke my nipples.

I moan instantly. "God, *lontra*. You know I don't wear undies. Your kid's gonna walk in any second and be traumatised by the hard dick and wet patch on my shorts, you know." Dominic's hand slides down and squeezes my penis. "That's hardly helping."

"I'm gonna help it in a few minutes, big bear."

"Dad, did you get my bed out?" A small voice grows nearer as footsteps bound towards the room, and Dominic relinquishes his hold on my crotch. Me and my erection turn away towards the wall and I ease myself out of the room as Oscar enters behind me. I re-establish my former relationship with the couch and settle back. I can hear the hushed, soothing tones coming from the study as Dominic begins to read a bedtime story. The tender routines of parental life tug hard at my heartstrings.

Dad used to do this for me.

I still miss him, nearly three decades later. My memories grow fainter with every passing year. It kills me that I can't hang onto them as tight as I'd like to. Dominic's gentle relationship with his son is exactly how things should be. How they were with my own father.

Dominic emerges, softly closing the study door. "Think we've earned ourselves a beer, mate." He makes his way towards the kitchen as I assess the deflated state of my crotch. May as well. All this parental reflection has doused the flame of my libido. Yeah, plenty of time for that later.

He joins me on the couch with two Coronas. We huddle together, sharing warmth and manly scent, enjoying each other's quiet company. The TV hums in the background, volume on low. This is the kind of domestic bliss I thought I'd never see again.

"Um, Dominic," I start, after sitting in silence for quite some time. "Does Anna know about us?" Now that Oscar's in the picture, this is something we need to sort out.

He turns his head, his gaze meeting mine. "Of course, she knows I have a boyfriend." His rich, dark eyes search mine for a moment. "That's what we are, aren't we?"

My heart does a little somersault at this confirmation. But that's not what I was fishing for. "I mean, about *us*."

He stares down at his stubby, running his thumbnail over the embossed logo. "I haven't gone into that, no. I guess that's nobody's business but our own." His eyes meet mine again. "Isn't it?"

I nod slowly. "Can we keep it that way?" I don't need anything complicating this happiness.

* * *

I'm waiting for the shower water to heat up, idly stretching the rear edge of my foreskin down, when Dominic walks in naked as a jaybird. His penis is in a full state of excitement already and he goes straight for my arse, delving his hand into my crack. "I've been dying for this all week," he mutters, as his finger rubs at the puckers of my arsehole. "Lucky I installed continuous hot water, eh? Now, get in." Dominic's tub is a tall old thing and it requires a decent scissoring of my legs to step over the edge. "Fuck, I will never get enough of this big butt of yours," he growls.

"Anytime you want it, *lontra*." The thrill I get over how much he adores my body becomes more intense with each passing day. We're voraciously sexual men. His physical admiration is testament to how deeply he feels about me. I don't need hearts and flowers. Just knowing how much I turn him on is direct validation of his profound love.

Love? It's a word with so many meanings. Of course, I love him. And I believe him when he says he loves me. He's my brother. He's part of me, part of my history, part of my present. But this is hardly a normal situation. Things haven't had the chance to develop in typical fashion. Does he *love* love me? Am I being too presumptive? How long do I wait till I allow myself to believe it, to accept it as gospel?

Dominic climbs in behind me, immediately soaping me up in long, firm circles. I bask in the decadence, soaking in the grand sensation of his hands running over me, a skilled masseur hard at work doing what he does best. I'm moaning softly, my head in a rush. I'm enjoying it so much it takes a while before I realise how selfish I'm being.

"Your turn, *lontra*." I come around to face him, taking careful steps to avoid slipping over. Once I've lathered him up, I'm not nearly as thorough as he'd been with me. I'm far too horny now. After a vigorous rubdown, I zero in on his best parts. In and out of his little arse crack I scrub my fingers, working the shower gel all around his anus till it's slick enough for my finger to gain entry. I wiggle the tip just inside his ring, rubbing it exactly the way he loves.

Dominic groans and shudders. "God, that feels so good." His face goes serious for a moment. "I'm sorry I'm so bad at taking cock."

"You're not. You're fuckin' amazing, Dominic. The two times I've ever fucked you are some of the best sexual memories I have."

He tries to smile, but I can sense frustration there. I hope it's not aimed at me. "See, that's what I mean. I worry that I'm not meeting your needs enough. But I can't just take a dick easily like you can. I wish I had that ability."

I'm still rubbing his anus and I'm not willing to stop, so I move my free hand to his cheek. "Do you ever hear me complain about how often you pound me like a bitch? I demand to be fucked, that's non-negotiable. And anything you want me to do with your arse thrills the living shit out of me. But I don't ever wanna put my dick in there unless I'm sure you're gonna love it, OK?" Dominic's eyes lower slightly. He's still not convinced. I slide my hand under his chin, lifting it so his gaze meets mine. "Never, ever doubt that sex with you is anything less than fuckin' spectacular. Ya got that?"

My candid sincerity has done the trick. Dominic smiles at me once more, leans forward and kisses me softly on the lips. "Bottom or top, two blokes like us are still gonna have a hard time shagging in this bloody tub."

I chuckle as I move my hands around the front of him, pumping my fist up and down his shaft. "And I'm guessing it's not a safe bet doing it in your bedroom?"

"Well, I suppose we can gradually work our way up to it sometime. When I'm sure Oscar isn't gonna disturb us."

I fairly burst with joy every time he speaks about our relationship in a future context. I don't really care about anal sex right now. I just need to get him off, then myself. Urgently. "Sit down, you sexy bugger." I give him a gentle push on his shoulders and he complies, grabbing the edges of the tub and settling on his arse with his knees spread.

In a split second I'm lying in front of him, my knees bent against the opposite edge of the tub, my belly pressed on the bottom. Dominic's long penis looms in my face and I suck it into my mouth straight away, swirling my tongue around hard as I Hoover and swallow with gusto.

"Fuuuuuck!" he cries, before dropping to a whisper. "*Oh shit. I've gotta remember to keep it down.*"

I snort through my nose as I toil on his knob. It's fucking delicious. I could suck this wonderful beast all day and never get tired of it. Dominic continues to vocalise, dialing it down to a steady whimper as he scrunches his hand in my long hair. He's always a perfect gentleman when I worship his penis. Not once has he ever pushed my head onto it. Any guy that does that is liable to get punched. Though, I'd probably make an exception for this man.

"Ryan, I'm not gonna last like this, I'm warning you."

Red rag to a bull. I double my efforts. I desperately need to taste that spunk; I'm dying to drink my sweet reward. I hump my hips, wiggling them on the bottom of the bath to coax my foreskin back. One hand is holding Dominic's penis steady and the other one snakes its way under me to start rubbing my knob. I haven't got any lube handy, but I've precome a ton so I should be OK. I need to time this perfectly; I'm so close.

"Oh, God, I can see your arse pumping, baby. It's so fuckin' beautiful." A sob escapes his throat and his hand tenses hard in my hair. A massive pain builds in my taint, my arsehole and the end of my dick as I feel Dominic's glans thicken against my tongue. His breath comes out in violent bursts. "I'm coming, big bear." His plaintive whimpers are what seals the deal. The heartbreaking sound of his pleasure causes my penis to start throbbing wildly, sending thunderous bursts of semen underneath me at the exact time Dominic floods my mouth with his life-giving seed. I don't even think, I just swallow it as it comes out: while my hand works the vestiges of my own orgasm, while my body jolts in ecstasy. Fuck, this was worth the several days' abstinence I imposed on myself.

* * *

When we return to the bed, Oscar is plonked on Dominic's side of it, under the covers, plumped against the pillows like royalty. "You take a long time in the shower, just like mum and Uncle Dennis."

I can't even manage to hold in my laughter. I have to clutch the tiny towel that's wrapped underneath my rounded belly, lest it falls to the ground and gives the poor kid an eyeful.

"What are you doing in here?" Dominic's stern, fatherly tone has made a swift return.

"I couldn't sleep," Oscar whines. "Can I stay here? Please?"

Dominic relents, his voice softening. "OK. But only for a *little while.*"

I'm suddenly glad we've both emptied our caches of sperm. I would have gone out of my mind. I struggle into my shorts surfie-style, shimmying them up underneath my towel and patting them around my balls to dry the remaining dampness.

Dominic, however, throws his towel aside in his typical, brazen style, rummaging around in his chest of drawers, his hairy buns flexing as he digs deep for the right garments. "Here you go," he says, turning around and tossing me a singlet, while his floppy dick swings away cheerfully. "This one's way too big for me." His smarmy grin goes wide as he eyes my hefty torso.

The damn singlet is still a squeeze to get on, but I know I have to make myself decent. Once we're both clothed, Dominic slides under the covers to the middle of the bed, holding them up for me with a smile.

As I snuggle in beside him, my immediate instinct is to cuddle him the way I normally would. I decide it's better to be on the safe side and keep my hands to myself, my belly pressed against his back. Dominic stretches over Oscar and switches off the light on the bedside table. In the dark, I feel his arm reach behind him. His fingers interlock with mine and he pulls my hand over him, clasping it against his svelte tummy. I'm safe. I'm secure. It's the last thing I think of as sleep overtakes me.

Chapter Eleven

My eyes open to the sunlight streaming in through the sheer curtains. I'm cuddled up to Dominic's warm, furry body in the same position I was in last night. Only now, the man I'm wrapped around is as naked as the day he was born. Lifting my head slightly, I notice we're alone. I glance round at the door to see it firmly shut. The cotton sheet over us is barely covering our hips.

Shuffling down the bed, I'm met by two small, hairy buttocks. I never need to pull Dominic's cheeks open, my face always sinks straight inside that shallow little cleft. I love the way he smells down here right now: scrupulously clean after a thorough shower, but with enough hours left in between to give me the manly scent I crave. I breathe deeply through my nostrils, letting it bombard my senses. It's almost a shame to wash it all away with my tongue, but I know resistance is futile. The second I've made contact, Dominic's anus wiggles against my snout.

"Mmmmm. My favourite alarm clock. You can wake me like that anytime you like."

I knew he'd give me the green light. He fucking loves the way I do this to him. I softly probe his puckered hole as he moans. He reaches behind me and presses my face into his arse, tightly aligning me with his heavenly little playground. Bliss.

It's right then that Dominic's phone decides to trill in the most annoying synthetic ringtone possible. "Fuckin' hell," he groans. I'm not ready to relinquish my glorious rimming session yet. I grab onto his hips, travelling with him as he rolls onto his stomach and reaches out to pick up the offending mobile. I don't even register what he's saying into the bloody thing. I'm too busy licking, swirling, pushing my tongue into that tasty little pucker.

Dominic hangs up with a sigh. "Bad news. I gotta go into the office for a few hours." He wriggles out from underneath me, leaving me there with my tongue still hanging out. "I'm so sorry, big bear. Please don't feel like you have to leave. I'll get Oscar packed up and he can come in with me."

"Don't be silly. I'm thirty-nine, mate. I think I can look after a kid for a day."

Dominic scoots down to face me and brings his hand to my cheek. "Really? You sure you don't mind?"

"Babe, it would be my pleasure." The touching look Dominic gives me is all I need to know how much this means to him. "Though I can't say I'm gonna be too thrilled sitting through four bloody Toy Story movies or anything."

He laughs out loud. "You may be surprised there."

* * *

I'm on the balcony, sitting down to my morning cup of tea and my first smoke of the day, when Dominic pops his head out the door. "I'm gonna head off now, mate. Oscar's up and dressed."

I smile as I take in the sight of him. He looks so handsome dressed in his casual work clothes: a Polo in striking green—the *genuine* brand, of course—crisp beige chinos, and R.M. Williams boots. "We'll be alright, *lontra.* You don't need to worry."

He comes out to me, squats on his haunches and places his hand on my thigh, staring at me fondly. "You know, I'm really grateful for this."

I slide my hand over his and give it a squeeze. "He's your son, mate. Of course I'm gonna shift my lazy arse and look after him. Now, bugger off before you give me another stiffy."

He chuckles, getting up and mashing his lips into mine. "I've left some money on the table if you want to grab lunch," he says as he straightens himself.

"No, mate, I won't hear of it—"

"Don't bloody argue," he cuts in. Ruffling my hair, he takes off back inside.

By the time I've downed the rest of my tea and stubbed out my durry, Dominic is long gone. I stroll back inside to find Oscar sitting on the couch, toast plate with discarded crusts on his lap, glued to an episode of 'King of Queens.' Hearing me approach, he looks up and his eyes go wide. "I didn't mean to eat on the couch. Dad says I can't."

The poor kid looks so guilty, I have no choice but to smile. "Are there any crumbs on there?"

Oscar shuffles off the couch at breakneck speed, plopping his plate on the floor and scanning the cushions. "No." He turns back to me, a look of worry on his little face. "You won't tell dad, will you? He says only adults can eat on there."

Ha! Typical lawyer, covering his own arse. "Well if there's nothing on the couch, then we won't mention it, will we? Now, pop your plate back in the kitchen and think about what you wanna do today."

"Oooh! Can we go to the beach? I wanna swim!"

Gee, what I wouldn't give to have that kind of childish enthusiasm once more. A fleeting pain seizes my chest. Images flood my mind: of my dad, of me at Oscar's age. The unbelievable ache of knowing how much I missed out on has never left me. "Well, go and get your bathers and I'll find us some towels."

Oscar scurries towards the study in excitement, before doing a quick reversal to retrieve his toast plate from the floor. *Good kid.*

With the little tyke safely stashed in his makeshift sleeping quarters, I stride down to the master bedroom and rifle through my bag. *Fuck.* I haven't brought any damn bathers with me. I glance over at Dominic's drawers. I doubt he's got anything I can squeeze into, but it's worth a try. After a quick rummage, I find several pairs of togs. There's no way my arse and package are going to fit into his slutty little speedos, but there's a pair of Lycra trunks that I may *just* about be able to get on. Well, they'll have to do.

I'm half-expecting Oscar to burst through the door at any moment, so I know I've gotta be quick. In two seconds flat, I've stripped naked. I turn my head around and catch the sight of me bent over in the huge full-length mirror. I'm intrigued. *This* is what Dominic sees when he's giving my arse all that close, loving attention. What his hands run over. What his face buries into. What he watches his cock thrust in and out of.

I stand up, still looking over my shoulder. My arse is large and thickly-furred. My butt cheeks are fat, but they're beautifully-rounded courtesy of the hard all-day slog in my building job. I pull one cheek outwards. The dark, hairy crack I see is the kind of thing I jerk off to whenever I indulge my bear porn addiction. Fuck, I don't do much of that anymore. What was once a daily routine has now dwindled in dramatic fashion. Every weekend Dominic's been servicing my arsehole—aside from all those times when we're so turned on by the kissing and sucking and rimming and fingering that we don't even make it to the anal sex stage. The rest of the week, I only manage a couple of masturbation sessions before I'm saving up my spunk for Dominic again.

I sidle even closer to the mirror, pulling both my arse cheeks right open. *Yeah, I can see why guys wanna eat that.* My hole is brown and taut and uniformly-puckered. I know how good it is. I've always received enthusiastic feedback.

I turn slowly, taking in the sight of my short, thick floppy penis. The wrinkled foreskin hangs down well below the fat knob it covers. I don't have a huge dick or anything. But it's fuckin' handsome. And I don't have low-hangers, either, but my furry nuts are plump and sit beautifully behind my stumpy prick. I'd do me. Bloody oath, I would.

Running my hands up over my bear belly, I try to imagine what other men—what *Dominic*—might sense as they touch it. I've given up feeling inadequate. I wasted far too much time worrying whether men thought I was fat. Fuck me, I'm a muscly bloke. My cuddly layer, my belly, my chunky arse, *these fuckin' big mounds on my chest*—they get me attention, they fuckin' do. My hands run up over my pecs. Yeah, they're covered in padding, but underneath that they're damn hard and brawny. And these nipples, these permanently-peaked pleasure spots the colour of burnt sienna, they can bring me to orgasm faster than anything else.

I move rapidly into hazardous territory as my thumbs start to strum my hardened chest-nubs. I feel that clear sensation, that ripple of moisture making its way down through my penis, that glorious substance that soaks my damn clothes whenever my rampant horniness is piqued. *Fuck, I need to start wearing underwear.*

Abandoning my nipples before my swollen dick makes a rapid ascent, I bring my hands to my thick, full beard. I've started growing it now. I want it to be a decent bushranger length. I spend a pretty penny going to a specialist barber in Redfern, this Leb guy who's an expert. And I spend about as much time grooming the bloody thing as a drag queen does on their makeup. But, *fuck me*, other guys love my face fur as much as I do. I turn my head left and right, surveying the few grey hairs in it. I'm a little alarmed at how fast they're emerging, but I've seen those block-coloured beard dye-jobs and I'm steering clear of that.

"Ryan! Ready to go!" Oscar's voice thunders down the hallway, his feet slapping the wooden floor. With a swift flick of my wrist, the door is locked. He doesn't need to see me like this: buck naked, my thickened cock at a forty-five-degree angle after a long, ego-boosting, mirror appraisal. The kid can wait.

"I'll be out in a sec!" My reply is enough to discourage Oscar from trying the door, and the slapping footsteps travel back up the hallway. I whip Dominic's trunks straight on, stretching them tight over my arse. Glancing again in the mirror, I give myself another once-over. I feel better; I feel validated.

With a bag packed and our towels ready, an impatient eight-year-old is bouncing around next to me. "We've got one more thing to do, little fella," I tell him.

"What's that?"

I lead him into the study and point to the metal filing cabinet. "We're gonna get rid of this heap of junk."

"Won't dad get all mad?"

"He's got no say in it. Now, you're going back to mum's tonight, aren't you?"

"Awww, no," Oscar moans. "It's boring there. Can't I stay here?"

I ruffle the little tyke's hair. "You can stay anytime you like. But *only* if your mum says so."

Oscar perches himself on Dominic's desk chair, swinging back and forth on it while I get to work. I strip his bed, fold it up and stash it in the lounge room for the moment.

Then I empty both drawers of the metal cabinet, carefully transferring every file into my jarrah masterpiece. Once the old heap of crap is loaded onto my trolley, I hand Oscar the beach bag and towels. "You can carry this on the way down, eh?"

As we pass through the lounge room, Oscar spies the money left on the table. "Wow! One hundred bucks! Can I have it?"

"No. It's your dad's and it's staying there, buddy." Typical Dominic. He's generous to a fault, but I'm sure he enjoys flashing his cash. How much damn lunch can an eight-year-old eat, anyway?

The cabinet is unceremoniously dumped next to the bins at the back of the apartment block. Sudden panic rises in my chest as I remember my ute is parked in a two-hour zone. I glance at my watch. Ten-thirty. Parking restrictions start at eight, so I'm only half an hour late.

"Are we driving to the beach?" Oscar says, as I check my windscreen, relieved to see there's no ticket on it. "Dad and me walk there when we go."

"Nah, mate. I'm just gonna move the car so the nasty man doesn't come and give me a fine. Hop in."

Oscar slides into the passenger seat and I walk around to my side. As I settle behind the wheel, he's looking around the cab. "Your car's really messy. Dad's is really clean."

"That's because your dad's a rich lawyer with a classic sports car and I'm just a dirty builder with an old truck."

"Hmmm. Well, I like your car better. It's really big and awesome."

"Yeah. I'm a big man, and I like my trucks big, too. Now, stick your seatbelt on, buddy."

I turn the key in the ignition and out blasts 'Modern Song' by The Numbers. I can't stand pissfarting around with Bluetooth and smartphones, so I've had my ute kitted out with a state-of-the-art tape deck. At least it's guaranteed to work without stuffing up. I need that kind of certainty in my life.

"Why do you listen to all this old music?" asks Oscar, as we circle the surrounding blocks for a new parking spot. The cool post-punk of The Numbers has now moved into the power-pop epic 'Gay Guys' by The Dugites.

I guess it is very old. Eighties and nineties Aussie pub rock has always been my obsession. It reminds me of a time when everything wasn't so bloody complicated. "I like it because it sounds like real people playing real instruments, buddy. It's almost as if you're in the room with them while they're performing."

Oscar considers this. "It's much better than the yukky stuff other kids play at school."

I like this kid even more.

As luck would have it, we nab an empty car space even closer to the beach than where we'd been before. Oscar ambles along beside me, rubbernecking at the hive of activity going on around him as we approach our destination. His excitement is infectious. I'm buoyed by his wide-eyed enthusiasm. It's the best kind of reminder for a man who takes life all too seriously most of the time.

Once we've found our patch of sand and spread out our towels, we pull off our t-shirts and I shimmy out of my shorts. "Your bathers are really tiny, Ryan," says Oscar, a little too loudly.

"That's because they're your dad's. I didn't bring any."

"My dad's much skinnier than you."

Cheeky little bugger. "Yeah, I know. I have a big bum."

Oscar giggles at my choice of words. If only he knew how much I was curbing my language right now.

We run down to the water, Oscar whooping it up as we near the edge. The waves are dead calm and there's hardly any breeze. "It's too cold!" he shrieks.

"Nah. It's a hot day, mate. Once you get in, your body will adjust." We wade out slowly, till I'm at waist level and Oscar is treading water. "Too deep for you here?"

"No. I'm a really good swimmer." He sends a huge splash my way, soaking the top half of my body. How did this skinny little kid get so damn powerful?

"Game on!" I growl, as Oscar squeals.

We tire ourselves out, splashing, dipping and dunking, swimming back and forth, then just floating and staring at the blue sky and the view around us. Quite a few people are here taking advantage of the late summer weather, but I'll bet nobody is having as much fun as we are.

"You know what I forgot, Oscar?"

"Sunscreen," he replies immediately. "Mum always says I have to put it on."

"And you didn't think to say anything?"

"No. *You're* the grown-up."

God, this kid can sass. "Righto. Out of the water. There's some in the bag."

Back at our towels, once we're slathered in greasy fifty-plus, I settle back to catch a few rays, my head propped on the bag. Oscar is quiet for a while, digging around in the sand. "I need to wee," he announces.

Opening my eyes, I sit up and look over my shoulder. "The dunnies are ages away. Just go down and wee in the water, buddy."

"I can't! What if people see me?"

"Just wade out a bit, squat down and do it. Don't tell me you've never pissed in the water before." *Shit. I've gotta watch my mouth.*

"Mum says I'm not allowed to wee anywhere except in the toilet."

I'll bet she does. "Well, you're a good kid. You do what your mum says. But when you're with me, you can wee in the ocean. Now go. I'll be here."

As Oscar scampers off, I take the opportunity to roll a durry. Once he's finished in the water, he barrels up the sand again, coming to an abrupt stop at my feet. "You shouldn't smoke, you know. It's bad for you."

I look up at his little face, an impertinent expression plastered across it. "No, really? Nobody ever told me that before." I finish the last of my cigarette and stub it out. My stomach rumbles. "Time for lunch, buddy. What do you feel like?"

"Oooh, Macca's! Can we? Can we?"

Another plus in my book, kid. "OK. Let's get packed up, then."

It's only a short stroll through the park to the McDonald's on Campbell Parade. Inside, I'm expecting a massive line-up, but it's not too bad and we manage to snag a two-person table. I stash our stuff underneath it and fish around for my wallet, then re-emerge to find Oscar sitting there, squirming with excitement. "Can I have a Quarter Pounder and McNuggets and mustard sauce and chips and a strawberry shake and a caramel sundae?"

I can't even stop myself laughing out loud. Where the hell is this little bloke gonna put it all? "You can have anything you want, buddy. But let's make a deal. You get through everything first and *then* we'll get you the sundae if you can still fit it in."

I end up buying some kind of family feast package. It has everything he's asked for and more. I'm a bloody pig, anyway, so I'm pretty sure we can make a good go of it. It's a special occasion.

And no, we never make it to the sundae stage.

* * *

After rolling our full bellies home, we both settle on the couch. Oscar switches on the TV. "Ugh. News. Boring. Why does dad watch it?"

Yeah, why indeed. It's depressing. I'm expecting Oscar to change the channel to some awful anime rubbish, some horrible action cartoon. Once again, though, he goes straight for my favourite classic comedy channel. Several episodes of 'Bewitched,' several of 'The Golden Girls' and a few of 'ALF' thrown in for good measure—and the kid laughs throughout. At one point, he cuddles up close, nestling against me the way he did with his dad. *My little nephew.* I instantly turn to mush.

Oscar doesn't even move when Dominic rushes through the door, charging up the hallway all a-fluster. "God, boys, I'm sorry it took so long!"

Oscar turns his head from where it's snuggled in the crook of my arm. "That's OK, dad."

Sweet kid. But somehow I think that apology was aimed at me. "Don't worry about it, Dominic." I look down at Oscar. "We had fun, didn't we?"

"Yeah, it was awesome!" He turns back to Dominic with glee. "We went to the beach and we swam and we went to Maccas and I had a quarter pounder and McNuggets and chips and a strawberry shake. But I didn't have enough room for a sundae." He looks up at me, a forlorn expression on his face.

"I promise we'll get one another time, matey." I don't wanna disappoint this kid.

Dominic's brows are raised in a dubious kind of amusement. I don't know whether he's upset about the junk food, but I couldn't give a shit. What else are secret uncles for?

Late that night, with Oscar back at his mum's, Dominic and I are cuddling in bed, our naked bodies pressed together, our hands roaming each other's skin, brushing over each other's fur. "I can't thank you enough for what you did today, Ryan."

He seems deeply touched. His brow is wrinkled and his mouth is set in a tiny upward curve. A gentle glow filters through the curtains and dances across his eyes, making them shine in the dark.

"*Lontra,* that kid is my nephew. He's family, and I'll do anything, alright?"

"You don't know how much that means to me, baby," he whispers. He takes hold of my hand and squeezes it. "Anna and I have been talking. She wants time alone with Dennis, so Oscar will be spending every second weekend here with me." He searches my face. "Will you be OK with that? It won't stop you coming to see me, will it?"

I reach up and stroke the back of my fingers against the dense softness of his beard. "Nothing will, *lontra.* Absolutely fuckin' nothing." I smile at him. The relief on his face is charming. "Anyway, that little bugger's well and truly stolen my heart."

Chapter Twelve

My fortieth birthday's approaching. It's May, the hot summer weather is now a distant memory, and even I have had to concede defeat. Forgoing my trademark tiny shorts, I'm now swanning around all day in equally-snug Hard Yakka cargo pants.

"God, your arse looks hot in these! You don't know what you're doing to me." My greeting from Dominic this Friday when I arrive for our usual rendezvous is to be pushed against the wall face-first. Two busy hands grope my buttocks all over. Kisses rain down my back, then a face is buried in my cotton drill-clad arse crack. Taking a huge sniff, Dominic growls on the exhale. "Fuck, I'm bonded to your scent, baby."

He jumps to his feet, spins me around and fairly flings his face into mine. His tongue barges into my mouth with a whimper. It roams around inside, exploring every nook and cranny, tasting as much of me as it can. I'm already panting. The relief flowing from Dominic directly into me is equally mirrored by the desperation I've felt at our separation. A week is too damn long, for fuck's sake.

Dominic pulls back, hand still clasped around the back of my head, and grins at me. "I know you're dead against having a party, so I'm taking you away for your birthday next week, big bear."

"Um… my birthday's on a Monday, mate. Neither of us are gonna be able to swing that."

"Uh, uh, uh!" Dominic admonishes. "We're celebrating early. I'm whisking you off for a dirty weekend in a beautiful little country town way out west."

"Oh. Where's that?"

"Grenfell. Near Young. Bit over four hours' drive. But it's worth it. Oh, and you're gonna need to finish early on Friday so we can get out there. Think you can manage that?"

My mind races through the coming week's schedule. "I'll call Marisa. I'll be starting early, so I could finish by two. Is that gonna be enough time?"

"Great. Pack your bags and take them with you. I'll pick you up Friday at two sharp from your office, OK?" Dominic grins gleefully and reaches down to my crotch. "We are gonna have *So. Much. Fun.*" He punctuates each of these last three words with firm squeezes on my dick.

Something occurs to me. "Meet me at the lunch bar over the road from my work, OK? I don't want those nosy bastards at the office bombarding me with questions on Monday."

Dominic raises an eyebrow. "So, I'm a secret lover, eh? You don't want me to meet your workmates?"

I can see how dodgy I sound. I'm scrambling to work out how to say this. "I keep to myself, Dominic. I'll definitely introduce you when the time's right." It hits me how insecure I'm still feeling about our whirlwind romance. Dominic's spot on. There's been a whole clandestine feeling to this arrangement. There are just so many variables, so many things holding me back from broadcasting it to the world. My feelings are deep. We spend passionate weekends together. But, he's still living with Anna. Oscar's thrown into the mix. And the thought of people prying into our family background…

Dominic is looking at me intently, and I can't even manage to come up with a feeble explanation. "I'm sorry, *lontra*. Really soon, OK? I promise. For now, I just don't want everybody getting all up in my business."

Getting up in my business. I realise the apartment door is still wide open. God knows who's seen the little arse-sniffing and face-sucking session we've just had. Dominic reaches over and shuts the door, then takes my hand. "I understand, big bear. Things are gonna change in the near future, you'll see. Then we'll be free to live the way we want to." An endearing smile illuminates his features. He reaches up and strokes my beard, then tugs at my hand, leading me down the hall. "I've got us a suite at a gorgeous old bed and breakfast there called Grenfell House. Full of antique furniture and beautiful bedrooms. You're gonna love it."

Grenfell House. I make a mental note to look it up when I get a moment. Dominic leads me straight through the lounge room and out onto the balcony. The air is chilly now that it's late autumn. I see the spa glowing, the lamps under the surface emitting a striking luminescence. It looks like the last thing I'd want to be doing right now in this weather, except for the fact there's steam rising off the rushing water.

Dominic spots me dawdling by the edge. "Strip," he orders, struggling out of his shirt. "You are not gonna make me wait a second longer."

"Oh? Am I holding you up?"

"Big bear, my dick is aching here. Get a fuckin' wriggle on."

I'm not keen on freezing to death. I'm also reluctant to lose the raging stiffy that's currently saturating my trousers. My steel caps are unzipped, my jumper and hi-vis polo are ripped off, and my cargos are shoved to my ankles at lightning speed. Dominic's already in the spa waiting for me. Shivering, I plunge into the water. The heat of the rippling eddy envelops me; a blissful, toasty-warm contrast to the frigid air my naked body has just been exposed to. I feel a tightening in my groin and I'm pleased to verify my ever-reliable hard-on is still intact.

Moving against me, Dominic wraps one hand around my penis and begins to stroke it. His other hand searches around the back of me. I spread my legs, arching my back so my arse is easily accessible. His confident finger moves in sync with me, finding my anus and rubbing it firmly. "No mucking around tonight, baby," he whispers. "I'm like a fuckin' geyser about to erupt. Now, turn around and give me a taste of that hole."

I'm momentarily reluctant to leave the safe haven of the hot water, but the second I've flipped over and presented my butt to him, his face is in there, his tongue pushing straight into my pucker. My moan is so loud, I'm sure I've disturbed the neighbours, but Dominic isn't deterred in the slightest. He's grunting with full force, eating me out with the roughness of a frenzied lion. I've just grabbed hold of my cock when he withdraws. A container is slapped down next to me. I shift back to get a better look at it. "Flora?" I chuckle. "I used to use this to wank with when I was a kid."

"And," says Dominic, his voice right near my ear, "it's gonna allow me to slide into that hairy cunt of yours underwater." He grabs a glob of it and I turn my head around to see him rise above the surface and slather it all over his penis. "Get up here and give me your cock," he orders.

I raise myself, bracing my hands against the edge of the tub, then turn around to face him once more. Dominic pulls back my foreskin, slicking another fistful of the oily margarine over my knob. The jolt of pleasure I feel almost brings on the orgasm I know isn't far away. God, I wish I'd masturbated this morning. I'm going to come at teenage speed.

He ushers me back around again, pulling me down under the water with my back to him. Grabbing my hips and using his knees, he pries my legs right open. "Straight in, big bear?"

"Please," I whimper. I feel his knob pressing against my sphincter and I push outwards, letting him slide inside me with one smooth shove.

"Oh, fuck," he groans. "How do you *do* that? How do you let my dick just *ram* up your hole?"

I want to laugh at the amazement in his tone, but I'm too busy moaning. "Dildos," I gasp. "I've got Adult World on speed dial, I've been in there so many times buying them."

Dominic growls, sliding his long prick in and out of my rectum. "Just for me, big bear? Really?"

"Yes, *lontra.* But I've gotta admit it's been a fun learning curve."

With a lusty chuckle, he begins to thrust harder. It's fucking heavenly. I really want to last, but I urgently need to touch myself. I grab hold of my dick with both hands, resting my head and shoulders against the edge of the spa. My knob is still beautifully greased-up, even though it's immersed in water. I can't believe I've never thought of doing this before.

I hear a snarl in my ear. "So, every night you're not with me, you're stretching this beautiful manhole of yours? Are you thinking of me while you do it?"

"Oh, fuck, Dominic," I moan. "What do you reckon?" He's right. Since I've been fucking myself silly with dildos, I just close my eyes and dream of the many times we've made love. I don't even look at porn these days. The vast bank of Dominic-memories I've got stored up is more than enough to bring me to orgasm now.

Dominic starts slamming into me with even greater venom. "You really fuck that hole while you think of me? Oh, God, hurry up, big bear! I can't hold off. I'm gonna come..."

My cock swells and my arsehole clenches. "I'm already there, *lontra.*"

Our wails happen at the same time. The pressure in my prostate detonates and my cock sends missiles of sperm into the swirling water. Dominic's clutching me tight as he convulses. I feel the throb of his cock against the rim of my arsehole, driving his potent nectar deep inside me. It's been our fastest fuck to date, but by God, it was exhilarating.

"Sweet Jesus, I needed that," Dominic sighs, as we cuddle up to each other afterwards. He turns and looks me in the eye. "I needed *you.*"

* * *

The next morning, I'm laying in bed, checking my phone while Dominic's in the bathroom. My stupid big thumbs fumble as I'm trying to text, and the damn thing falls on the bed, skidding off and tumbling to the floor. Cursing to myself, I lean over, hanging from the edge of the mattress, groping for the wayward gadget. Out of the corner of my eye, I spot something. A book, with a crumpled hand-towel next to it. Forgetting about my phone, I reach under the bed to retrieve both articles. I flip back up again and settle against the pillows for a closer inspection.

It's a battered porn paperback. On the front is a cleverly-drawn picture of a dark-haired, bearded man with a red-faced grimace. He's wearing a schoolboy's blazer and tie and he's bent over, with the edge of his bare, hairy arse visible behind him. And there, in the background, is a stern-faced headmaster holding a cane.

A naked Dominic saunters back into the room, his dick flopping happily as usual. Seeing me propped up in bed with his secret stash, he stops dead in his tracks. I watch in amusement as his face turns scarlet.

"'*Fifty Grades of Ché?*'" My eyebrows are raised and I'm trying my best not to snigger. Pressing the small towel against my nose, I take a deep sniff. The unmistakable scent of Dominic's semen infiltrates my senses. "Mmmmm. Is there something you wanna tell me?"

Dominic's mouth is open. He's lost for words. I decide to try a different tactic. "Is this something that turns you on, Dominic? Something you want to explore?" He chews on his lips, still not sure what to say. "*Lontra,* this is a judgement-free zone. You tell me what arouses you, and I'll make it happen."

With some hesitation, Dominic comes closer. He pulls the book from my hands, turns the cover to face me and points directly at the red-faced schoolboy. "This."

I want to tease him more, but my dick is stiffening right now. I have to make sure I've got it right. "The schoolboy is you?"

My heart pounds faster as Dominic's head tilts ever-so-slightly in assent.

* * *

"Um… have you got any canes? Like for schoolboy/headmaster play?"

Bradley, the manager at Adult World, doesn't bat an eyelid. "How hard do you like it?" he asks.

I chuckle nervously. "Nah, mate. You've seen the kind of stuff I buy." I can feel my face flushing. I shouldn't be embarrassed. Pretty much all of us poofs like things stuck up our arseholes, don't we? I clear my throat. "This isn't for me, it's for my boyfriend." Fuck, I love saying that word out loud. I'm getting used to it now, but it still gives me a little thrill every time it passes my lips. "Oh, and no. He's a beginner. Just wants to indulge his curiosity."

With a knowing smile, Bradley minces to the rear corner of the shop, leaving me to lumber along behind him. "A cane is pretty painful," he trills in his camp, funny tone. He passes me a flat wooden article. I look it up and down, turning it in my hands. I have no bloody idea. "Try a paddle," he says. "It'll hurt, but it won't kill him. You could also use a wooden spoon, but it's not really appropriate for a schoolboy fantasy. Not unless he wants to get spanked by Aunty Maureen in the tuck-shop during recess."

I shift nervously, letting out a goofy laugh. I sound like a total dickhead. "Yeah, I reckon I'd look better in a tweed suit than a cafeteria lady's apron. But… I think it's gotta be a cane. You know, to make it more authentic." I cast my eyes over the range of them hanging against the wall, running my fingers along the surface of each one. "Do they all hurt just as bad? I mean, is one a bit less severe?"

Bradley picks a slightly thicker-looking sample off the rack. "This would be better. The thin ones are for more experienced play. But remember, go easy on him at first. Use your traffic lights and safe words."

All this jargon is hurting my brain. "Um… I don't wanna sound all uncool and clueless, but can you dumb it down for me?"

Bradley gives me an indulgent smile. *Fuck. He knows way too much about me already.* Ticking each point off with his fingers, he launches into Spanking 101. "He says 'green' it means he loves it and he wants more. He says 'orange' it means he wants you to slow down and ease up. He says 'red' and it means he wants you to stop."

"And the safe word?"

"Tell him to think of something he hates. Something random, like his least favourite food. And you make sure you both remember it. The second you hear him say that word, it's over. You understand me?"

Locking that information into my brain, I thank Bradley and he leads me back to the counter. During our journey, I spot something on another wall rack. "Those," I blurt.

"These?" he asks, pulling down the leather handcuffs I've indicated. He passes them to me and I inspect them closer. They have all these buckles and straps. You could probably get yourself out of them, but it'd take you a while. And in between the cuffs, there's another long leather strap. Seeing my quizzical look as I fondle this part of the getup, Bradley says, "that's for attaching them to a bedhead. Or a bedpost, or whatever else you want to tether him to."

My face is crimson as I hand over my credit card for the expensive purchase. I remind myself that Dominic is worth the dent to my dignity and my bank balance. I'll do anything for that cocky bugger.

I wander up King Street a couple of blocks to St Vincent de Paul. I'm not sure if I'll find anything, but there'd have to be some portly old codger who's donated his suit. As luck would have it, some old codger did. A daggy vintage tweed jacket and brown trousers, to be exact. I squeeze myself into the tiny dressing room, drop my daks and pull on the trousers. The waist fits fine, but they're kind of tight around my arse. I look over my shoulder into the mirror. On second thoughts, my arse looks *hot*. And the rear seam chews right into my crack. Dominic's gonna love them. The jacket smells a bit like naphthalene. But the buttons do up over my tummy without too much difficulty. That'll be good enough.

I start hunting for a costume for Dominic. I know it's a long shot, but I'm hoping there's some eighteen-year-old whose mum has gotten rid of his old uniform or something. My heart sinks as I flick through rack after rack, finding only bloody tiny sizes of anything remotely suitable. In desperation, I look back over to the men's suits and jackets. There, I spot the sleeve of something hideous and way-too-blue sticking out. I pull it from the crammed rack and look it over. It's a blazer with horrible piped edges down the front. On the breast pocket are the embroidered words: *St Thomas Aquinas Boys' College.* Bingo.

A daggy pair of wire-rimmed glasses, an ugly brown tie and an equally foul navy-and-red striped one complete my shopping haul. This is gonna be epic.

Back at home, I pack my clothing purchases neatly at the bottom of a large sports bag. There's no time for dry cleaning and I'm not going to reveal my surprise by carrying a suit pack with me. Assessing the length of the cane, I manage to fit it in over the clothes on the diagonal. From the power point next to my bed, I unplug a sex toy I ordered online. It looks hot and I actually bought it for myself, but I haven't put it anywhere near my arse yet. It'll be far more interesting to use Dominic as my guinea pig.

Settling back on my bed, I Google Grenfell House. It looks gorgeous, exactly as Dominic described. When I dial the number, an older gent by the name of William answers. "Uh, hi, William. My name's Ryan and my boyfriend Dominic has booked us into your B and B this weekend."

William doesn't even need to look it up. "Ah, yes. Two of you next Friday and Saturday night. I've got you in the honeymoon suite."

"Oh, wow!" *Honeymoon* suite. "I can't wait." I'm trying to gather my nerve. Here goes. "Um, William, it's kind of a special celebration for us. And we like to be a little, uh, *rowdy* in the bedroom." After my session with Bradley in the sex shop earlier, I'm on a roll. I may as well get all my ducks lined up in a row.

If William is amused, I'm certain he's doing his level best not to show it. "I dare say you'll have no issues. Your room is downstairs at the end of the corridor. There's just myself and one other couple staying upstairs in the rooms on the other side of the house. So you won't be disturbing anyone."

Perfect.

Chapter Thirteen

After slipping out of work a bit before two on Friday, I lug my sports bag over the road to the lunch bar as planned. The place is nothing flash, just a no-frills takeaway aimed at all the tradies and other workers in our industrial area. The food is cheap, the staff are nice and it's refreshingly unpretentious. There's a distinct chill in the air, but I plonk my arse down on one of the plastic outdoor chairs in front of the shop to roll a durry while I wait.

I've just about finished my smoke when Dominic pulls up. Chucking the butt in someone's abandoned takeaway coffee cup, I sling my bag over my shoulder and stroll towards his waiting sports car. If I'm gonna be honest, I'll admit to feeling a twinge of envy every time I see the immaculately-restored 1969 MGB roadster. The British racing green duco is *so Dominic*. He winds down the passenger window and warm air wafts out from the interior. "We're only going for two nights. What the hell have you got in there, Princess?"

"Never you mind. Paris Hilton's gonna stick this in the boot, so pop it open." I haul my luggage round the back and squeeze it in next to Dominic's more modest-sized but expensive-looking bag. I also take the opportunity to shove a couple of Butter Menthols in my mouth. It's only polite not to reek of tobacco when you're in such close quarters with someone.

I love riding shotgun at times like this. Dominic holds my hand the whole way, fondling my fingers and stroking my palm. Of course, there are gear changes involved in a manual car like this, but I can predict every one of them. As a tradie, having a ute that isn't a manual is akin to admitting you have no testicles.

When we arrive at Grenfell several hours later, it's already dark. Grenfell House is lit up, the outside lamps casting a beautiful glow around the porches and garden. It's a picturesque homestead, the kind of stately mansion you'd imagine seeing on an Aussie period TV drama. We park around the back and I follow Dominic, trudging over the loose stone path that winds through the lush garden beds to the front of the building.

William greets us at the door. He's a kindly gent, I guess maybe in his early seventies. "Continental breakfast is served in here between eight and ten," he announces, showing us into a lovely-looking dining room to the right. The antique furniture and vintage decor give it an elegant old-world charm. "And behind this is the guest sitting room." He leads us further down the hall to show us a large, exquisitely-furnished lounge, decorated with lush couches, intricate cabinets and a large occasional table. My weary body instantly wants to sink into one of those couches with Dominic, but I have more pressing things planned for tonight.

We follow our host down a long corridor to the other side of the building. "You have your own bathroom on this side of the hallway," William says, indicating a door to the right. "And here," he opens a door on the left, "is your suite." He turns to look at me. "I think you'll find you have all the privacy you need." The corners of his mouth turn up ever-so-slightly.

The room is stunning. It's huge, with a raised living area on one side and a spacious bedroom area on the other. I push my hand against the mattress, which feels like a cloud. God, we are gonna sleep well tonight. "We've even got our own courtyard," chirps Dominic, opening a French door and poking his head out. "But it's a bit bloody cold right now." He ducks back in and closes the door, keeping the warmth from escaping out into the frigid night.

I heft my bag onto one of the luggage racks, then saunter over to Dominic. Pulling him into my arms, I kiss him long and hard on the lips. "You go and shower first," I say.

"Are you telling me I stink?"

Chortling, I pull up his arm and bury my face in his pit. "Mmmmm," I purr. I've got him well-trained. No nasty deodorant, just pure *man*. "You always smell so good, I get hard just thinking about it," I growl. "But I have a surprise to get ready. So, fuck off and do as you're told."

With Dominic gone, I get to work. Unpacking my sports bag, I start with the cane, which I hang on the hook behind the door, underneath one of the terry-towelling bathrobes. Then I unpack my brand new sex toy, slipping it into the drawer of the bedside table, along with a tube of lube. Taking out Dominic's blazer, tie and one of my button-up shirts, I smooth them down and arrange them on the bed. And finally, I gather my folded costume and cover it with my towel, leaving the bundle on top of my bag. Slipping into my down parka, I open the French door and step outside, braving the cold for a well-earned smoke while I wait.

Just as I'm returning from the courtyard, Dominic wanders back into the suite with a towel wrapped around his waist. I stride over to him and rip the offending article off. My cock starts to thicken as soon as I spot his lengthy prick, which is still pointing at a downward angle but well on the way to a chubby. Set underneath his furry torso and hairy bush, it's spectacular in its brazen masculinity. I very nearly squat down to get a taste, but I restrain myself.

Adopting a stern tone, I bark out my orders. "Your clothes are on the bed. Make sure you're wearing them by the time I get back." Turning on my heel, I scoop up my towel-covered bundle and exit to the bathroom.

It's steamy and hot in there. I pamper myself in the elegantly-appointed shower, getting my undercarriage prepped and squeaky-clean. I know how much Dominic loves my natural scent, but it just feels so good washing away the grime of a long day. There will be plenty of time to indulge in sweaty manly fragrance later, anyway. It takes two towels to dry myself enough so that I can slip into my suit. I pull my hair back into a tight ponytail and slip on the ridiculous wire-framed glasses.

When I enter the room, Dominic is sitting on the edge of the bed, legs spread, dick dangling down, wearing his schoolboy blazer, shirt and tie. "What the hell have you come as?" he laughs, taking in my tweed monstrosity.

I deepen my voice. "I've come to punish you for being such a little shit." Dominic stifles a giggle. "I mean, a hooligan. No—a *delinquent.*"

"Where are my pants?" he retorts, flipping his cock and balls up and down with his hand. The low-hanging gonads jiggle and I see that he's starting to stiffen again.

"Delinquents like you don't get pants. They turn over and show me their bare arse so I can inspect it before I spank it."

Dominic shoots me an amused little smirk, then rolls over onto his stomach, his legs hanging over the edge of the bed. I kneel down on the carpet between his ankles. Running my hands over his furry, spread-out rump, I bury my face straight inside. Dominic groans in anticipation, but there's going to be no tongue right now. This is for *my* pleasure, not his. He's scrubbed clean, but I can still detect his manscent. I run my nose up and down, sniffing in his pheromones till my head starts to spin. The hair in his crack caresses my nose and cheeks. My cock is straining inside the tight trousers. I can feel it starting to leak.

"Now, I'm going to give you some instructions, young Dom."

"Don't call me that. You know I fuckin' hate it. Anyway, aren't I meant to be a bloody sub?"

"Quiet!"

Dominic is unperturbed, cocky as ever. "I'll start calling you 'Rye.' See how much you like sounding like a loaf of fuckin' bread."

I'm giggling under my breath, trying not to break character. This is getting ridiculous. "Silence," I snap, giving him a small slap on the arse.

Dominic moans and wiggles his little butt. "Do that again."

"SILENCE!" I yell, giving him another slap, a little harder this time. "Now, listen closely. If you say the word 'green', I'll know you're not remotely sorry and you'll get another spank. If you say the word 'orange', I'll know you're thinking about how bad you've been and I'll do it lighter. If you say the word 'red', then I'll know you've decided you'll be a good boy and you won't get any more spanks. Are we clear?"

"Yes."

"What's the food you hate most in the world, young Dom?"

"What's that got to do with the price of fish, *Rye*?"

"Answer. My. Question."

Dominic laughs. "Roast pumpkin. Especially the way your mum did it. Made me fuckin' puke."

God, yes. It was revolting, that's for sure. "Listen carefully. If I hear you say 'roast pumpkin,' it's all off. Finished. *Do you understand me?*"

"Yes, sir. Hurry the fuck up and punish me. My cock's about to burst, here, *Rye*." Dominic's insolent little sing-song tone has me snorting with mirth again, trying not to lose my shit entirely.

I stand up and stride over to the door, fetching the cane from under the terry-towelling robe, and grabbing the leather handcuffs from the vanity flap in my suitcase. "Lie in the middle of the bed," I order. Dominic scuttles into position straight away. "Hands out."

Grabbing his wrists, I clamp the leather around them and do up the series of buckles firmly. I pull his arms over his head with the long middle strap, then buckle it to the centre bedpost. "Now," I bark in my deepest tone. "Here is what I will be punishing you with." I hold out the cane. "Consider this carefully. Do you think you deserve to be spanked?"

Dominic eyes the cane, one eyebrow cocked. "Yes." He looks up at me with a smarmy sneer.

"Are you *sure?*"

"I'm a little cunt. I need a hiding, *Rye.*"

Oooh, it's on. "Turn over and show me that little cunt then, young *Dom.*"

Not wasting a second, he swings himself onto his stomach. "Like this?"

"Up on your knees!"

He hops onto all fours, sticking his arse right out as far as he can.

My dick thanks me as I peel off the tight trousers, springing out to dance in the warm air. I grab the lube from the bedside table and move around behind Dominic. His cheeks are open so wide they've disappeared entirely and his wrinkled hole is virtually level with the surface of his arse. The sight of it is so divine that my cock flexes hard. Quickly, I squirt a huge glob of lube into my left hand and spread it over the fingers of my right. My left hand goes around my knob, soothing my raging erection as I slick it up. The fingers of my right hand smear the viscous gel all over Dominic's anus, working it in well. He starts to moan as I apply pressure, slowly entering his muscular little ring, rubbing around the inside rim where I know I'll get the most rapturous response. Soon, there are two fingers in there and Dominic starts to whine. I advance them further, gently breaching his hole till I'm buried up to the last knuckle.

"Oh, God," Dominic whimpers, as I start to rotate and stretch my fingers apart. I'm well-prepared. I've filed and buffed my fingernails down to the quick. It doesn't take much effort to get a third finger into him. Dominic squirms as I twist them around, bumping the pads of them against his hard little prostate. He's yelping so softly and plaintively I take pity on him and reach underneath to grab his hard dick. Making a circle with my finger and thumb, I stroke it up and down over the ridge of his knob, relishing the way his cock jumps each time.

"Fucking torturer," he cries.

"Torture? You want torture?" I withdraw my fingers, admiring the way Dominic's anus springs back to a moist gape. I'm on my knees in a flash, my angry knob pressing on his open hole. "Push that little cunt out against me, young Dom. Now!"

He groans hard as I feel his sphincter loosen further, expanding around my throbbing glans. With seamless choreography, I've countered him and the entire thing has slipped inside. "Fuuuuuuck!" he yells. "Oh, God!"

"Colour!" I bark.

"Are you fuckin' kidding me? Green! Fuckin' green!"

I push a little more. The fiery, dank heat of his manhole feels incredible around my dick. I'm a gluttonous bottom, most of us poofs are. But this is priceless. Being inside Dominic's arse is a rare, heavenly treat and I'm going to relish every blessed moment of it.

Once I'm buried to the hilt, Dominic collapses his chest onto the bed. His wrists are still trussed up above him and his arse is now a flat plane with a stretched hole in the middle stuffed tightly with thick man-meat. The restraints on his arms upset me. I want him to be free, to be able to show me love in any way he needs. But this—all this rigmarole—is for Dominic. I desperately need to please him. *Shut up, Ryan. No negativity.* I move my eyes down and focus on the splendour of his arse instead. The wide invitation he's extending to me, the vulnerable exposure of such a personal place, makes for a potent and celestial vision. It's sheer manly beauty and I will never forget it for as long as I live.

I'm revelling in the power I feel as I'm buried deep in Dominic. It's a shame we have to move into the second act. *This* right here—this is what I love: masculine, animalistic sex. Wildly sensual, deeply loving men enjoying each other's bodies. But there's a task I have to complete. A promise I made.

I pick up the cane and run the cool wooden surface across Dominic's hairy flank. "Should I punish you now?"

"Yes!"

"Colours!"

"Fuckin' green! Green, ya bastard!"

OK, then. I start to pump my rigid prick into Dominic's rectum. Once I've got a good rhythm going—and a stream of high-pitched moans from my submissive victim—I raise the cane. I'm wincing. *How fuckin' hard do I have to do this? I'll try and go really easy on him.*

Thwack! The cane lands fair on his left arse cheek. "Aw, FUCK!" yells Dominic.

I rub his buttock with my free hand, thrusting my hips forwards. "Colour?"

"Green," he whimpers.

OK. Here goes again. Raising my arm, I land a blow on his other arse cheek.

"Green!" He's sounding breathless.

I thrust my dick into him a bit faster and raise my arm a third time, bringing down the cane even harder.

"Yes!" Dominic cries.

I'm spurred on, encouraged by his reaction. I gather more strength in my arm and drive down the cane with force. *Thwack! Thwack! Thwack!* Three successive blows land and Dominic screams, his guttural howl morphing into sobs.

This can't be good, can it? "Baby?" I say, my voice full of worry. "Please tell me what's going on?"

"Crushed pineapple—" he chokes out. "Fuck! *Roast fuckin' pumpkin!*"

I throw the cane across the room and collapse onto him, grabbing him tight. "Oh, God. I'm so sorry." I kiss his shoulders, the back of his neck and move around to his ear. "Are you OK?" I whisper.

Dominic's panting slows down to rapid breaths, then he lets out a low moan. His face is turned to the side and I can see tears on his cheek. "I'm alright." He swallows. "And you're so fuckin' wonderful for indulging me. But can we never, *ever* do this again?"

"Oh, thank *fuck!*" My sense of relief is palpable. "I hated hurting you, *lontra.*"

Dominic cranes his neck around, trying hard to catch my eye. "I love you, big bear. You really are the nicest man in the world."

I run my thumb under his eye, wiping away his tears. "I love you, too. So fucking much."

A warm smile works its way across Dominic's face. His damp eyes shine in the lamplight and his white teeth glint through his open lips. "You know one good thing? After that hiding you gave me, my arsehole is so bloody slack it feels like heaven with your cock inside me."

I'd almost forgotten about that. I cast my mind down to my dick, which is still hard and hot and wet inside Dominic's special place. "Um… in that case, I've got another surprise for you. This one I *know* you're gonna like."

I slide my cock out of Dominic. It's a rude shock not being submerged in his toasty warmth anymore, but I'm too curious to see what he'll think. Grabbing the toy from the drawer, I usher Dominic to flip over onto his back again. "I'm not gonna set you free of those cuffs just yet. But I reckon this'll blow your mind." I hold up the black silicone object.

"What on earth is that? Some kind of weird butt plug?"

"It's a Love Honey Rotating Prostate Massager," I state with authority. "And it's going right up here." Reaching between his legs, I slide my finger into his arsehole. "OK?"

"Bring it on," Dominic grins.

After I've slicked the toy with lube, I gently push the tip into Dominic's twitching anus. "Have you used a butt plug before?"

"No."

"Well, you know how it gets wide, then your hole kind of slips over that part and secures it in place?"

"Uh, yeah."

I twist the toy slightly, angling it, coaxing it inside Dominic. I'm anticipating a slow entry, but Dominic's greedy hole practically gobbles it up.

"Oh, fuck, Ryan. That feels so nice."

"You ain't seen nothin' yet, *lontra*." I grab the small remote from the drawer. Shooting him an evil grin, I press the button.

Dominic's eyes bug out. "Oh. Oh! Oh, shit! It's like... it's like it's fucking me hard!"

I chuckle as I bend down and slide Dominic's cock into my mouth. He's now fully erect again. God, it's such a pleasure sucking him. He's always fucking delicious and he loves the way I savour his knob and foreskin. He's whimpering now, a rapid barrage of tiny little yelps, his hips squirming and his thighs tensing over and over.

"Jesus, mate! You're gonna make me come so fuckin' fast!"

Those are the magic words. I start rubbing my aching cock. It's still all slick after its frolic inside Dominic's butthole. And—fuck me—the sensation of my skilful hand is twice as intense after all the stimulation my knob's been getting tonight.

I pull my mouth off Dominic's dick and he whines in protest. "Why'd you stop?"

Scrambling back up to my knees, I squeeze out some lube and jam two fingers in my arsehole. "Because it's my birthday and I deserve a little present, too, don't you think?"

I lift my leg over Dominic's waist, straddling him, then reach behind me, grab his cock and descend straight onto it in one smooth flourish. It's my turn to groan, now, as the burning in my ring merges with the wallop to my prostate when Dominic's knob grinds into it. I'm overwhelmed with urgency. It's been days since I've come. I've spent hours and hours with this beautiful man beside me, touching me. And it's been one long session of me getting up-close-and-personal with his naked body. I *need* to come. The situation is fucking dire.

I tighten my arsehole around his dick and ride him like a fucking jockey. My right hand yanks my foreskin to the base of my shaft and my left hand squishes hard up and down over my knob. I can feel it coming on already. My thighs are on fire, I'm humping so fast. I look down and see Dominic, open-mouthed, brow contorted with intensity. It's enough to send me spinning out of control. Blood-curdling roars rip through me as I seize up. A small stream of spunk spurts out onto Dominic's furry stomach. Then I seize up even harder. The pressure in my cock and arse reaches a level I never knew possible. A spine-rattling convulsion wracks my body and a second shot of spunk skates across Dominic's chest, hitting his chin. The floodgates are now open and squirt after squirt follows, my prostate pumping hard as I keep bouncing.

Dominic is wide-eyed, his face in a divine grimace. His whole body shudders and he chokes out a strangled grunt. His cheeks turn red and his eyes screw up. I can feel the pulsing of his shaft against my sphincter. He's marking me, making me his own.

And I *am* his. There's no doubt in my mind.

Chapter Fourteen

After a relatively early night and a long, sound sleep, Dominic and I are freshly-scrubbed and in the dining room for breakfast soon after eight. The elegant dining table is beautifully set, and there's a full continental array on the large serving buffet. Dominic busies himself with the coffee pods, fixing his usual double espresso. I can't stand the stuff, so I'm pleased to see the range of teas available.

"How did you enjoy your first night?" asks William as he ferries in a tray of pastries. I'm so busy eyeing them off, my polite response doesn't make it out in time before Dominic chimes in.

"It was a learning curve. I think we discovered that some fantasies should just remain in the wank bank." He grins like a Cheshire Cat as he helps himself to a croissant.

My face turns red. I catch Williams's eye as he laughs. It's all the more embarrassing after our little phone discussion the other day. "Um, it was very comfortable, thank you. I love the room and the bed was fantastic." I cast my mind back to last night, wrapped around Dominic in our cosy cocoon. "It was a nice surprise because Dominic's also got an amazing bed at his place. I'm a bit spoilt."

"Oh, so you two don't live together?" asks William.

"Not yet," replies Dominic, shooting me a wink. "I'll make an honest man of him one day."

I'm blushing again. Is he trying to tell me something, or is he just being his usual cocky self?

We're spared any further discussion when a couple enter the room. The woman is curvy and funky, well-dressed with impeccable make-up and a platinum-blonde Roxette hairdo. The man is a tall, striking redhead with a well-maintained ginger beard. He smiles broadly at me and Dominic as the two of them move past us to the buffet table. Dominic's head turns in their direction and my eyes follow his. He's looking at the man, and I can see why. Ginger Otter is skinny and wiry, with a body similar to Dominic's. He's wearing a tight-fitting green polo tucked into beige chinos. And his little butt is so cute—two small, square glutes, dimpled in at the sides. Those glutes separate beautifully as Ginger Otter bends over the table to reach for things.

I turn back to Dominic and see him watching me with a smug grin. *"Nice arse,"* he mouths, with a wink. I try my best to stifle a giggle and end up snorting like a pig instead.

Roxette passes by us, giving Dominic and I a warm smile. Ginger Otter, however, strides up to me, plate in his left hand, and extends his right. "Hey guys, I'm Oliver." I put down my tea cup and shake his slender, long-fingered paw. He then leans across the table to shake Dominic's hand, too. I can hear Dominic introducing us, but I'm not paying attention. I'm fixated on Oliver's lip-smacking skinny arse, which is mere inches away from my face. Oliver stands up straight again. Passing his plate to his right hand, I feel his left arm slide across my shoulder. My eyebrows shoot skyward as I catch Dominic's gaze. "And this is my wife, Melinda." He points his plate towards Roxette, who gives a friendly wave amid mouthfuls of Danish.

Oliver joins Melinda at their seats further down the large dining table and I turn back to Dominic, who's grinning again. *"Bi,"* he mouths to me, and it's all I can do not to laugh again.

As we work our way through the bounty of toast, cereals, fruit, yoghurt and baked goods, Dominic and I get chatting with the friendly couple. They're from Tasmania, travelling through New South Wales visiting friends. Oliver works as some kind of engineer and Melinda is a public servant. They're off to visit a place I've never heard of for the day.

"What have you two boys got planned?" asks Melinda.

"Absolutely nothing," chirps Dominic. "We've been so bloody busy, we're due for some downtime. We're gonna laze around in the sitting room, enjoy the sunshine in our courtyard, maybe take a nap. Then we'll probably walk into town for dinner later on."

God, he knows this lazy Taurean bull so well.

Our day of decadence works out just as Dominic promised. I've never been one for naps, but now I'm ensconced in a love nest with this gorgeous otter, I'm only too happy to strip off and hold his naked body again for a long afternoon cuddle. We sleep for so long, there's not even time to have sex before we have to get ready for dinner.

When we're freshly showered and dressed, Dominic grabs my hand and we brave the chilly night air to take our stroll into the centre of town. Grenfell is a small place and it's less than ten minutes before we're in the hub of it all. "Come on," says Dominic, leading me to a pub called the Criterion Hotel. "This place is right up your alley. I've read great things about it."

I'm dubious. It looks nice, but I'm expecting drunken, rowdy yokels. *God, I really have become a city slicker these last seven years.* It's a pleasant surprise when we meet the bar staff: two very trendy girls and a young, pony-tailed gay guy named Harry. You'd think we were in some Sydney hipster wine bar, save for the fact these guys are super-friendly—unlike the painfully-disinterested bartenders back in our city.

Outside, there's a large beer garden, complete with tall outdoor gas heaters. Dominic and I spot a free barbecue table and bench, so we settle there, side-by-side next to one of those towering infernos. After devouring our huge steaks and several schooners, Dominic looks around the beer garden. "There's our breakfast buddies," he says. I glance up to see Oliver and Melinda at a round bar table over the other side of the courtyard. Melinda is busy chatting with two women, but Oliver spots us and gives us an enthusiastic wave.

It's not long before Oliver meanders over to us. "Mind if I join you guys for a while? It's Girls' Night Out over there."

"Sure, pull up a pew," says Dominic, reaching down and pinching my thigh.

"I'll just go get us another round," I say, sliding off the bench to stand up. "Cooper's OK?"

When I return with the schooners, I notice Oliver has taken my seat next to Dominic on the bench. They're laughing away, having a great old time. The alcohol's kicking in and I'm beginning to loosen up, so I decide to roll with Oliver's forthright move. Plonking the schooners on the table, I slide onto the other end of the bench next to the ginger greyhound. "Sorry, didn't mean to steal your seat," he says, his red beard splitting into a charming grin.

We're now huddled together, three-in-a-row, under the tacit pretext that we need to be as close to the gas heater as possible. By the end of our schooners, Oliver has one arm across each of our shoulders. He seems to be every bit as merry as the two of us. Not drunk, just a little tiddly. "You know," he says, "you two are a *hot* couple." He turns his head to me, then to Dominic. "Are you getting what I'm saying?"

Dominic shifts sideways, leaning his elbow on the table, resting the side of his head in his hand. "What are you proposing?" His eyebrows are raised and he's got an almighty smirk on his dial.

Oliver glances from me to Dominic once more. "The three of us," he blurts.

"But what about..." I point over to where Melinda is still chatting away.

Oliver erupts into an open-mouthed laugh. "Oh, no. We're open. And both bi. *She's* the one who's been egging me on to talk to you."

Dominic leans forward, one eyebrow cocked, staring at me. His face screams '*I told you so.*'

Oliver stands abruptly, lifting his long, lithe legs over the bench one by one. "I'm going to get us all another beer and leave you guys to discuss this for a moment." He strides off and I stare at his taut little buns as they disappear inside with him.

Dominic shuffles up to me and grabs my crotch, squeezing my hard penis. "You fuckin' *want* it, don't you." It's a playful accusation, punctuated by a shit-eating grin.

I reach over and clasp my hand around his equally-roaring erection. "So do you. Bloody hypocrite."

Dominic's still grinning like a sly dog. "He lives in Tasmania. We'll never see them again." His eyes grow serious and he moves his hand up from my throbbing dick to cup my chin. "And you and I will be together. That's the most important thing?" It's a question as much as an observation. The fact he's seeking my approval crushes me in the sweetest way.

I lean forward and kiss him gently. "Together," I mumble against his lips.

By the time all three of us have drained our glasses, our inhibitions have well and truly left the building. Melinda and her gal-pals have conspicuously departed. "Back to our hotel room?" Dominic asks Oliver.

We stagger along the main drag, not because we're pissed, but because Oliver has his arms slung over our shoulders. Speaking of piss, though, my bladder is bursting. "I need to take a leak," I announce.

"Me, too," says Oliver.

Nodding in agreement, Dominic follows us as we duck down the side of a building. Sweet relief washes over me when my pee hits the side of the brick wall. I glance to my right. Oliver's next to me, and the glow of a street lamp infiltrates the dark alley we're in. His penis is in his right hand and my view is unobstructed. Much like his body, it's long and slender. And it seems to be ever-so-slightly engorged with excitement as he begins to urinate. I'm gripped by a sudden wave of fascination. Without thinking, I reach my right hand over and wrap it around his dick. Oliver relinquishes control immediately. His shaft is smooth and silky. I pump his foreskin up and down, making the spray of watery, clear piss shoot in all directions.

"You're getting it everywhere!" Oliver laughs.

"Yeah, but it looks fuckin' hot, mate." I'm so mesmerised by the sight, I slide my thumb around the end of his knob, distorting the high-pressure stream gushing out of him.

"Jesus Christ!" Oliver's voice is a mixture of shock and amusement. If I had any doubt as to the nature of his response, it's made all too clear as his cock grows firmer in my hand.

Before Oliver's even close to finishing, Dominic swivels him around and crouches down in front of him. I don't even need to see what Dominic's doing. I can hazard a guess from the surprised yelps escaping Oliver's throat.

Not wanting to be outdone, I squat behind Oliver. Reaching around his slim waist, I undo his belt buckle and the top button of his trousers. One swift tug of my hands has all his lower garments down to thigh level, and I'm confronted by his gorgeous arse. It's the same delectable shape as Dominic's. His cheeks are smattered with ginger hair, which is also bursting from his furry crack. Gripping these taut little buttocks, I wedge my face straight between them. He's beautifully musky in there. I breathe deeply, seducing myself with his manly scent. *Oh, my fucking God.* My tongue goes to town on him straight away. He tastes as good as he smells. All over his pert, puckered hole I slather myself, gorging my senses on his divine little playground. I grab his hips harder, grinding my face right into him, and shove my tongue fair up his tight quoit.

Oliver bellows, but cuts himself off short, clearly mindful of where we are. "My God," he laughs. "You guys are fucking *dirty!*"

Car lights approach all of a sudden and we scramble to our feet, quickly tucking ourselves away. All three of us breathe a sigh of relief when the intrusive vehicle turns and heads down the street. Dominic catches my eye and shoots me a sly smile. "Let's continue this somewhere that we're not gonna get arrested, eh?"

* * *

Back at our hotel room, we waste no time ripping off our clothes. Dominic and me eye each other with a smile as we undo our belts and slip our jeans down, our commando cocks flipping right out to stand tall. I glance across to see Oliver, his back turned, pushing his trousers and undies down to his calves. He pauses there, bent over, his flattened arse cheeks splayed open to show us the ginger beard surrounding his anus. But he's not tantalising us; he's fiddling with something in his front pocket.

"Oh, guys," he says, standing up and turning to face us. His chest has a lovely rug of rusty orange fur, which extends down to his stomach in a finer fashion. The same orange hair snuggles in a thick patch above his long, majestic prick, which is waving at the ninety-degree mark. "I came prepared." His face is decorated with a charming blush as he holds up a strip of condoms.

I'm profoundly grateful that he's addressed this. It's a load off my mind. Dominic catches my gaze with a slight waggle of his eyebrows.

He seems to know what I'm thinking and I'm relieved. "Thanks, champ. Ryan and I don't take PrEP anymore, so frangers are perfectly fine with us."

I'm still standing next to the bed, naked as a jaybird. "How do you want us, Oliver?" I say.

He doesn't even need to ponder. "Both of you on all fours. I've gotta get acquainted with those hot arses."

In perfect sync, Dominic and I clamber onto the bed and assume the position. Oliver's right behind us; I can feel his hands pulling my arse cheeks apart. "Fu-u-u-ck!" he chortles. "Such a big, sexy bear arse!" Those last words are muffled as he dives right into my crack. I can feel his hot breath against me and his warm tongue starts firmly licking my hole.

Moaning, I reach under myself with my left hand and shuffle my foreskin back and forth. I don't want to get into a proper wank just yet—if I have my way, there will be a whole lot more activities on the agenda. Oliver grunts like a foraging pig. I can feel his vocal appreciation vibrating against my pucker. His tongue is so busy and rapid that my balls retract and electric shocks zap right through my nether regions. Suddenly, I can feel him breaching my hole. His tongue seems every bit as long and slender as his cock and it pokes right inside me, thrusting further than any man has ever done before. It's like I'm being fucked, and I'm literally hollering with how good it feels.

Dominic turns and kisses me. "Enjoying that, baby?" he whispers, his lips buzzing against mine. I can't even answer, I just chuckle in between pants.

My left hand is still around my cock, squeezing it, pumping my long hood up and down. I lower my chest and head onto the pillow, reaching out to Dominic and pulling him down with me. Sliding my arm over his shoulders, I draw him close and thrust my tongue into his mouth. We pash hungrily, moaning and grunting as we battle for dominance.

Oliver's face vacates my arse and I feel the mattress move as he leans back. "Oh, my fucking God, what a beautiful sight."

With Dominic and I still on our knees, and our faces and chests planted on the bed, our arses are pushed out in the most wanton way possible. I'm thrilled Oliver's enjoying the view so much.

Dominic groans right into my throat. I can hear the moist, sloppy sounds of Oliver's mouth and I know he's giving Dominic's arse the same treatment he gave mine. Dominic begins to whine—one gorgeous little sound of pleasure every second. "Nnnnnngh!" he groans suddenly.

I pull my lips slightly away from his and laugh. "You've just discovered how long his tongue is, haven't you?"

Dominic just smiles, squeezing his eyes shut and groaning again. His shoulders are jiggling as his arm jerks furiously, working his cock underneath him.

There's a light slap on my arse, then the sound of one on Dominic's, too. "Get up here, guys," Oliver growls.

Dominic and I scoot around, coming to a kneel facing Oliver. We've barely righted ourselves when he's pulled our heads in for a three-way kiss. It's hot, it's nasty and it's wild. Tongues dart around in a messy melee. Three bearded mouths mash together, turning this way and that. Hot breath, saliva and manscent are rampant. Our arms clutch around each other, holding us up, binding our three bodies together in tight unison. Down below, torsos press against torsos, fur rubs against fur. And underneath that, I feel two cocks prodding into mine, grinding back and forth with the slight movement of our hips. I've never been so overwhelmed. The raw animal lust is sending me into a brutal headspin.

Oliver takes the lead once again, pushing Dominic and I backwards with surprising force. We plonk our freshly-rimmed arses down on the pillows, our backs leaning against the bedhead.

"You know what I want now," Oliver says with a lusty chuckle. He flops his lanky frame onto the bed, grasping my dick in his left fist and Dominic's in his right. With a snarl, he clamps his lips over my cock and sucks hard. Inside the hot, wet depths of his mouth, I feel him slowly edging my foreskin back, stretching it right down as he bombards my knob and frenulum with his tongue.

"Oh, fuck, you're good at this," I pant. My thumbs have made their way to my nipples and they're stroking with featherlight precision, sending lightning bolts of pleasure down to my dick. My erectile muscles tense hard. I'm pumping precome right into Oliver's mouth and I can see him swallowing rapidly as he slurps.

I glance sideways at Dominic. He's relaxed back with his eyes closed and a wide smile on his face. Oliver's hand is stroking Dominic's dick with rhythmic ease as his mouth toils away on mine. My God, this man can multi-task.

Just when I think Oliver's going to go too far, he gives my dick a final suck and moves straight onto Dominic's. Oliver's hand lets go of my shaft and I see it slide underneath Dominic, whose breath catches violently. I know exactly where Oliver's just put his finger. I get precisely the same reaction when I do it to that Latin stud.

"Ah… ah… ah!" whines Dominic. "Jesus Christ, you're gonna have to stop."

Oliver's ginger eyebrows raise as he looks up at Dominic, his mouth still full of cock. Slowly, he retreats, letting his lips slide off Dominic's glans, forming them into a sly grin. "Was I that good?"

Dominic chortles. "You know exactly how fuckin' good you are, mate. But if you want any action, best not to make me blow."

Oliver's face lights up. "Wow. Does that mean one of you guys will fuck me?"

I look at Oliver there, lying on his stomach, propped up on his elbows. The lithe muscles on his skinny physique extend in two ridges down his back, eventually arriving at his tasty little butt. "Bloody oath, we will."

"Which one of us do you want?" Dominic says with a leer.

Oliver comes up to a kneel, taking each of our dicks into his fists again. "No offence to either of you, but I'm gonna choose Dominic. Your cock is way too thick, Ryan. You'll rip my arse in half."

"Good choice, mate. Ryan pounded the living daylights out of me last night and I'm still bloody sore." Dominic looks across at me with a smirk.

"Oh?" says Oliver, his eyes locking on mine, his forehead wrinkled in a cutely-inquisitive expression. "Are you the top?"

I practically guffaw. "I'm totally vers, mate."

"*I'm* the top," Dominic chimes in. "I only let Ryan's cock up my arse on special occasions."

Oliver eyes us off with a sudden thought. "Well in that case, I've always wanted to be the meat in the sandwich."

None of us need any further encouragement. We're instantly scrambling into position, lying on our sides. Oliver reaches over me, grabbing the condoms from the bedside table. While he and Dominic busy themselves covering their cocks, I scoot over, delve into the drawer and retrieve the lube. Squeezing out a glob, I rub it over my anus, my right fingers giving it a cursory prod. Seeing as Dominic's prick always goes straight up my hole with no trouble, Oliver's is not going to be any different.

I turn around to see Oliver stroking his condom-clad cock. It's pretty much the same length as Dominic's, and the rubber only comes two-thirds of the way down his shaft. I look into his eyes as I reach around his body. Slowly and gently, I push my middle finger amongst the fur in his crack and straight into his arsehole. It's tight, but it doesn't fight me. Oliver's brow screws up as he looks at me with intensity. But he's panting, whimpering, shuffling his hand over his cock. I know he's enjoying it. With a deft manoeuvre, I've partially slid out my middle finger, twisted it on an angle and inserted my fourth finger in alongside it. He moans loudly, his hand speeds up on his cock, and his sphincter squeezes around my inserted digits.

"I'll take over from here," pipes up Dominic, catching my eye with a wink. He moves forward, shifting Oliver's lissome body so it aligns with his own. His hand disappears behind Oliver. I can guess what he's doing by the way Oliver's eyes widen. A stifled, breathy holler escapes Oliver as Dominic thrusts forward in slow-motion.

I give them a moment, letting Oliver adjust, studying his face as pain turns to pleasure. His hand slides up and down his prick, keeping it nice and hard. I can't wait any longer. I roll over again and slither back towards him, reaching behind me for his dick. The snake-like appendage is hard as a rod and I guide it straight inside me. It's perfect. There's no pain, only bliss. It keeps on sliding up and up into me, penetrating me in the deliciously deep fashion I've become so used to in recent months.

How on earth we're going to actually move in this position is beyond me. I'm busy considering this when Dominic makes the decision for all of us. He starts ramming into Oliver, in turn sending Oliver's lengthy penis thrusting right up into my backside. Oliver's almost shrieking. "Fuck! This is incredible!" Dominic's grunting hard with every shove. As for me, I'm whimpering like a fucking baby. I'm rolling my foreskin hard, too scared to rub my knob. I want this to last at least a bit longer.

Clamping my sphincter muscles onto Oliver's dick, I start pushing my hips backwards to counter Dominic's thrusts. We are literally banging this redheaded otter from both directions and he's crying out with each impact. Dominic and I fall into a steady rhythm, ramming against Oliver at a rapidly accelerating rate. "Euh! Euh! Jesus, guys, I'm gonna come!" Oliver cries. With an evil chuckle, Dominic quickens his pace, going into overdrive. I squeeze and squeeze my arse muscles as I feel Oliver start to shake. His wails become wild and uneven. With one final jolt, his body slackens between us.

Dominic pulls out of Oliver, lying on his back and stripping off his condom. "Your turn, Ryan."

Oliver's still way up inside me and I'm absolutely enamoured with his dick, but it's time for me to get rogered into oblivion. It takes a substantial move upwards to get all of Oliver's inches out of me. He lifts his lithe limbs over my body and props himself up, staring down at my face with a grin. "I'm gonna swallow every drop of your load, buddy."

As soon as the coast is clear, Dominic's right behind me, pushing me to my side in the same position Oliver was just in. We're well-rehearsed in this. He grabs my hip and guides his erection straight up my arse.

A set of lips wraps around my cock and I glance down to see Oliver's ginger hair, his head already bobbing as he sucks with rampant hunger. When Dominic starts to thrust into me, I completely surrender. I lie there in a state of utter euphoria as two men take care of me in the most exquisite way imaginable. My arse is in seventh heaven as Dominic's knob pummels my prostate. Every time he drives into me, my cock flexes hard, immediately met by the firm rubbing of Oliver's tongue, and the hot, wet suction of his mouth. It's too much. I don't know what kind of sound I'm making. I don't have the coherence to give a warning. I'm in ecstasy as the most delicious pain hijacks my being. Higher and higher the pressure inside me builds until I detonate. Colossal contractions send my seed shooting into Oliver's mouth, flooding him as they project time and time again. I'm now acutely aware of Dominic's high-speed thrusts, his warm breath strafing the back of my head, and the sudden, guttural roar that barrels from his throat as he clasps me tight and convulses.

Dominic and I collapse onto our backs, catching our breath. Oliver rises up from my right side, licking his lips. "Fuck, your load tastes so good." He leaps over me, nimble as a cat, and settles his slim body in the small space between Dominic and me. I roll over to face Oliver, sliding my arm underneath the pillow. My hand finds Dominic's hand, tucked underneath his own pillow. I reach over Oliver and grasp Dominic's other hand, bringing it across to rest with mine on top of Oliver's warm, flaccid penis. We form a perfect circle there, breathing deeply, sinking into the mattress as we fall asleep.

It's some time later before we stir. The bedside lamps are on, bathing the room in a subtle light. Somehow we've switched places. I now have a lanky otter underneath each arm, and two heads are snuggled against my chest. My hands are extended down. Apparently I've been stroking their arse cracks in tandem as I slept.

"Mmmmm. What time is it?" our redheaded friend asks.

"One a.m," says Dominic, checking his Rolex.

"Oh, man. Guess the fun had to end sometime." Oliver sits up, rubbing his eyes and stretching. "I'm sure I'm way past my curfew."

When he's dressed and at the door, he turns to us with a wistful smile. "Thanks, guys. That was a ride I'll never forget." And then he's gone.

I feel a sharp twinge of sadness. I don't know anything about bisexual open marriages. But I do know how empty it feels when you leave a mind-blowing hook-up, all too aware that it will never be repeated.

Dominic shuffles closer, pulling me into a hug. "Are you OK, big bear?" he says softly.

"Yeah. That was really fun." I turn my head to look into his dark eyes. "But only because you were there to share it with me."

I can see Dominic thinking, searching my face, trying to find the right words. "Ryan," he starts, "I don't want a full-on open relationship. I don't want us trawling the apps, breaking our dates to hook up with randos. I don't want to imagine you out somewhere doing it with other guys." He grabs my hand and brings it to his mouth, planting a gentle kiss before continuing. "But on the odd occasion, if we find a willing guy like we did tonight…"

When Dominic's voice trails off, I step in to finish his thought. "Then we act like horny gay men and we enjoy every second. But always with the two of us together."

Dominic lets out the breath he's been holding, his face softening in tender affection. "*Always* together, big bear."

* * *

By the time we've packed our bags the next morning, it's nine-thirty and we only have a short time left for breakfast. Dominic goes out to settle the bill while I scan the room for anything left behind. Over near the wall, I spot the cane I threw across the floor on Friday night. I dare say it's no use to us now. I walk over and retrieve it, noticing for the first time a large harlequin doll on a cabinet in the sitting area. Chuckling to myself, I straighten the bed, plump the pillows and sit Harlequin against them. And across his lap I place the cane, arranging his hands over it.

Here you go, William. Our gift to you.

There's no sign of Oliver or Melinda at breakfast. Maybe they've already checked out. As Dominic and I make our way down the stone garden path to leave, Melinda strolls in the side gate. She looks stunning as usual, sharply dressed and made up. "Did you have fun last night, boys?" she asks, cocking an eyebrow.

I turn crimson instantly. "Uh, yeah. It was great." Fuck, that was a dumb response. But what the hell else can I say?

Dominic doesn't miss a beat. "Yeah, thanks for the loan, Melinda."

She laughs out loud. "No, thank *you.* He always performs so much better after he's been serviced."

* * *

The next morning I'm in at work by seven. Unusually, Marisa's already there, organising the office. As soon as she sees me, she drops the papers she's holding and rushes up to give me a huge hug. "Happy birthday, Ryan!" She pulls back out, clutching my shoulders. "How was your weekend?"

"Thanks. It was—"

"A man." She's scanning my face. "No. *Men.* You dirty little tart!"

Wow. Spot on. "Yeah. Busted."

"Who? Who were they?"

"Nobody you know," I chuckle. I've studiously avoided her on Monday mornings, after the high of my weekend flings with Dominic. I don't need her reading me like a book. To date, it hasn't been hard, because I start work earlier than she does and I'm off on site long before her arrival. Nevertheless, I feel bad keeping these big things from her. She's a friend as well as a workmate. One day soon, I'll sit her down and tell her all about Dominic. Well, not *all.*

"I came in at this ungodly hour because I wanted to catch you before you left," she says in a breezy tone. She turns and saunters over to her desk, her jewellery jangling as she digs into a drawer. Coming back up to me, she hands me a small, beautifully-wrapped oblong gift. I remove the paper with great care. I always feel bad destroying it when someone's gone to so much effort with their presentation.

It's a box with weird pictures on it. "Tarot cards," she pipes. "You can't buy them. They don't work that way. You have to be given them."

"Wow. They're beautiful. How do I use them?" I'm clueless.

"That's where I come in. I'm gonna sit down and do yours."

I shift uncomfortably, but I can only smile at her enthusiasm. "Thank you so much." I turn the cards over, studying the intricate designs. I'm genuinely touched. "We might have to do it another time, though, or I'll be late."

I give her slight frame a big bear hug, then busy myself getting my stuff organised to leave. It's a narrow escape. I'm definitely not ready to share my secrets just yet.

As I hop into my ute, my phone chimes with a message.

»Happy birthday, big bear! I know you're busy, so I'll leave the sexy phone calls till you knock off tonight. Just wanted to give you a heads-up—be really careful driving into your back courtyard when you get home.

I'm intrigued. If I was on a site anywhere near the inner west, I'd duck home to see what Dominic was on about. But I leave it till I finish work at three-thirty. Pulling up in the laneway behind my house, I switch on my hazard lights and hop out to open the gate. Just inside is a massive teddy bear. He must be four feet tall. And tied to his hand with a neat red ribbon is a small gift with a tiny tag on it.

"A big bear to love for the big bear I love."

In the gift box is a top-of-the-range G-Shock watch. It must have cost hundreds and hundreds of dollars. What crushes me most, though, isn't the amount of money he's spent. It's the way he knew exactly what I'd like. Dominic is impeccably-dressed and flashy, all expensive suits and Rolexes. But me, with my scruffy tradie clothes and copious tatts—well, this gift speaks volumes. If I could cry, I would.

Chapter Fifteen

A week and a half later, Dominic calls me on Thursday about our regular weekly rendezvous. "Hey big bear, sorry to do this to you, but I've gotta go to Melbourne for work and I won't be back till early Sunday morning. We could spend Sunday together and you could stay over that night, if it suits?"

I have to think for a moment. There's something important I've got planned Sunday evening and it can't possibly be moved. "Um, I'd love to. Any time I get with you is a bonus, *lontra.* But… it's Owen's birthday. I've got a sort of ritual I do every year. If you don't mind, I could go take care of that and come back again."

"Oh, baby." Dominic's voice is gentle. "Do you want to do it alone? Can I come with you, or is that gonna intrude on your space?"

It will, actually. It's going to be an emotional minefield for me and I'd hate for Dominic to witness it. But… I can read between the lines. He wants to be there to support me. How can I say no? "Sure. I mean, if it won't make you feel uncomfortable."

"Big bear, if you can't lean on me, then what use am I? You know I'll do anything for you, don't you?"

* * *

There's a biting chill in the air as we head down the block from Dominic's apartment to my ute late Sunday afternoon. As he climbs in the passenger side, Dominic notices the bunch of yellow roses I have stashed in a small bucket on the floor. "These are beautiful," he says softly.

The drive to Lane Cove is sombre. Dominic chats away and I make sure to smile at regular intervals. I'm hyper-aware I have to put in an effort. Maybe his buoyant mood will help prevent me from slipping under.

I pull up my ute next to the park flanking the cove. Reaching across the console, I lift the bouquet of flowers out with great care. Dominic and I stroll through the tree-lined park. The scent of wood smoke permeates the cold evening air. Part of the park is closed off for construction as we near the water. We walk around the taped-off fence, and the splendour of the cove hits us in full technicolour.

The sun is low on the western horizon, casting ripples of golden light across the surface of the bay. At the water's edge, there's a small dinghy tethered. Dominic gives me a quizzical glance. "Are we going out on this?"

"Only as far as the boat." I point out towards a series of buoys, where different sizes of small vessels are anchored. "Barry's one of my bosses at work and he loans me his when I need to… you know." Keeping my word count low is crucial right now. Every one that tumbles from my mouth makes me a little weaker.

Barry's speedboat is one of the more modestly-sized ones. You could probably lie down in it, though that's about it. Under different circumstances, I'd be imagining how wonderful it would be to fuck Dominic in it, way out in the harbour as it bobs around. But I can't think about that right now.

We chug out further into the bay, till we're a good distance from anyone. I'm never sure exactly where to go when I do this, but I always know when I reach it. "Owen and I used to go sailing on Fannie Bay in Darwin all the time. It was the place he felt happiest." I pick up the bunch of yellow roses and pull a handful of petals off, holding them over the edge and letting them flutter down to settle on top of the water. "And these flowers held a special significance for us."

* * *

I woke up later in the morning than I usually did, so deep and peaceful was my sleep. Emerging from my fog, I realised I was at Owen's apartment. I groped around for the slim, warm little body that was almost always touching mine in one way or another.

Slowly, I raised myself to sit up against the bedhead, getting my bearings, rubbing my eyes. When I opened them, in walked Owen, completely naked. His big, thick penis flopped around between his slender little hips, its wrinkled foreskin pointing slightly to the side like a shy child. My endless fascination at his manhood distracted me momentarily from what he was holding in each hand: a large mug of tea in the left and a massive bunch of yellow roses in the right. "Happy twenty-first, my gorgeous teddy," he sang, his smile shining as bright as the morning sun.

"Jesus," I said, flabbergasted. "These must have cost a bloody mint!"

"Not really," he replied, sliding the tea on the bedside table, handing me the obscenely large bouquet and giving me a hug. I didn't believe him for a second, but I wasn't going to push the point. I was far too moved. I couldn't have imagined anything more special. "They just delivered them," he continued. "I don't know what they're supposed to signify, but I think they look nice and sunny."

Yeah. Just like your personality.

"They're perfect, little man. I love them." I wrapped my arms round his

body and pulled him against me, my face nuzzling into his shoulder. "Thank you so much. It's the best birthday present ever."

"That's not all," he said, breaking free and kissing me on the lips. "Time for you to get up so I can take you out to breakfast."

I shifted the bouquet, then grabbed his body again and rolled him on top of me as he giggled. Mashing my lips against his, I pushed my tongue inside his mouth, licking him where he tasted incredible, hearing his light whimpers as he responded in kind. "Maybe we have time for a little fun, first?" I purred, in amongst the tonsil hockey. My penis definitely agreed with that suggestion, but Owen had other ideas.

"Drink your tea," he said, sitting up and handing it to me. "I swear I will do whatever you want me to do to your body later on. But right now we got a schedule."

Breakfast was at an upmarket hotel buffet. We were both ravenous, as usual, so the all-you-can-eat aspect was particularly awesome. No surprise for me, given my big, solid body. But for such a slightly-built guy, Owen could sure pack it away. When we were stuffed and fully sated, Owen grabbed my hand. "Next thing coming up now."

He wouldn't tell me where we were going, but we hopped into his old van and he drove up to Fannie Bay, turning into the driveway of the sailing club. "We're going out on the bay," he announced.

"Since when did you own a boat?"

"Cor, I wish, mate!" he laughed. "I just hired an outboard dinghy for the day. Bay's really calm, so we'll be fine."

He drove round to the boat park and pulled up next to a small aluminium number. It was a cosy little thing; just big enough for a couple of people. "I gotta admit I know nothing about boating," I said, marvelling at the ease of which he hitched the trailer.

Owen looked up at me, grinning proudly. "Well, I hope you're gonna like your present, then."

He manoeuvred the boat down the ramp with studied ease. Before long, we were in the water and I couldn't hide how impressed I was. "You're an old hand at this, Owen. How'd you learn it all?"

He started the motor up, a wistful look on his face. "My dad. He was a real nasty piece of work. Abusive bastard. Took off when I was thirteen. Boating's the only nice memory I have of him, really. Dad taught me a lot and I hung onto that. Started doing it again when I got a bit older."

I remembered Costa's cruel, tasteless jibes about the abuse Owen and his mum suffered. I never pried. This was the first time Owen had mentioned it and I felt so special that he trusted me enough to talk about it. When we were a good distance out, he cut the motor. I drew him near and hugged him close to my heart. "I'm so sorry all that shit happened to you, Owen. Thanks for opening up to me."

Owen didn't reply, he just nuzzled me, kissing my neck. It was a difficult topic for him, clearly. Moving back out, he smiled. "Look, Ryan. Nobody's here."

I cast my eyes out in front, around and behind us. The coast was way back, and we were surrounded by miles of still, blue-green water. I pulled Owen's t-shirt off, then hooked my fingers under his waistband, sliding his shorts and undies right down. His penis was fat and rapidly hardening, and he fondled it as I took off my own clothes. "God, I love watching you touch yourself, Owen."

He grinned at me, bringing his other hand under his balls and playing with his arsehole a little. He knew just what I wanted to see. My dick was sticking straight up in full flight, my foreskin still wrinkled at the end. I pulled it back, exposing my angry red knob, and stroked it a few times. But I had greater needs. Bending forward, I brushed my nose over Owen's testicles. He didn't shave them, which pleased me. And despite Owen having showered this morning, they were already nice and musky thanks to the hot weather. I moaned with pleasure as I took in his natural fragrance. "I love the smell of your balls, Owen."

He gave breathy whines as I trailed my nose and lips up his girthy penis, *slowly drowning in his scent. My mind flashed back over the previous few years. Since losing Dominic, I'd been on my own, so deep in the closet I'd nearly found Narnia. Seedy blowjobs at beats had been my sole contact with men, and I'd encountered more than a few horror dicks. But now, I had Owen, and his upstanding prick was divine. Clean, piquant and so very male. "And fuck, I'll never get enough of your cock."*

Owen ran his fingers through my long hair, gently massaging my scalp. "Every part of your body down there drives me fuckin' nuts, Ryan. Dick, balls and arse."

"Oh God, your arse!" I growled, lifting his legs right up so his little cheeks spread open and exposed his hole. Ducking down, I sniffed hard against the puckered aperture, rubbing my nose around. In seconds, I'd added in my tongue, pushing hard into his taut ring, which he relaxed a bit for me. "You don't know how beautiful your little arse is." My words were muffled because my snout was still buried against his wide-open cleft. I slathered my tongue round more, growling him out good and proper, getting him nice and wet. Coming back up, I grabbed his great big dick and slid it greedily into my mouth. My tastebuds rejoiced at the subtle, salty flavour.

Owen whimpered hard as I began to suck. I had quickly learnt exactly what he liked: the amount of pressure and rubbing with my tongue; the way he liked his foreskin to be alternately pulled tight and then let slacken so it rode down over his knob; the super-sensitive little spot on his frenulum.

Owen and I had also learnt that we both liked a finger or two up our arse while we were being sucked. I'd already discovered that pleasure with Dominic, of course, but I loved seeing how pleased Owen was when he made me come hard like this—sucking firmly on my knob and steadily pumping multiple fingers into my anus, bashing them against my prostate.

Right now, though, it was Owen's turn. My middle finger made its way straight into his warm manhole. "Jesus!" Owen shivered, his cock jumping in my mouth. "More, please mate. That feels so good!"

Fuck, I loved playing with his little mancunt. I loved the way he wriggled and writhed. I loved the worried look on his face, the way he whimpered, the way his cock got so fucking hard. And his arsehole was getting very experienced now, given all the time I'd spent worshipping it. There was no difficulty at all slipping my index finger straight in alongside my middle finger. I let them dance over his g-spot, advancing in and out of his pliant sphincter while I dined out on his cock. Owen almost cried. "Ohhhhhh... mate, you're gonna make me come so fast!"

You fuckin' beauty, I thought. I moved into fifth gear straight away, pumping and rotating and corkscrewing my fingers inside his moist chute, bombarding his fat prick in every way I knew how. Owen's moans rose sharply as I felt his cock expand. This part of the game never failed to thrill me; the anticipation, the thickening of his glans, the marked swelling of his prostate, the quick peristaltic movement as his warm sperm propelled out of his penis all over my tongue. Owen's body went rigid with the aftershocks and he was still whimpering. I swallowed his gift, milking his urethra, licking every drop out of the slit in his knob. Gently sliding my fingers from his hole, I rolled his foreskin back into place, then kissed the penis that had given me so much pleasure.

I gathered Owen into my arms and pushed my tongue into his mouth, brushing it over his own tongue, offering him the vestiges of the load he'd blown. He licked his lips and brought his hand to my cheek, stroking it slowly. "Time for you to come, sexy man,"

He immediately moved into place. He knew exactly what to do. Owen had discovered something about my body I hadn't even known. I thought every man had sensitive nipples. Mine were so sensitive I'd never even regarded them as sexually pleasurable. Owen, however, had latched his lips onto them one day, sucking and licking gently, and I had practically hit the roof, rubbing my cock for about ten seconds before I shot right into the air. Christ, it was amazing. All this time I'd had these hot buttons, something to drive me into new planes of ecstasy, and I'd never exploited them. But, by God, Owen did. He loved seeing the way I squirmed and cried when he did his nipple thing.

Right now, slicking two fingers with spit, Owen pushed them straight into my arsehole, which was so horny it welcomed them with no hassle whatsoever. When Owen's lips started to suckle my nipple, I began to whine and I didn't stop. Holding my long hood right back, I spat into my free hand and stroked it hard up and down over my knob. Sensory overload made me nearly wail as I rapidly ascended to a magnificent climax. Spunk rocketed up over my stomach while my legs shook, my arsehole and cock convulsing in sweetly painful spasms. Owen worked like a Trojan, not letting up until he knew I'd finished the last of my orgasm. As soon as my body relaxed, he chased every drop of my load with his tongue, licking it off my stomach, then swallowed as he grinned up at me. "Happy birthday, teddy," he said.

After checking where we were to make sure we hadn't drifted too much, Owen settled on the bench seat. I sat on the floor of the boat with my back to him, nestled between his legs. In the warmth of our afterglow, I was seized with an affection so potent that I had to voice it. Owen had to know how fucking special he was to me. "You're my light, little man." I said, caressing the hair on his legs either side of me. "You work so hard to make me happy. I can't ever remember a time I smiled this much. Don't ever change."

Owen didn't respond for a moment, and when he did, his voice was small. "You make me feel like I'm worth something, Ryan. I always found it difficult to make friends. Mum would say to me, 'Be as nice as you can to people and they'll like you back.' I tried hard, I really did. I didn't know what I was doing wrong."

I turned around to look up at him—lounging back slightly, his floppy hair and tanned skin looking browner than ever against the bright midday sun. I saw the sadness in his eyes and immediately felt the lump in my throat, the start of tears welling. My whole life I'd subsisted on just a few friends. I was a quiet guy and that was all I needed. But it seemed so important to Owen that he was liked, and it was a crying shame people didn't realise just how much he had to offer.

Guilt hit me like a ton of bricks: gut-wrenching, all-consuming guilt. I'd failed him in the worst way. "I'll never forgive myself for not sticking up for you with those fuckers at work, Owen. I was so pissweak, petrified they'd twig and realise I was gay." Tears began to spill down my cheeks. I couldn't handle the fucking shame of it all.

Owen glanced down at me and his face contorted with worry. "Don't cry, teddy. Please, mate. You really did stick up for me. Each time they hassled me, you gave them a shitty look and walked off. Before too long, if they were giving me a hard time and you rocked up, it was all, 'fuck, here comes Ryan', and they'd stop straight away."

Really? He was giving me credit for that? His generosity knew no bounds.

"Plus, that was some awesome black eye you gave Costa."

And just like that, he turned my tears into laughter. He was a perfect ray of sunshine. God, how I adored that handsome little bugger. "Owen, you're gonna meet so many people who see the real you and they're gonna love you every bit as much as I love you." Owen was silent for a moment. I gazed into his eyes. An ache formed deep within my chest as I noticed tears starting to run down his own cheeks, now. I grabbed hold of his hand and kissed it. "That's right, Owen. I love you. I really do, mate. Sure, it's only been a few months, but I know it in my heart. You're all I ever needed."

He slid down off the bench, folding his lithe legs around me, giving small sniffles as he hugged me tight. "I love you, too, Ryan. I'm pinching myself that I get to have such a fuckin' awesome man in my life."

I moved my head round, kissing the tears off his cheeks, tasting the salt of his emotions. "These are the only kind of tears I ever want to see on you, Owen. Happiness from here on in, OK? I have so much to look forward to, and it's all gonna be with you. I fuckin' love you so much, little man."

Our mouths came together and the heavens collided in a kiss unlike any I'd ever experienced. The honesty was raw, the joy overflowing. We just couldn't get close enough. The heat of the day combined with the heat of our passion, and Owen's natural scent filled my nostrils, causing a fire to ignite in my soul. We were both panting so heavily it wasn't long before we collapsed against each other, chests heaving, arms clutching. I held my little man so fucking tight; his naked, sweaty skin merging with mine, a slick tangle of pure love out there on the water, all alone in our slice of paradise.

"Ryan?" Owen piped up later, as we reclined in each other's arms, gazing out over the bay towards Mandorah in the distance. I turned my head to look at him; our faces were comically close. "Would you wanna move into my flat with me? I know it's all daggy and houso, but I promise I'll do everything I can to make it a nice home for you." The earnestness in his expression went straight to my heart.

"Wow! Oh God, Owen. Yes!" I pulled his head to mine, squishing our cheeks together, before moving back out to stare into his deep blue eyes. "But just the invitation is amazing enough, OK? You don't need to sweeten the deal."

"I want to, though. I want you to always be as happy as I am. I gotta express my love, teddy."

Owen averted his eyes, his head slightly bowed, seemingly overwhelmed by the sincerity of the moment. I leaned forward and kissed his forehead with all the reverence I had in me. "I need to spend every second I can with you, little man. I'm fucking thrilled you wanna live with me. And I'm gonna give you all that love back and more."

Tomorrow, I'd make a start. Pack up all my stuff. Get the caravan in tip-top shape so mum could sell it. Fly the coop at long last and land softly in the arms of the man I loved.

The water lapped at the sides of our little boat. The bay was calm and a slight breeze wafted its warm fingers over us. "This is my favourite place in the world, Ryan." Owen turned and smiled at me, his face as radiant as the fierce sun above us. "When we're old and my time comes, I want you to scatter my ashes out here. Will you promise me that?"

"Of course I will." I gathered him closer, hugging him as hard as I could. "But I'll be six feet under by then. They say that the happiest people live the

longest. So you, little man—" I pecked him on the lips, "—are gonna live to be a hundred."

* * *

My guts are churning. I feel like I'm going to be sick. But I plaster a smile on my face for Dominic as I let the very last few petals go. All that remains now is the bunch of thorny stems. My sunshine is gone.

We drive home in total silence. I can't bring myself to say anything. Dominic's hand is on my thigh the whole time, a constant reminder there's still something good in my life.

By the time I pull the ute up near his building, it's well past dark. Dominic leads me through the lobby, up the elevator, then into his apartment. Steering me straight to the bedroom, he helps me out of my jacket, peels off my shirt and slides my jeans to my feet. As I stand there naked, he pulls off my boots and socks then frees the bunched-up denim from my ankles, one leg at a time. Clasping my bare body, he buries his head into my chest and sniffs deeply. I hold him tight, my arms around his shoulders, my hand stroking the back of his head. This is what my soul so badly needs. And this incredible man had no trouble working that out.

* * *

I wake in the middle of the night, shivering in violent, uncontrollable spasms. The quilt has worked its way right down, leaving me covered in only a thin cotton sheet. I yank the thick doona up as fast as I can and curl into a ball, willing the rampant trembling to stop. When it finally dies down, I grope around to my right, trying to find the warm man next to me, but he's not there.

Slowly, I psych myself up to move. Pulling the doona off the bed, I stand and wrap it tightly around my naked body like a shawl. I tiptoe over the frigid floorboards, making my way across the room and down the hall. There is Dominic, stretched out on the couch covered in blankets, softly snoring away. An indescribable hurt claws at my chest. *I've driven him away.* I stand there in the doorway, watching him, trying to reason with my anguish. I've laid a heavy trip on him. *Yes, that's what's happened. Things will be OK in the morning.*

But, come daylight when I open my eyes again, there's no sign of him anywhere.

Chapter Sixteen

ominic texts me regularly throughout the week. On the surface, everything seems normal again. But I can't help feeling his messages don't have the same warmth as usual. I'm probably just being a paranoid dickhead. Still, something is off. There's a detachment, I can sense it. One of the invisible threads that joins my heart to his has been severed.

On Thursday, I find myself in Burwood Westfield shopping centre on a reno job. During my break, I take a wander around the shops. Out of the corner of my eye, I spot a Zing Pop Culture store and I immediately think of Oscar. I'm beginning to love that kid, with his cheeky quips and his quiet manner. We sit for hours watching comedies, we take regular walks down to the beach all rugged up in our jackets, and we frequently go and stuff our faces with whatever junk food we feel like. Oscar's only too thrilled to have an uncle figure who's as childish as he is when it comes to diet. Dominic even turns a blind eye. I'm sure he's just glad to have an hour or two's peace when he has work to do in his study.

I take a cautious stroll into the Zing store. I'm bamboozled by all the stuff in there. Most of it I've never heard of. Scanning the upper shelves at the back, something slaps me in the face. It's an ALF toy. And it's not some little kiddie-style cuddly thing, it's a huge plastic figurine. I pull it down from the shelf and look over the box. It even talks, apparently blurting out the sassy one-liners ALF says in the show. It's *perfect.*

I don't even check the price, though I'm relieved it's not too exorbitant when they ring it up at the register. This kid is worth it.

When I'm back home in my little house after work, I get to and start packing my usual weekend bag in preparation for tomorrow. In go my toiletries and all the clothes I've had done at the laundromat—yes, I'm a lazy prick and get someone else to clean my duds. On top of it all, I place the ALF figurine.

Maybe I should have wrapped it?

No, don't be silly. No need to make a big deal out of it. It's just some token to make the little kid happy.

Just as I'm doing up the zipper, my phone chimes with a message.

»Sorry, mate, I've gotta call off this weekend. Family dramas.

That's it. No further explanation.

»No worries, lontra. Everything OK?

I wait for a few minutes, my heart pounding with confusion, stress, hurt, I don't know the fuck what. Finally, there's a reply.

»Nothing for you to stress about. I'll speak to you later, mate.

It's so damn cold. He's not his usual self. I can feel the heat rising rapidly in me. I'm getting upset too fast, too hard. I need to calm the fuck down.

Crestfallen, I open my bag and take out ALF. I can't help thinking there's more shit in store for me.

* * *

Texts keep coming from Dominic, but they're almost perfunctory.

It's like he's doing his duty, keeping me on-side out of a sense of responsibility. We barely had a day together the weekend before last, then we skipped the next weekend. It's been well over a week since I've touched him. This has never happened, not since we reconnected five months ago. I'm worried fucking sick.

See, this is why I don't get close to people. Why the fuck should I? You get fucking stomped on, I tell you. Fortunately I'm a reserved, aloof prick in general. Nobody's gonna notice anything different about me at work. Well, so long as I avoid Marisa.

* * *

I'm close to breaking point by Wednesday afternoon. If anyone crosses me, I'm gonna let fly. My life has turned to shit. Dominic kicked me in the fucking balls when I was at my most vulnerable.

I'm just packing up my stuff for the day, when I get a text.

»*Hey, big bear. I'm sorry I've been so absent lately. I promise I'll try and make it up to you. Will you meet me for dinner tomorrow night? Should I book us a table at Churrascaria?*

It's the Brazilian steakhouse in Coogee I've wanted to go to for ages. He's thrown out the lifebuoy. Anger drains from me in an instant.

»*Don't worry, lontra. I'm off work now so I'll make the booking. Seven-thirty?*

»*Perfect! See you at the restaurant, big bear.*

* * *

The next night I sit at a window table at Churrascaria. I'm dressed in my nicest shirt. I've groomed my beard, I've got my hair pulled back, and I'm clutching a huge bunch of flowers I bought on the way over here.

I wait and I wait. With every passing minute, my heart sinks even further. Finally, I give up. I stand and throw a couple of bills on the untouched table, turning to see the hovering waiters looking over at me. The utter humiliation I feel is eclipsed only by the sense of dread clawing its way through my body.

Walking back to my ute, I pass by a steel-framed rubbish bin. With an almighty roar, I smash the bouquet repeatedly against it. Petals and leaves fly everywhere. I don't stop until the cunt of a thing is obliterated as badly as my fucking heart.

* * *

There's no word from Dominic until the following afternoon.

»*I'm gonna be off work earlier than I thought. See you at my place, OK.*

What the fuck? Even if he completely forgot our date last night, surely he must have remembered it by now?

I try to remind myself that people are fallible. Sometimes they do forget. Dominic has been busy and maybe it's slipped his mind.

Bullshit, a little voice says. *Dominic's the most organised person you know.*

I could give him the benefit of the doubt and accept that it really *did* slip his mind. Maybe I should. But he needs to grovel as soon as I arrive at his place tonight. I don't see any other way of avoiding some sort of confrontation.

In typical Bondi style, I trawl the streets, eventually finding a park two blocks away from Dominic's apartment. When I arrive at his front door, he opens it as he's putting on an expensive-looking button-up shirt. I see him do a double-take at my worn old jeans and Adidas hoodie. "Are you ready to head straight off?" he says, his brows knitted in a dubious expression. His manner seems brusque; he's clearly stressed and preoccupied. "Did you make the booking, Ryan?"

I frown at him, confused. "What do you mean?"

I can see him visibly losing patience. "The booking for Churrascaria, remember?"

"That was for last night, Dominic."

His nostrils flare. "Why on earth would it have been for last night? You know I'm at home Thursdays."

I bristle at his use of the word 'home.' "You called me on Wednesday and said to make the booking for 'tomorrow.'"

"Oh, for Christ's sake, Ryan. You knew what I meant," he snaps.

I can't even fathom what's happening. I'd expected some level of contrition, but I'm being spoken to like an errant child. My hackles are raised and I'm finding it near impossible to control my emotions. "You blew me off last weekend for some unspecified reason, Dominic. Then you said you'd make it up to me, remember? So, naturally, I thought that's why you asked me to dinner on Thursday. I made the booking. I rushed home after work, got dressed up, bought you flowers and drove across town through peak-hour traffic. Then I sat there alone for nearly an hour, taking up a table while waiters looked on like vultures." My voice is starting to waver. "I was so looking forward to seeing you, Dominic, and you dogged me. Do you understand how demoralising that was?"

Dominic is unmoved. He speaks in a patronising, sing-song tone. "Well you could have saved yourself the embarrassment if you'd just called me. You've got a phone."

"How long was I supposed to wait before I did that, Dominic?

Where's the cutoff point? Ten minutes? Half an hour? I kept thinking *he'll turn up. He's just running late.* I never imagined you wouldn't show. And I *did* call you, just before I left. I was worried sick that something bad might have happened to you. Anna answered and said you were in the shower."

He stands there with his hands on his hips. "Well, she never told me that."

"Because I asked her not to, that's why. I didn't need to be any more bloody humiliated than I already was. On the one hand, I was relieved you were OK, and on the other I was gutted that you'd forgotten me. I expected an apology, Dominic. I think that's only fair, don't you?"

Dominic's voice raises a few decibels. "Stop this shit, Ryan! I have enough on my plate without being lumped with your petty moods. I'm already dealing with a massive workload, two different homes, a child, a wife…" I see a flash in his eyes. He knows he's gone too far.

I'm so close to losing it, but I pull hard on the reins, keeping my voice even. "A *wife*, Dominic? So Anna's the First Lady and all I am is a *mistress*? How the hell am I supposed to compete with that?"

"Fuck, Ryan. The situation isn't perfect. *I'm* not perfect. But you think you've got it tough having to compete with my family? I'm having to compete with a FUCKIN' DEAD MAN!"

My mouth falls open. I've been booted so hard in the guts, I can't breathe. When I finally manage to find my voice, it's tiny. Defeated. "Well, you won't have to do that anymore, Dominic." I turn on my heels and flee down the corridor, desperate to be as far away as possible.

"Jesus Christ! Stop being such a bloody drama queen!" His words are stones, pummelling me, kicking me when I'm down. I can hear him following me, but I've already reached the stairs. "For fuck's sake, come back! Please, Ryan!"

Those last two words may have been enough to make me stop in my tracks; to turn around and go to him. But there's no hint of supplication in them. He isn't begging me to stay. He's still barking at me like I'm some petulant adolescent.

I run down the last few flights of stairs several at a time. Busting out of the front door, I pound down the road, covering the two blocks' distance in mere seconds. When I reach my ute, I double over, fall to my knees and vomit. Over and over I retch, long after there's anything left to come out. My skull throbs in agony. I'm seeing stars.

Numb with disbelief, I stand up and my head spins so violently I stumble and fall hard against the ute, bashing my temple against the tray. The agonised yelp that escapes me is fraught with heartbreak and devastation. I grab onto the metal edge, hoist myself up, fumble for my keys and drag myself into the driver's seat. I sit there for an eternity, my head slumped against my arms on the steering wheel, vaguely aware of the incessant vibrating in my pocket.

Too late, Dominic.

Back at home, I make my way indoors, still in a daze. Staggering into the bathroom, I piss on autopilot, then take all my clothes off and crawl into bed. How the fuck am I supposed to sleep? Through the fog of my distress, I remember my one and only flight to Adelaide. *The Xanax.* Rummaging in my bedside table for the box, I take one, two, three, four of them. Maybe if I pass out for the entire weekend, this nightmare will go away.

* * *

I don't sleep as long as I hoped I would. I awake in the darkness, unsure of where I am, who I am, what bloody day it is. I scramble for my phone. Saturday, seven p.m. I've been asleep all night and all day. There's a bunch of missed calls and texts. All from Dominic.

Oh God, I'd almost forgotten. The sick feeling rushes back to me and I want to puke all over again, even though I haven't eaten in well over twenty-four hours.

With shaking hands, I go to my contacts list on my phone. *I have to do this.* Working of their own accord, my fingers block Dominic's number. Then, going into my messages, I swipe delete on the entire thread of his texts. I don't want to read any of them. Then I type one last message.

»Do not contact me anymore.

When I'm sure it's been sent, I put his number on the SMS blacklist. *Loud and clear, Dominic.*

There's no coming back after last night. I realise now I was never gonna be anything more than a bit on the side. Weekend entertainment. Dominic has endless ground to cover before he'll ever be able to have another relationship. And I've been way too invested already. The only way to deal with this is to make a clean break.

Sitting up in bed, I let my eyes adjust to the room. *Bang.* Right in front of my face, there is big bear. Smiling his cheerful smile, taunting me with memories of those halcyon days when I thought I'd finally found happiness. I can't look at him anymore. But I can't bear to throw him out. Struggling out of the bed covers, I pick him up and turn to leave the room. But something else catches my eye and I nearly cry out in pain. *ALF.*

Oh, fuck. Oscar. My dear little friend. If my heart was broken before, it's torn to pieces now. I am never gonna see that kid again.

Scooping up the glossy box with my free hand, I carry both creatures into the kitchen. It takes several huge garbage bags and half a roll of gaffer tape to wrap them up properly. When they're fully encapsulated, I haul the whole package out to the shed. *Welcome to your new home, my furry friends.*

I take a long shower, which helps a little bit. There's a chilly wind outside, so I dress in jeans and a jacket and force myself to walk up to King Street. The pavements are full with the bustle of Saturday night crowds. The excitement, the happy energy, the sense of fun in the air is a cruel juxtaposition to the intense misery that's clouding me. I know it's only going to get worse when the shock wears off. I can feel it starting already.

I stop in at Clem's Chicken shop to order takeaway. I don't feel like eating, let alone cooking. But I know I have to get something in my stomach. Maybe then the incessant churning might stop.

Back home, I settle under a blanket on the couch, swigging Coke straight from a two-litre bottle, scoffing down chips and gravy and staring mindlessly at the TV. I never watch free-to-air, but I can't deal with Netflix or Prime or Stan. I have no mental capacity for making choices right now.

Hours fly past. I don't know what I'm watching, I don't know what I'm thinking, it just seems like a struggle to stay alive. At some ungodly hour, I drag myself to bed. Fishing around in my drawer, my hand lands on a plastic pill bottle. I pull it out and scan the label. *PrEP*. I may as well. Looks like I'm on my own again for good. The realisation is a sickening stab in the gut. I wash down one of the pills with a huge glug of water, hoping it'll help ease the searing pain. Then I reach for my trusty box of Xanax, swallow another two and knock myself out cold again.

Chapter Seventeen

They say that you don't get quality rest when you take benzodiazepines like Xanax to sleep. The tablets just trick your body into relaxing, but you don't enter a deep slumber. They were right. By Monday morning, I'm as wretched as if I've had no sleep at all.

I could have got out of going to work, but I've been left alone to stew in my torture chamber long enough. I can't stand another day of my own company, tormented by the thoughts running through my head. I'm feeling like death warmed up, but I sorely need a distraction.

The moment I walk in, I run smack bang into Marisa. *Jesus, it's seven a.m., for fuck's sake. What the hell is she doing here so early?*

She's onto me in an instant. Eyeing me up, she blurts, "Something terrible happened to you!"

"No, Marisa. I'm just really bloody tired. I haven't been sleeping well." I try to smile. I even have a go at a chuckle, but it's pathetic. I know she sees right through it, but she graciously backs off, perhaps aware she's dipping her toe into hazardous waters.

Not that I'd snap. Or get abusive. I'm not like that. And although I'm terrified I'll break down in front of people, in reality I know I'm no longer capable of it. See, a normal person would have bawled their eyes out after what had happened on Friday. I, on the other hand, let it get so bad that I spent a whole twenty minutes chucking up in the gutter.

This is me now. I am so stunted. I have no outlet. I can feel myself festering on the inside. Pretty soon the rot will work its way right through me and there will be nothing left.

* * *

I throw myself into work. I don't talk to anyone, except for the minimum communication required to get the jobs done. If anybody notices, they don't say anything. I'm hardly a fuckin' social butterfly anyway, so I guess there's no effervescence for them to miss. Of course, Marisa is the exception. She sees everything.

After five days of working like a robot and four more nights of torrid sleep filled with hideous, indecipherable dreams, I'm finally running on empty. When I get back to the office on Friday afternoon, I sit slumped against the steering wheel, bent over in the same position I was in a week before. Right when it had all gone to shit.

The passenger side door to my ute opens and a patchouli-scented body slides into the seat next to me. "It's a man. You love him but you can't have him for some reason. Something's blocking the connection and it's his fault."

I look over at Marisa. "Fuck, you're good. Spot on. I haven't even said a word to anyone."

She doesn't look smug, even though she probably has a right to. Putting her delicate hand with its two dozen-odd rings and fifteen bracelets against my arm, she smiles gently, radiating genuine compassion. "You could, you know. It might help."

Maybe she's right. I can't do any worse than I'm doing right now. I'll give her the abridged version. "He was my first love, when we were teenagers. He moved away and I was heartbroken. I never saw him again till this summer when I did the kitchen in his rental place. He's bi, married with a kid, but separated a year and a half ago when he came out to his wife." I glance over at Marisa, who's attentive, non-judgemental. This is where my story gets dodgy. "Unfortunately, he still lives with his wife. For their son's sake, he says. I got to see him on weekends at his rental—"

"Oh, sweetie. You were the other woman."

"Yes, I was." God, I've deceived myself for so long. I feel ashamed. Dirty. Tainted by the tawdriness of it all.

"Ryan, you're suffering. You're devastated and you're pining for something you know deep down won't ever be yours." She sits up and taps my arm decisively. "You need a diversion. There's truth in that old cliché…" Pausing a moment, she looks me in the eye, summing up whether to say what's on her mind. "The only way to get over someone is to get under someone else."

** * **

Marisa's right. I need to fuck Dominic out of my system. Or, more accurately, get him fucked out of my system. As if possessed, I drive straight to Darlinghurst and find a one-hour park in a back lane. I'm exhausted, but I've tapped into some strange reserve of nervous energy I didn't know I even had.

With my heart in my mouth, I walk the short distance to the sauna. In the past, I've studiously avoided sex-on-premises venues, but desperate times call for desperate measures. I can't go on like this any longer. I'm willing to try absolutely anything to escape this fucking torture.

After swapping my money for a towel and locker key, I venture into the seedy bowels of the change room. The whole place throbs with ugly, auto-tuned dance music, the air thick with the smell of chlorine. Avoiding any glances, I strip naked and stash my stuff in the locker, then wrap the paltry towel around my waist.

Well-aware I'm less than fresh after a hard day's slog, my first stop is the bathroom and the showers. As I soap myself from arsehole to breakfast, I try my best to breathe deeply, willing myself to relax. Once my racing heartbeat is lowered and my crotch is gleaming, I dry myself off and brave the labyrinth of halls and rooms.

Overdramatic screams and pseudo-porn wails sail through the air: fake, femme affectations that made me decidedly queasy. Random men walk past, no doubt doing laps, busy averting their eyes, fiendishly holding their abs in the highest state of flex in the vain hope they'll score as far above their station as possible.

As a burly, hairy bear, I'm used to garnering a modicum of attention whenever I go out. I'm certainly much lower in the pecking order than your typical Muscle Mary—given my padding and belly—but definitely brawny enough to attract the cubs, the bear-curious and the twink-like chasers. And here lurk the latter: the young, waxed posers, scattered throughout the dark corners of the maze, reaching out with limp wrists to brush their hands over the fur on my chest, then spewing brief, bitchy flourishes when I fail to react to their advances.

More power to them, I think. But they aren't what I'm looking for. I'm hoping to find…

What the fuck am I hoping to find?

When I'm at the point of turning and fleeing, a huge muscle bear steps out of a doorway. Six-two or three, I estimate, definitely on the 'roids, given the hard swell of his upper abdomen and the almost comical mass of muscle that cloaks his frame. Apparently not one for gentle introductions, he grabs my arm and yanks me into the room he's just appeared from, a predatory trapdoor spider snatching its juicy prey.

Once inside, with the door swiftly locked, I'm thrown onto the padded bench in the centre of the dank cubicle. Straight over my face, a sweaty, musky and decidedly hairy arse lands with a thud. Immediately it starts to gyrate, grinding across my snout in heavy, hurried strokes. I dutifully stick out my tongue, aware of what's expected of me. Normally, I would be in heaven eating an arse like the one that's suffocating me right now, but this presentation is a pure insult intended to establish dominance. There's no voicing of pleasure, no synergy, no appreciation from this brute. I am merely providing a source of human friction for his horny hole, a living Scotchbrite to tease his nether regions.

As quickly as his massive, muscular arse has arrived to smother me, it's gone and I'm yanked to the floor on my knees. A huge paw grabs my hair and a fat, fat, fucking *fat* cock is jammed into my mouth. I thank whatever deity may exist that this man's length does not nearly match his massive girth, because I have no choice but to endure the chunky monster ramming repeatedly down my throat. *Can't even be six inches,* I think. I can tell, because it doesn't go down far enough to make me vomit. If it had, I would definitely be aspirating puke with the ruthless way he's battering my tonsils.

Things go from bad to worse as he starts pulling on my hair, yanking me towards him while his hips thrust forward. My ire shoots skyward as my scalp starts to scream. I fucking hate it when men do this. I wonder whether to grab his balls and squeeze the living shit out of them, disarm him just long enough to break free. My boxing skills aren't honed like they used to be when I was young, but I'm sure I could get in a few good punches.

Mercifully, my hair is released, though my freedom is fleeting and I'm immediately tackled onto the bench face-down. My arse cheeks are pried apart, then wet, sloppy goo is slapped against my hole. A couple of thick fingers force their way inside, giving a cursory jab, no doubt for his own ease of entry, certainly not for my comfort. I hear the squishing sound of his hand rubbing against his cock, priming it for attack. He pulls back roughly on my hips, slamming the fat monster against my pucker time and time again, impatiently trying to force his way inside me. For my own sake, I push my arsehole outwards as much as possible, fearful of the imminent pain and desperate to make it more bearable.

But bearable it isn't. I scream as his ultra-thick dick breaches my sphincter, getting my head slammed down against the bench by a hefty hand as punishment. No sooner has my face registered the shocking impact than the hefty hand yanks hard on my hair.

So this is what I'm reduced to, I think, as he starts savagely pounding into my arse. *I've finally hit rock bottom.*

I can't move. I'm completely numb, paralysed as I stare straight ahead, my body lurching forward each time his massive hips collide with my arse. All I can do is struggle to focus on the wall in front of me as I'm systematically raped into the bench. I can feel the fissures forming in my arsehole, forewarning me of the inexorable wreckage, the agonising rectal devastation I will be left with for weeks to come.

His hand yanks my hair harder and I gather every ounce of brawn in my neck to counter it. This obviously displeases my rapist, who begins to hit me viciously across my arse, my back, my shoulders, my head. The excruciating pain strafing my body is eclipsed only by the indignity of it all. *I am powerless. I am pissweak. I am a fucking piece of shit who's getting exactly what's coming to him.*

I can no longer cope with this in a conscious state. The wall in front of me becomes distorted and I begin to dissociate. *This is not happening to me. This is someone else's nightmare.* Everything goes blank. My desperate struggle for breath resounds in my head. I'm underwater, listening to his muffled screams of rage. The heavy blows to my back are now dull and aching, the agony in my arse is a slow throb.

A final roar, a final yank to my hair and a graceless jolting against my arse brings me back to the surface. My assailant comes to a standstill, pulsating, vibrating, filling my rectum with his vile seed.

A rough dismount leaves my anus gaping, bleeding, completely raw. Shell-shocked, I remain there on my stomach, my face buried in my arms, hiding my shame, my weakness, my deplorable fragility.

Footsteps come from behind me, around my side and stop in front of my head.

Oh, my God. Wasn't that enough? What the fuck could he want now?

Dread forms inside my gut as a warm splatter rains down on my head. Another yank on my hair forces my face upwards as a thick spray of piss hoses me like a Gerni. *The final insult.* The hand that's been yanking my hair moves down to pinch my nose hard, compelling me to open my mouth so I can gasp for breath. No sooner have I sucked in air than his gushing cock is thrust down my throat. I clench my stomach, bracing myself for the acrid onslaught. A twisted sense of gratitude hits me as I realise he's been drinking beer—the torrents filling my mouth are nothing more than warm water tinged with hops. But in a reflex act of defiance, I widen my mouth and spit it all out the sides.

Thwack! His hand lands a Will Smith-sized wallop across my temple. My head flies to the side, wrenching my already-tortured neck. The stream of urine continues to pelt down the side of my face and my guts heave over and over. But it isn't the lingering taste of his watery piss making me sick, it's Dominic's words screaming through my consciousness:

"Maybe someday we can chug down half a slab of beer and turn that latent fetish of yours into a real one, eh?"

Well, I've certainly been given my introduction now, haven't I.

As my assailant's deluge slows to a trickle, I hope to God that's the end of it all. A vicious shove on my head signals he's had enough and the sound of a door opening and slamming confirms his departure.

It's over.

Relief floods my body, only to be swiftly overtaken by disgust and disbelief.

What the fuck is wrong with you, you pathetic cunt? Why the hell didn't you fight him?

My body heaves with fresh waves of nausea as the truth slaps me right in the fucking face.

Because you're worthless, Ryan. Look at yourself, you filthy slut. You don't deserve love. You don't deserve anything.

* * *

»Marisa, I really need to speak to you.

I send the text the following morning, my fingers trembling. I've been in a daze since the door to that cubicle slammed last night. Vague flashes of memory come to me: doing my best to walk straight down the hallway past all those naked men, scrubbing myself over and over in the shower, somehow making it home, passing out in a foetal position.

Numbness pervades every part of my being. My brain is travelling slower than my body, each movement dragging through my conscious-ness, my vision smudged by the mental lag. A chime on my phone cuts through my fog.

»This is a face-to-face thing, isn't it Ryan. I'm walking up to Newtown shortly. Meet you at Bacigalupo in half an hour. No excuses.

Dear, dear pushy Marisa. I almost crack a smile. Thank God she took the decision-making out of my hands. I struggle to get up and hobble to the shower. I can feel the sore spots all over my back and shoulders. I can feel the dull ache in my arse. I stop to look in the bathroom mirror, assessing the visual damage. I see a bruise on one side of my forehead from where he slammed my skull into the bench. I see a deep gash on the other side from where he walloped me. I try to crane my neck to assess the state of my back, but I cry out in agony. He's jerked my hair so hard, so many times, that I can barely turn my head. For the first time in my life, I consider taking clippers to my scalp and getting rid of the lot. It'll be like losing my identity, but maybe that's appropriate. I am nothing now.

The cold air has me shivering, so I jack up the hot water in the shower. I stand under the stream, letting it hit my battered back, bracing myself against the tiled wall as I piss down the shower drain. I feel sick as I wonder what state my arse is in. Pumping some body wash into my hand, I reach round and gingerly touch my hole. *Thank God*. It's a bit swollen and it aches like hell, but at least it isn't like the mouth of a Saint Bernard.

Back in my bedroom, I dress in my baggiest trackpants. I'm glad I never wear undies, because just the thought of them wedging up my tortured arse make me shudder. I pull on a loose t-shirt and consider what to put over it. There's no way I can handle the friction of a jacket with the bruises on my back. After settling on a large fleece hoodie, I pull a thick beanie over my head to hide the injuries there. Before I leave the bedroom, I give myself a once-over in the mirror. I look like shit, but maybe I can pull it off. An attempt at a smile makes me wince and I quickly turn away from my reflection, gather my stuff, and set out for the short walk up to King Street.

Marisa's already waiting for me at the café. She looks me up and down as I enter, no doubt taking in my stunted gait, the careful way I sit down. "Somebody hurt you," she blurts. "Like physically, mentally and emotionally." She goes to pat me on the shoulder and I recoil automatically.

"Sorry," I say, noting her alarm. "Yeah, you're right."

"Oh, my God, Ryan. You were bashed. No… *even worse*." Marisa's eyes go wide with horror.

"I really can't talk about it." My voice is shaking.

"It's OK, it's OK," she soothes, reaching out and placing her fingertips on mine—the barest of physical connections, but enough to let me know I'm being supported. "What can I do for you, Ryan? Please let me help you."

"I need a week off, Marisa. I can't go to work like this. I've got leave, I know it'll be OK with Barry. But I'll need your help rescheduling stuff."

"Of course I will, sweetie." Her brow is twisted with concern. "But what will you do while you're off?"

I shrug my shoulders. "Sit at home and try to recover."

Marisa's frown deepens. She picks up her phone and starts texting frantically. Glancing back up, she appraises my face, trying to read my expression. "You know my girlfriend, Rani?"

I look at her blankly. Marisa is the most promiscuous lesbian I've ever met.

"Come on, Ryan! The new guitarist in my band? We've been together nearly *four months*!"

"Oh yeah… Rani. I remember her now." I don't.

Marisa looks proud. Pleased as punch. "Well, she does some volunteer work at a meditation retreat in the bush. They've got a seven-night program starting tomorrow. They're always booked solid but sometimes people drop out at the last minute."

The lag in my brain is still fierce, and all I'm seeing is dollar signs dancing in front of my eyes. "Thanks, Marisa. It's a lovely thought, but I can't afford some fancy yoga resort."

"No, Ryan! It's a meditation retreat run by the Buddhist society. The cost is minimal. Simple cabins, humble vegetarian meals and silent meditation for a week." She reaches out again, this time grabbing both my hands with urgency. "This will help you heal, Ryan. Please consider it."

I know she's right. I can't just sit in my house and stew in my misery. I need to escape, to take drastic action. "Do you think there's a way I could get in?"

Marisa taps the table with her palm and grabs her phone again, whisking herself outside in a flurry of jangling jewellery. I watch her through the window as she talks animatedly, gesticulating while she paces back and forth. When she ends the call, she looks at me through the window and gives me a double thumbs-up.

Chapter Eighteen

The Buddhist Meditation retreat is in a pocket of bushland in southwest Sydney, near the National Park. I've never been to these parts before and it's surprising such a wild environment is tucked away so close to the urban sprawl. I pull my ute up into the car park and collect my bag and the sack of bed linen I've brought with me, as per their instructions.

I've arrived fairly late in the registration period and this is a good thing. I didn't fancy standing in a queue for ages. Frankly, I don't feel like being around people at all. After paying the suggested fees, I'm given an info sheet and written instructions on where to find my cabin. It's a tiny little one, set much further back from the main area which is full of larger cabins. That suits me fine.

Inside it's very clean and basic. There's a single bed, a tiny table and chair and a small wardrobe. I get to work, making my bed and hanging my clothes away. Once everything looks a little more homely, I settle back on the chair to read the information sheet. Various things catch my eye as I scan it for a quick preview.

"This is a silent retreat. We ask that you refrain from talking for the duration of the stay."

Sounds like bliss. I don't like too much chatter at the best of times. And right now, I have nothing to say to anyone.

"Meals served here are vegetarian. We ask that you refrain from

consuming any meat."

That's fine. My guts can do with a break from all the junk I've been eating.

"First meditation sessions start at five-thirty a.m. and we ask all to attend..."

I always get up that early for work. No problem.

"We ask that you do not indulge in any sexual activity..."

I almost laugh. I have absolutely no desire to touch another man and it's going to be a long while before that changes.

"...either with others or whilst alone."

Ha! No bloody chance. I'm not changing a twenty-eight-year-old habit. I know how to be quiet. What are they gonna do? Sit by my bedside all night and slap my wandering hands away from my crotch?

"We ask that you refrain from taking any non-prescription drugs..."

No problem there, I never touch them.

"...alcohol..."

Fair call. I can hardly imagine there will be any mates to crack a beer with here.

"...or smoking."

Oh, fuck. Just when I needed one. Maybe I can duck out to the car park. That's not really cheating, is it?

Plonking the info sheet on the table, I stand up, pat my pocket to check for my tobacco pouch, then venture outside. In the distance, I can see a couple of people sitting next to their cabins, plumes of smoke rising and dispersing into the air above them. *Well, what's good for the goose...*

I sit down on the bench at the front of the cabin and roll a durry. Lighting it, I suck in a deep drag, relax back and close my eyes. I recall seeing a movie with Sissy Spacek where she talks about this. I can't remember exactly what she says, but it's something about smoking always being the same. It's constant; it doesn't ever change. I need that. All this change is fucking with my head.

I hear the crunch of a footstep on twigs and my eyes fly open. An androgynous-looking—*woman? Non-binary person? I don't know*—is making their way towards me. I jump a little, glancing at my cigarette, but the person holds their hand out, signalling me not to worry. They come to stand next to me. I'm not sure what to do, so I stand up as well. The person points to a name tag on their shirt. *Rani.*

Holding her arms out, she pulls me into an embrace. It's a shock, but I guess this is that kind of touchy-feely place, maybe? My discomfort subsides immediately. I can sense the energy flowing from her into my body. I'm no longer tense. I feel stronger.

Rani releases me and sits down on the bench. I'm relieved she's taken the lead here. I have no idea what the etiquette is and I can't open my trap to ask. I plonk my big arse next to her, staring at the dead butt of my durry. I'm looking around for somewhere to put it, when I hear the flick of a lighter. I turn to see Rani choofing away on a cigarette and it's the first time I crack a smile in God knows how long. *Guess I can roll another one, then.*

* * *

The following morning I'm awake at five a.m. It's dark, but it's not hard to get up. My internal body clock is still set this way, despite the earth-shattering shit that's been happening to me lately. I'm trying not to think about it.

I'm immensely glad I took off to the communal shower block yesterday evening and scrubbed myself clean. There's no way I'd be able to face the frigid temperatures in that bathroom at this time of the morning.

When my room is tidy and my bed is made, I throw on my parka and go outside for a smoke. I can hear the faint sounds of people rustling about in the distance, but it's strangely calm with no conversation clouding the air. Pretty soon, the birds will start singing their morning chorus, untainted by the raucous intrusion of human voices.

When my durry is down to the end, I notice Rani approaching. Maybe she's doing the morning round-up, making sure all these lazy bastards are out of bed. She beckons me and I stand up, following her through the grounds and into the main building. People are shuffling into what seems to be a large hall or something, but Rani leads me into a room down the corridor. She arranges bolster cushions on the floor and gestures for me to sit. Guiding me gently, she adjusts my posture till I'm in a comfortable position. Then she sits opposite me, takes my hands and closes her eyes. I'm not sure where this goes from here, but something tells me to do the same.

Apparently, I'm right, because we sit there. And sit there. And sit there. My body protests, but with the bolster under my arse, it's not too bad. And all this silence—there's not so much crap flying round inside my head. I notice my thoughts slowing down. I feel heavy, but it's in a good way. I'm not tired, I'm... *serene.*

∗ ∗ ∗

Every morning this happens. Rani's there at my cabin before five-thirty, she takes me to the room and we spend ages sitting silently. I also attend all the group meditation sessions and read a stack of the literature. I don't understand a lot of it—academic stuff never was my strong point—but I reckon I'm getting better at it. The shitheap that is my life seems to be growing smaller, shovelful by shovelful.

And the food, to my surprise, is great. I doubt I could do it long-term, but it's like a cleanse. I'm not craving any junk. I'm still a fuckin' pig, though, but I'm not gonna go beating myself up about it.

My sex drive is coming back, too. I break the rules every night, making ample use of the massage oil and extra towel I brought with me. I don't care about that fucking rule, anyway. It feels good and it's something just for me.

* * *

Saturday morning comes and I go outside for my first smoke of the day. There's an envelope on the bench outside, weighted down with the tin can of stones that I—and sometimes Rani—use to ash into. Inside the envelope is a business card stapled to a short note.

Rani Gupta, Psychotherapist, MA, PACFA

Hi Ryan—just wanted to say thank you for letting me get to know you this week. I'd really love to work with you further. Ignore the address on the business card, that's the rooms where I see my private city clients. I also run counselling sessions two nights a week at the LGBT centre in Newtown. It's a funded service and it won't cost you anything. I'll leave the decision in your hands, but I hope to see you there.

Rani.

PS. I'm under strict instructions to tell you to turn up to our gig at the Townie tomorrow night. Marisa says she will have your guts for garters if you fail to show up, and we don't want that, do we?

* * *

I remember seeing a TV series hosted by the comedian Judith Lucy where she stayed at a retreat like this. As soon as her time was up, she was outside in front of the cameras, talking fast and clearly exhilarated. I can relate to the feeling of exhilaration—I'm streets ahead of where I was a week ago—but I'm not remotely tempted to talk to anyone. I just pack my stuff up, tidy my room and leave. Maybe I'll come back again in the future, whenever life gets too much.

Chapter Nineteen

There's a distinct buzz in the air as I get to the Town Hall Hotel that night. Locals call it the Townie, and it's where the Sydney bears gather every weekend. Today, though, it's lesbian central. Marisa spots me as I approach the stage. She drops whatever setup task she's in the middle of and runs over to give me a hug. "Was it an amazing experience? Do you feel cleansed? Isn't Rani fabulous?"

"Um, yeah to all of those. Especially the last one. She meditated with me every morning. She's an awesome person."

I'm feeling a bit uncomfortable—not with Marisa, but with the busy, packed environment. I'm hoping it's just because I've spent a week in peace with nothing to crowd my mind. I don't have a lot of perspective right now—I literally ran away from all my shit and I'm worried that I'll nosedive now I'm back to my normal life. Right at this moment, I'd love to just sink onto a bar stool near the wall and quietly enjoy the show. But it's not gonna happen.

"Hey, Lezzo," Marisa calls over my shoulder. "Get over here and take care of my friend, Ryan." Marisa steers me around and I come face-to-face with a heavily-pierced woman. She doesn't seem remotely perturbed by Marisa's slur. *Is it a slur if another lesbian says it? Is it like gay boys saying 'Yass, queen'?*

I'm bustled through the room to a table in the centre near the dancefloor. "Um, you're fine with her calling you that?" I ask along the way.

Pierced Girl gives me a wry grin, raising an eyebrow. "My name is Lesley Van Dyke. For real. Did I ever stand a chance?"

Two other girls arrive at the table right then, plonking down a round of beers. I glance up towards the crowded bar, assessing it for a gap.

"You can have this one," says Lesley, thrusting a schooner over to me. "It was for Marisa, but she's buggered off backstage again."

I must admit I'd been dreading this social interaction, but Lesley and her friends Jodie and Vicki are like rowdy blokes. It's pretty much a lad's night out and their bawdy humour makes for easy company. I'm trying not to be a stick in the mud, and I guess their infectious energy is rubbing off on me.

I also feel like the worst friend in the world. It's been months since I've seen Marisa's band. And it's not like it isn't my thing—I know my classic Aussie rock. Any song these guys pick up, I'll have a bar-by-bar familiarity with. I'm actually excited to hear their new set.

I've loosened up with a couple of beers by the time the five Big Girls make it to the stage. Only now, there's just three. Monique, Vanessa and Meg are built like tanks. Back when Marisa took over lead vocals after their last singer left, they were landed with a svelte, femme frontwoman who had way too much talent to ignore. That concession is now stretched to Rani, who, as their new guitarist, is built like a handsome, wiry athlete.

Nevertheless, the audience go wild as they launch into the chant at the beginning of their signature song. The Electric Pandas' 'Big Girls' is a crowd favourite and the dancefloor area is filled by the time the chant moves into the guitar intro. The frenetic rock moves seamlessly, with Monique pounding the drums, Vanessa thumping the bass, Meg strumming away on rhythm guitar and Rani twanging on lead guitar—complete with eighties-style solo in the middle. I couldn't think of a better song to showcase the group's collective talent, with four bandmates singing prominent *'ooohs'* in the background, morphing into a more elaborate chanting reprise at the bridge. The whole thing powers through to the end, with high, sustained belting notes bringing the song to a crashing conclusion. It's a joyous intro, and life just seems that little bit better for witnessing it first-hand.

Without waiting for the cheering to die down, the band dives straight into QED's 'Everywhere I Go.' Meg ditches her axe for keyboards in the synth-heavy song, leaving Rani to handle the jangly guitar part on her own. Vanessa's bounding bass intertwines with growling low synth notes, as Marisa belts out the tune in a surprisingly-accurate representation of Jenny Morris's original vocals.

The keyboard rock continues as the hard-hitting slap-bass intro of Sharon O'Neill's 'Physical Favours' cuts through the crowd. Marisa raunches it up in her tight rock-chick gear, growling through the angry, defiant vocal line as Meg's sea of synthetic brass blasts behind her. The whole thing descends into a raucous 'woah woah' chant, belted out with footy-crowd verve by four bandmates, as Marisa ad-libs over the top. It's a masterful piece of musical choreography.

After several bombastic numbers, it's time to take it down a notch. Marisa swaps angry for sultry and Meg swaps faux brass for faux strings as the band move into Kim Hart's 'Love at First Night.' The slick disco number gives the sexy frontwoman a chance to show off another side, as she slinks around the microphone, simpering like a kitten.

It doesn't last long, though. Disco Diva morphs into Desperate Drama Queen when the band goes dark with Divinyls' 'Pleasure and Pain.' Marisa does a mean version of Chrissie Amphlett's video antics, writhing and grinding on the floor, then up on her knees humping the air, a picture of a woman driven to the edge of her sexuality. Her commitment to the cause is admirable and I'm amazed she's not exhausted.

My confusion is piqued when the distinctive open-hihat-crashing intro to The Models' 'Out of Mind, Out of Sight' starts.

"I thought this band was all about Aussie and Kiwi rock *chicks*," I yell into Lesley's ear, trying to be heard above the din. "I'm pretty sure James Freud had a dick."

"Aaaah… you're forgetting Kate Ceberano sang on this. *There's your rock chick.*" She waves towards the band, prompting me to pay attention again.

As the cacophony of fake brass rings out from Meg's Roland synth, I feel arms tugging mine. "Come on, let's dance!" It's Jodie and Vicki.

I laugh with embarrassment. "Nah, I don't dance. I'm bloody terrible."

Jodie looks disappointed, but Vicki has already made her way into the throng of gyrating bodies, so she smiles and shrugs before chasing after her friend. I watch them jumping around, flailing their arms with wild abandon. They're having so much fun that I can't help but feel a twinge of envy. I wish I could let go like that, I really do.

I look back up to the stage. Marisa has relinquished the spotlight and is bashing away on a tambourine in the background. Then Rani steps up to the lead mike and lets rip with a low, smoky croon. I'm mesmerised. I've spent the last week with her, yet I've had no idea what her voice is like till right now. She sounds like she's downed a litre of whisky every day for the past decade. Deep, manly, gravelly and seductive.

Marisa's rest period is short-lived as she pelts out Kate Ceberano's backing vocals in the chorus. Her ringing tone slices through the band, owning the soundscape with complete authority. I suddenly notice I'm bopping away at the table. My immediate self-consciousness is overridden by the realisation that I'm actually having *fun.* Fuck everything, fuck everyone. I need to give myself permission to enjoy this.

The second Rani has growled out the final words of her song, she moves to the background. Meg has returned to her guitar and strums out the long, sustained first chords to Maybe Dolls' 'Nervous Kid.' My face lights up and my mouth falls open. *My favourite fucking song ever.*

Marisa comes back to the lead mike, a huge grin on her face. "OK, guys, this is our last one. And it's especially for our guest of honour tonight, my dear friend Ryan." She points directly at me and a host of faces turn my way. My cheeks are on fucking fire.

"Come on! You're not gettin' out of this one." It's Jodie. She drags me through the crowd with full force and doesn't stop till we reach the front. Clamping her hands onto my shoulders, she begins to thrash up and down and I join her. I don't give a shit anymore. I'm fucking *free.* We toss our heads around, flinging our hair in all directions, throwing our arms in the air while the song rages along. Rani rips into a killer slide guitar solo; Marisa belts with all her might; the four others interject in perfect vocal harmony; both guitarists grind out the grungy main riff with gusto. By the time Marisa gets to her final, breathy acapella moans, tears of joy are streaming down my face.

I catch Marisa's eye and she leaps off the stage, throwing her body against mine, her hands tightly cupping my cheeks.

"*Welcome back*, Ryan," she says.

Chapter Twenty

It's the following Friday afternoon at three-thirty. It's been a long week but I've been getting through it OK. I know there's a shit ton of baggage left to unpack in my fucked-up brain, but I feel like maybe I've made a start.

Marisa's waiting for me in the parking lot outside my office when I pull up in the ute. She leans in the window, trying to act all cool, but I know she's reading me. "You seem a little bit better, Ryan."

Yeah, I know you know. "Ha. So, Rani told you I had an appointment with her last night, I gather."

Marisa's face tells me this is news to her, but it falls short of surprise. "She never said. She might be unorthodox, but she's a true professional like that." All of a sudden, Marisa's a dreamy, lovestruck teenager. "She's the best, isn't she? You know, she gave up her cabin for you last week. Bunked in with some other girls so you could go to the retreat."

I feel instantly bad and profoundly moved at the same time. "No, I didn't know that." What do I say? How do I thank someone who has given me so much, someone who doesn't know me from a bar of soap? "I think she saved me, Marisa." I gaze into her eyes. They're overflowing with kindness and compassion. "So did you, for that matter."

Marisa leans in further and gives me a kiss on the cheek. "Come on inside. There's a woman waiting to see you." She pushes herself away from the window and starts back to the office.

"Who is it?"

"She never said," Marisa calls over her shoulder.

Inside, perched on one of the chairs in the reception area, is a small, slender woman with dark hair. As she stands to greet me, I sense an eerie familiarity. "Hi, Ryan. I'm Anna."

My stomach instantly ties in knots. *Not now. Please. Not when I'm just starting to get back on my feet.*

I have no choice but to face this. But I'll be buggered if it's going to happen here. I manage a weak smile. "Um… Anna, there's a takeaway place over the road. Can I get rid of all this stuff and meet you there?"

The lunch bar is just winding down, but it's still open. Anna's sitting at one of the plastic outdoor tables, fidgeting nervously. "Hi Anna. Sorry about before, there are a few nosy people in that office." I sit down, pull out my tobacco pouch and start rolling a durry.

"Oh, um… do you mind?"

I glance up, expecting her to ask me not to smoke. *No bloody way.* But she's pointing at the pouch. "Sure. You want this one?" I hold out the smoke I've just finished making.

"Nah, it's fine." She delves into the pouch and rolls an expert cigarette in seconds. "Sometimes I pinch one when Dennis or Dominic aren't looking." She lights up and takes a long drag, visibly trying to calm her nerves. "Ryan, I'm not sure what's happened between you two, but I need you to know it's all my fault." I begin to protest and she cuts me off. "No, please hear me out. Dominic and I have been fighting for weeks. I've told him I want to start divorce proceedings and sell the apartment in Cronulla. I'm going to take Oscar down to live with me and Dennis in Wollongong. It's time to move on."

I sit there in silence. I don't know what I'm supposed to say, but it doesn't excuse the way Dominic treated me.

"I'm not one of those bitchy, punitive ex-wives, Ryan. I know he's terrified he's going to lose his son. But Oscar will still spend every second weekend with Dominic. I've even taken on a class at our campus in Circular Quay, so I'll be teaching in Sydney every Friday evening. Dominic will be able to spend a few hours with Oscar on the off-weeks, too."

I still don't see what this has to do with my relationship, I want to say.

Anna stares at me, smoking furiously, begging me with her eyes. "Please contact him, Ryan. He's fallen apart. I hear him crying in his room at night when he thinks I'm asleep."

It hurts to hear Dominic's suffering, but it's not enough.

Anna tries one more time. "I'm reluctant to use my child as a bargaining chip. But Oscar is devastated. He can't understand why you've gone."

This is tipping me over the edge. That poor kid has done nothing wrong. I miss the hell out of him and it's a damn sight more complicated than Anna thinks. I'm not just some floozy his father's broken up with. He's my *nephew,* for fuck's sake.

"OK, Anna. I'll give it some thought. I can't promise anything, though." It's the best I can do right now.

* * *

I'm still stewing over all this when I get back home. I park my ute, secure the rear gate and walk through the house from back to front to collect the mail. There's a power bill, a bulk letter from our member of parliament and a handwritten envelope with no return address. *I never get these.* Wandering back inside, I toss the other two letters and open the last one.

"Dear Ryan,

Please PLEASE read this letter—I'm begging you. I promise it will be my last attempt to contact you. Instinct tells me to keep at it, to never give up hope, but I'd hate for you to think of me as a parasite, some kind of stalker. I couldn't bear it if that was your final impression of me.

I was wrong, so wrong, Ryan. There's absolutely no excusing the way I acted. I let things get on top of me and I took it all out on you—the most beautiful, loving soul on this earth, the person who so least deserved it.

I should have been crawling, begging for your forgiveness when you showed up at my place that night. The thought of you sitting at that restaurant, dressed beautifully for me, handsome as ever, holding flowers you bought for me, watching the minutes tick by as you waited for a man that never showed up—it haunts me, Ryan. I want to sob every time I think of it.

Your thoughtfulness, your generosity never fails to amaze me and I callously disregarded it. And instead of giving you the apology you were entitled to, I attacked you in the most gutless, cowardly manner possible. I took every cheap shot I could and I'm disgusted with myself.

I see you struggle with depression, Ryan. But I also see you doing your darndest not to let it affect our time together. I see you bravely smiling, riding out the pain and sorrow because you'll do whatever it takes to please me. You don't burden me with mood swings, not ever. I can't believe I threw that in your face. It wasn't just untrue, it was unthinkably cruel of me.

And I truly hate myself for making that quip about Owen. You've never lorded Owen's memory over me; you've never treated me as if I'm second-best. You've dealt with your tragedy in a dignified and honest way and I kicked you in the most vulnerable place I could. I wouldn't blame you if you never spoke to me again. I can only hope to God you're a better person than I am and you find it in your heart to do so.

As for Anna, it's now over. I'm moving into the Bondi place. That's not just lip service, I've been taking stuff over there every night. Anna's only too happy, she wants me out of the way so she can step things up with Dennis. But, more importantly, I need to cut the cord. It should have happened months ago. I should have shown you the respect you deserved. It was grossly unfair of me to expect you to wait around each week until I deigned to see you. It's true, I treated you like a mistress and I should never have degraded you like that.

This move, Ryan, it's not just because of you, I swear. I'd never put that kind of pressure on you. But I still pray there's a chance you might come back to me. And I want you to know that if you grant me that chance, I'm ready to devote my life to you. That man, that fucking arsehole who treated you like shit—that's not the real me. You have my solemn oath you'll never, ever see that man again.

I'm not in lawyer mode now. I'm not composing an airtight argument. I'm down on my knees, pleading with you. I've never cried like this in my life. I love you so fucking much it hurts.

Please, big bear. I'm bleeding here. My heart's in a million pieces and you're the only one who can put it back together.

You have my love forever, beautiful man—Dominic."

I'm blinded. Hit for six. Snatching my bag and keys, I'm out the door, in my ute and on the road in a flash. The traffic is a blur. I'm driven by an inexorable need—to get there as soon as fucking possible.

Barging up to the apartment building's entrance, I come face-to-face with dear old Joyce from downstairs as she's opening the door. "My, you're in a hurry, Ryan!"

I smile at her, holding the door for her as she makes her way through. "Yes, I'm running very late. Lovely to see you, though!"

I'm not waiting for the bloody elevator. I bound up the stairs two, three at a time, the letter clutched firmly in my hand. As I knock at the apartment door, I try to catch my breath, but my heart is beating way too fast. The door opens and there's Dominic. He's a mess. His eyes are shrouded in dark circles, his skin is pale and he looks like he hasn't slept in a week.

As soon as he registers who it is, his face crumples. *"Big bear…"* he whispers. I barely catch him in my arms as he collapses against the wall, sobbing. Guiding him down to the floor, I kick the door shut and squeeze his body as hard as I can, pressing his head to my chest, rocking him as he cries.

How the fuck did I ever think I'd be able to live my life without him?

Somehow, we've made it to the bedroom and we're lying on the bed in the same position. Dominic is cradled in my arms and I'm stroking the back of his head.

"I will never, ever be able to express how sorry I am for what I did to you, Ryan," he whispers. "But I'm gonna try my absolute best."

"It's fine. Truly, *lontra*. You said it all in the letter."

"Nah, one letter isn't going to cut it, big bear. You need a shit ton more than that. You're so fuckin' special. I can't tell you how much your love has changed me. I treasure it, mate."

I lean down and bury my face in his hair, drowning in that special smell of his. I can't even bring myself to move away, it's like a drug. "I know you do, Dominic," I murmur, as my lips move against his scalp, my hot breath dispersing in a warm, comforting cloud between us.

"You give so freely, Ryan. And I've blindly taken from you. You deserve nothing but the best, and I owe it to you to be that man. Every day, mate. Every fuckin' second I'm gonna show you how privileged I am that you choose to be with me. You're my fuckin' heart."

Slowly, he repositions himself, running his hand down my back to land on my arse. It's such a natural move for him, and he probably doesn't even know he's doing it, but I immediately recoil. Dominic looks like I've just slapped him hard. He quickly pulls his arm away. "God, I'm sorry, Ryan."

I feel terrible. I have no idea how to explain why I just reacted like that. But my beanie has slipped upwards.

"What the hell happened to you?" Dominic says, eyeing the gash on my upper forehead. It's pretty much healed now, but there's still an angry red line there.

I know I have to say something. There's no way of moving forward otherwise. My eyes fix on the wall opposite me. *Fix on the wall.* "After it all fell apart with you I was incredibly fucked up, Dominic. I really believed I was never gonna see you again. Some well-meaning person suggested a random hook-up might take my mind off things. I was ready to try anything to escape the nightmare I was in. So, I went to a sauna."

Dominic's voice is deathly quiet. "And?"

"Some massive bastard bashed and… raped me." I swallow hard, and slowly look down to see an expression of sheer horror on Dominic's face.

"Jesus, Ryan! Did you fight back?"

Gut-wrenching shame hits me and I'm catapulted back to that very dark place. I screw my eyes up. I can't look at him. At anything. "No, I didn't."

"Why? Why didn't you punch the shit out of the cunt?" His voice is seething with rage. I know he's shocked. But I can sense I've come down a peg or two in his opinion of me as a man.

"Because I felt like I deserved it."

Dominic goes silent. I can hear his rushing breath. I can feel him shift on the bed. Something wet hits my lips. I open my eyes again to see him bent over me, his face red and twisted in agony as tears spill in torrents down his cheeks. "That fuckin' cunt hurt you? He fuckin' dared to hurt my big bear? I'll fuckin' KILL him!" He's openly weeping now, pawing at me, touching my face delicately all over, checking the state of my long-repaired damage.

It's not my outside that's broken now, mate.

Wrapping his arms around my head, he crushes it against his chest, shaking with stifled sobs. I feel every shudder of his rib cage against my face, driving the pure and potent empathy from his soul into mine.

"I'll kill him I'll kill him I'll fuckin' kill him." His turbulent mantra buzzes at my crown. He's protecting me. It's too late, I know. But I can sense his fierce determination to keep me safe. And I need that so desperately right now.

Dominic's sobs give way to wavering breaths. The whole time, he clutches me against his heart, the strong beat of it reminding me we're alive, we're real, we *survived.* Taking a long sniff of my hair, he pauses, then speaks very softly. "If you want to report this, then I'm there with you every step of the way, baby. I'll use every connection I have to ruin this bastard."

"No… please, mate, I'm just starting to get on with my life. I'm seeing a therapist. I can't deal with all of that shit, too." I lift my head up, fixing my gaze on his. "I love you for wanting to help, but I *really* need you to understand this."

His expression softens. His eyes are glistening. Slowly, he reaches up and strokes my beard. "Of course I do, big bear." He stops short, searching my face. "I'll do absolutely fuckin' anything for you, baby. I'm on your side, no matter what. One day, I hope I'll earn your trust again and maybe you'll think about coming back for good."

The earnestness in his eyes cuts right through me. I pull his lips to mine, whispering against them. "I'm already back for good, *lontra.*"

Chapter Twenty-One

"Hey, big bear, do you really have to shoot off?" Dominic's busy tapping at his phone. It's now Sunday arvo and we pretty much haven't left the bed all weekend. The relief I feel having him back in my arms again is so powerful I don't think I've stopped touching him the entire time. "Anna says Dennis is staying over tonight, so I think I'll just go to work from here tomorrow morning."

The thrill I feel at this extended invitation instantly turns to knots as I remember something I've been trying to put out of my mind. "Um… I'd love to, but there's something important I really have to do."

I look down at Dominic. His head is craned back as he gazes up at me. His brow is creased with concern, and I know he wants me to say more. Still, he simply nods and gives me a small smile.

I feel bad. I'm well aware I have to communicate more; there have been way too many secrets lately. Letting out a deep sigh, I decide to spill the beans. He needs to hear this. "Owen died today. Five weeks after his thirty-third birthday. I always take the boat out again to… you know."

Dominic scuttles up the bed and wraps himself around me. "Oh, God, big bear. I'm so sorry," he whispers. "Do you want to come back here afterwards? I hate the thought of you being alone."

He's so kind. I squeeze him tighter, soothing myself with the compassionate energy he's imparting. I urgently need this extra strength. "It's a wonderful offer, *lontra*. But I'm not gonna be in the best condition." I'm sure of this. I feel a great sense of foreboding. Everything is coming to a head and I've never been quite so terrified.

He reaches up and strokes the back of my hair. "OK, Ryan. I understand. But if you need me, I'll be there for you as fast as I can, alright?" He moves out, cups my face in his hands, and looks deep into me. *"I love you,* baby."

* * *

The sun is rapidly descending as I stop the boat in the centre of the bay. The air is frigid, my rapid breath sending clouds of condensation into the atmosphere. I'm clutching my yellow roses as my chest trembles.

"Hey, little man. Here we are again. Seven years, mate. I still can't believe you're gone." I pull off a few petals, letting them go over the side of the boat, watching as they see-saw downwards, settle on the water and slowly drift away. Taking a huge gulp of air, I hold my ribs out, straining to settle the hurricane of emotion raging inside me.

"There's something I have to tell you." My heart is racing, thumping hard. "It's a man, and he loves me." I gather another handful of petals, setting them free over the edge, my eyes following them as they leave me, taking a part of my soul with them.

I'm teetering on the brink of a precipice. I don't know what's going to happen, but I force myself to carry on. "The thing is, I love him, too." My eyes are brimming over. A tear escapes and rolls down my cheek. "I feel like I'm betraying you, buddy. I don't want you to think I love you any less."

I'm starting to sniffle and my breath is becoming jagged. I look

233

down at the paltry bunch of flowers. Somehow, I've managed to strip them almost bare. I pull the final few petals off and hang my arm over the edge of the boat. My fist closes around them. I just can't seem to open it. I can hear the thickness in my voice as I say the words I'm dreading the most.

"I've gotta let you go, little man."

My mouth opens and a scream hurtles out of me. At long last, my heart implodes as the final few remaining pieces of Owen I've managed to hold onto fall from my palm. My body begins to heave as howls tear through my chest cavity, ripping me to shreds. I collapse onto the floor of the boat, curling into a ball, convulsing with every new lungful of agony. My world is spinning so violently, my anguish is so excruciating that I don't want to exist anymore. I weep over my years of loneliness and desolation, I weep over my violated body, I weep over the crushing, overwhelming loss of the wonderful little bloke I'd treasured, the man who had given me everything and never expected anything in return. I cry and cry without stopping, until my body can no longer cope and I slip into a state of unconsciousness.

A bright light shines in front of me. It's so blinding I have to shield my eyes, but I can't bring myself to look away. Through the white haze, a shape begins to take form. It's Owen. Dear, sweet little Owen in his tight tradie shorts, his tanned, hairy legs clad at the bottom with his trademark woolly socks and chunky steel-capped boots. His face is an urgent contortion of worry, and as he approaches me I see the tears in his eyes. Slowly, he crouches down in front of me and touches a hand to my head. A powerful warmth surges through my body. It's a pure and untainted energy: a potent mixture of sincerity, unwavering devotion, boundless compassion and all-encompassing love. I remember this. I recall every nuance of the incredible connection I shared with my little man.

"You gotta be happy, Ryan. It's breakin' my heart seeing you like this.

You got a great man, a real chance to move on with your life. I want this so much for you, mate. I can see how madly this bloke loves you. So just let him do it, OK? Let him take you in his arms and care for you the way you deserve. Please don't let me hold you back, it fuckin' hurts me so bad. Anytime you need me, just look up. I'll always be here for you. Always."

Owen stands up and smiles, the tears now running rivers down his cheeks. I reach out for his hand. I've never needed to cling to something so desperately in my whole life. I'm crying out, my voice so loud it's growing hoarse. I'm grabbing frantically at his outstretched palm, but I can't feel it. That gentle, calloused hand that soothed me for twelve years grows fainter and fainter as Owen's body fades. His beautiful, sunny smile is the last thing I see.

Gradually, my eyes open. The boat is rocking slightly and the darkness of night is stretched out above me. You don't often see stars in inner Sydney. I don't know why. They say it's pollution, they say it's something to do with the light. But right now, in the dull, cloudless sky, I can see just one. It's large, it's bright, it's positively resplendent in its brilliance. As I watch it there, shining like a beacon, Owen's voice resounds in my ears.

"Always, teddy."

Chapter Twenty-Two

The following Saturday, there's a knock on my front door as I'm walking down the hallway, fresh out of the shower. I swing it open wide, standing there naked as I finish drying my hair. "Hey, *lontra,* am I late?"

"No, sexy man. I'm early." He grabs my penis as he leans forward, giving me a kiss. I start to harden immediately. As usual, I haven't masturbated for days and I'm like a time bomb ready to detonate any second. "Mmmm… but unfortunately I'm not early enough to take care of this monster." Steering my shoulders, he slaps me on my bare butt, sending me off to my room.

He follows in my footsteps, collapsing onto my bed to watch me as I dress. "Still no undies, eh?" he says, as I pull my trackpants over my naked crotch.

"Never. You know that."

Dominic chuckles. "Well, your commando fetish has rubbed off on me, now. You wanna see?"

I growl at him as he slides the pants of his designer tracksuit down, his naked, mostly-erect cock bouncing out and flopping sideways across his abdomen. "Unless you want me to ravage that dick, Dominic, you're gonna have to put it away right now."

With a smirk, he shimmies the elastic waistband back over his hips, reaching down to tuck his hard willy back in. "Hey, I want to make a little detour before we go down to see dad, OK? But it's a secret, so I don't want you asking any questions."

I glance back over to him, languorously propped against my pillows with his hands behind his head. "OK, *lontra*. You have my word."

* * *

I know where we're going. I recognise all the streets we turn into, the bridges we cross. There's only one destination it could be. When we arrive, Dominic switches off the ignition in the MGB and sits there, looking at me. "Ready?" he says softly.

We walk through the park towards the water's edge, but Dominic stops short when we're on the grassy verge. Taking my hand, he leads me along a short distance. The construction fence that's been there for ages is now gone, and in its place are new benches and a barbecue table or two. Coming to the first bench, he runs his hand over the brand new wood, his fingers landing on a small, gleaming plaque. There, in black letters against the brass background, I see five words.

"In memory of Owen Kendrick."

My heart stops. "How?" I whisper.

"Money talks, big bear. I saw the construction, I made a few persistent phone calls, I greased a few palms."

I'm speechless. I slowly sit on the bench, turning to trace my finger over the plaque. Dominic takes a seat beside me, staring intently at my face, trying to read my reaction.

"Owen was laid to rest out here, Dominic." I lift my head to gaze across the water, admiring how the gentle waves shimmer in the early afternoon sun. "When we went sailing over Fannie Bay in Darwin for the first time, he said he wanted me to sprinkle his ashes there when he died. But after he was killed, the authorities held his body for fuckin' ages. I'd already run away to Sydney by then and I couldn't face the thought of going back." I start to shake. Tears are already spilling down my face. "I had his ashes sent down here to me and I scattered them…" I can't finish my sentence, I just wave weakly towards the water. "I… couldn't even fulfil his final wish." I gasp in lungfuls of air, holding my breath as hard as I can, but my body starts heaving with stifled sobs. I thought I'd got this all out of my system last weekend. I'm so fucking disgusted with myself.

Dominic moves over, clutching me from behind, squeezing my body tight against his. It's the only thing keeping me grounded right now. He knows I'm a physical person. He knows I'm a man of few words. All I need is his touch, his warmth, to feel that I'm loved and cherished. And he gives this to me in spades. There's not a moment gone by in his presence lately that he hasn't reached out to me, instinctively aware that this is how I communicate.

His fingers brush through my hair and he places a gentle kiss on my crown. "Big bear," he starts quietly, "I never knew Owen, but I do know this. He'd be so glad you kept him close by."

I slowly sit back up, wiping my eyes. I know Dominic's right. That kind little bloke only ever wanted me to be happy. I'm doing him a disservice by not living life the best way I can. I look at the man next to me, the here and now. This is what I need to focus on.

"Now you can come here anytime, Ryan. You can sit on this bench as long as you need. I know it's not much, but I hope with all my heart it's a way to help keep that special connection alive."

* * *

"My boys!" Joe's eyes light up as we enter his room at the nursing home. I'm shocked to see how old and frail he looks. But the smile on his face is radiant as he holds his hands out towards us. I'm not quite sure what to do here. I haven't seen him in decades. But as I approach the armchair he's sitting in, he seizes my hand and pulls me into a hug. Releasing me, he glances over my shoulder. "Where is *netinho?*"

"He's with his *mamãe*, dad." Dominic's standing in front of Joe with the calm demeanour of a doting son.

"*Mamãe?*" Joe looks back at me, his eyes full of confusion. "No, no, no." He points to the plastic chair beside him, beckoning me to sit down. Once I've parked my arse, he squeezes my hand again. "Where is *your* son?" he says, searching my face. "Where is Oscar? Why you not bring him?"

"No, dad. Oscar's *my* son. He can't come today, it's his birthday and he's down in Wollongong. I promise he'll visit you soon." Dominic's voice is patient and kind, but Joe ignores him, continuing to look into my eyes. "Next time you bring your boy, you hear?" He pats my hand resolutely, giving me another smile.

"You got my word on that, Joe." I know he's muddled, but his genuine affect is touching.

Joe looks to his right, fumbling for something on the table beside him. Handing me a battered paperback, he says, "You read to me, please? My eyes are not so good anymore."

I glance at the cover of the book he's given me. Stifling a smile, I notice it's an old copy of 'Valley of the Dolls.' So, I spend the next fifteen minutes or so narrating the salacious story of drugged-out, pill-popping Hollywood actresses. It's surprisingly addictive, and by the time I look up from the small print, I see Joe has drifted off.

Noticing that my voice has stopped, his eyes slowly open. "Thank you, *filho*," he says. I remember that word. *Son.* He used to say it to Dominic way back when we were kids. He cranes his neck towards the door, then turns back to the table beside him, picking up an alarm clock with large numbers on it. "Tea time. They are late. Maybe they forget?"

Dominic rises from the chair near the window where he's been sitting quietly, listening to my ridiculous storytelling. Giving me a wink, he turns to Joe. "I'll go and find out what's keeping them."

Joe's eyes follow Dominic as he walks across the room. The second he's disappeared down the hall, Joe grabs my hand once more. With a look of grave sincerity, he squeezes his fingers around my palm. "He's a good husband to you. He loves you very much and he make you so happy. You look after my Dominic, *você entendeu?*"

You understand? And yes—of course I do. Joe's blessing moves me in a way he'll never truly know. "I promise, Joe. I love him very much, too."

* * *

"There's only one pile of clothes left to collect, big bear," says Dominic as we approach Cronulla. "But if it's OK with you, can we hang around for a while? Anna and Oscar will be back from his birthday party soon."

"Dominic, I haven't seen the kid in seven weeks." I don't expand on this, I just let it sink in. I'm not trying to make Dominic feel bad; I'm just pointing out the collateral damage caused by our rift.

Nevertheless, Dominic goes silent for a while. A good thirty seconds passes before he quietly speaks. "Yeah, that was a bit insensitive of me."

"You know I only took you back because of him, don't you?" I give him a playful punch in the arm and he yelps defiantly, turning to see the huge grin on my face.

"You bloody cunt! That fuckin' hurt!" he laughs. Holding the wheel with his injured arm, he reaches over and rubs his deltoid where the punch landed. "But seriously, are you gonna be OK with him staying at my place all next week while Anna moves out?"

"Do you want another punch?"

Dominic laughs again. I'm glad he can see the lighter side of all this. I'd fully intended to see Oscar, anyway. I miss the fuck out of that little tyke. "I know you're planning to work from home as much as you can while he's there, but I've organised with Marisa to take two or three days off to help out."

Dominic glances at me, his face awash with emotion. "Fuck, big bear. You never cease to amaze me." He reaches for my hand, giving it a squeeze. "I'm really scared to ask you this, but..." his voice dies off.

"But what?"

"Nah, it doesn't matter."

"Tell me, you prick, or I swear you'll get another fuckin' dead arm."

We pull up at a traffic light and he turns his head to gaze at me. The look of sheer hope in his eyes makes me want to agree with anything he proposes. "Do you think we might become a family?"

I'm hit for six. It's all I've ever dreamed of. In my heart, though, I know we found this happiness months ago. "We already are, *lontra.*"

* * *

"Is there enough space for all your stuff in the boot?" I ask, once we've pulled up in Dominic's underground car park.

"I think so. I can wedge a few things behind the seats if there isn't."

"Pop it open for me and I'll check."

Dominic does as he's told and I walk around and rummage through the boot, pushing the few random things in there aside. "Yeah, looks like plenty."

He turns to head towards the elevator and I discreetly grab the bag I've brought with me, shut the boot and saunter off after him.

Up in the apartment, I stash my bag on a dining chair and follow Dominic down the hall. I poke my head into doorways, having a good old sticky beak. I've never been here before, and it's a really nice place. Every window seems to have either a view of the sea or the urban landscape. I know we've reached Dominic's old bedroom when I spot the empty little den. Its plush carpet is marked by furniture impressions and the only thing remaining is a large pile of shirts and trousers on hangers.

Dominic's staring wistfully out the window at the ocean in the distance. "I'm gonna miss this place," he says quietly. "Anyway, onwards and upwards. I've got a new life with the perfect man." He turns to smile at me and notices I've scooped up the bounty of garments. "Hey, you aren't here to play removalist, baby."

"Too late," I grin, turning and carrying his wardrobe back through the apartment. I dump it on the dining table, craftily obscuring my bag on the chair.

"Hey, Anna just texted and said they're half an hour away. Is that OK? We could sit in here and watch something if you like?" Dominic is standing in the entrance to the living room. The light from the overcast sky is shining from behind him, creating a halo around his body. He's removed his tracksuit top, revealing a form-fitting white t-shirt. His limber frame is more stunning than I've ever seen before. I can think of something I'd like to do for half an hour.

I join him in there on the large couch. I can tell who picked it. It's a chick's lounge suite. Expensive and stylish, but the kind of thing one perches on with propriety. Dominic's overstuffed couch at his place is way more comfortable, the sort of thing a bloke can sink into with a beer after a hard day's work.

He leans forward, falling onto his knees and stretching out to the coffee table to reach the remote. "Let's pick something you like," he says. I'm not really listening, because his slender butt is spread wide in front of me.

My hand automatically shoots out and begins to rub his anus through his stretchy tracksuit pants. "Ohhhh," he sighs. "You can keep doing that. But remember, I've got no undies on for you to steal this time."

I move behind him, coming down to kneel on the carpet. "I could easily slip my dick in here, you realise." I push my finger firmly at the entrance to his hole, the fabric giving way to the pressure.

"No bloody chance!" he chortles. "You fucked me last week, remember? My arse ached for days afterwards."

Growling, I reach up to his waistband and yank the trackies down to his lower thighs. There in front of me is the splendour of his wiry little arse, full forest of fur decorating his taut, wrinkled manhole.

In a flash, I've bent down and pressed my nose against it, drawing in his intimate manly fragrance. My tongue shoots out and begins to lick up and down his taint. "Fuck!" Dominic gasps. "Oh, Jesus! Why haven't you done this before?"

"You like it?" I murmur, my lips buzzing against his furry perineal ridge.

"Do I fuckin' ever!" He's panting now. As my tongue travels from the rear of his balls upwards, I feel his body jiggle with the furious masturbation going on in front of him. "I want you to do this all the bloody time, big bear."

"It'll be my pleasure," I chuckle in between broad, wet strokes. "I get to sniff this beautiful pucker while you jerk that long dick of yours."

A good few minutes pass as I lazily move my tongue up and down, tickling his taint with the tip of it one moment, slathering it with full force the next. Dominic keeps on whimpering and his arsehole continues to bump against my nose as he wanks like a horny teen.

I'm fully expecting to bring him to a rousing climax like this, but Dominic has other ideas. Flipping over, he thrusts his salty prick straight into my mouth. "Suck me hard, big bear. Get me nice and wet so I can shove every inch up your hairy fuckin' cunt."

Oh, my bloody God. I'm onto it immediately, pulling his hips towards my face, ramming that long, slender fuckstick as far down my gullet as it'll go. Dominic's hands scrunch in my hair, tightening every time his dick flexes against my tongue. The vigorous pounding has saliva pouring out of me. Reaching down, I pull my dick free of my trackies and slather my knob with the rampant moisture from my mouth. I'm stroking hard and fast in an instant. I'm so trigger-happy, I know I'll lose my load in no time flat. That's more than fine with me. I'll swallow anything Dominic wants to pump down my throat. There's plenty of time for him to service my arse later.

Pushing my head away, Dominic throws himself on the couch and rams his trackies down to his ankles. "Ride me like a bronco, big bear. I'm about to shoot."

I scramble to my feet, shoving my own trackies down. There's no time to remove them, I'm practically in the middle of an orgasm already. Turning my arse towards him, I bear down and spear myself onto his prick in one quick descent. Dominic groans and begins to drive into me without mercy. My sphincter is burning from the sudden intrusion, but I don't care. I can feel myself tightening inside, ready to reach the crest of the wave. Frantically rubbing my knob, I bounce against his crotch as he thrusts upwards.

"Ah… ah… ah! I'm coming, big bear!" Dominic shudders violently, his fingers digging into my burly butt cheeks. I can feel the throb inside me as he releases his seed, breeding me over and over. It's such a potently exciting sensation that my hand moves faster, my arsehole constricts and an almighty pain rips through my undercarriage. "I'm gonna blow!" I yell.

"Quick, turn around!" Dominic slaps my arse cheek as I feel the surge starting within me. I only just make it, thrusting my cock straight into his mouth as the first deep spurt comes careening out of me. Holding his head, I unload into his mouth one, two, three, four, five more times. My body keeps convulsing, my prostate pumping long after there's nothing left to come out.

The sound of voices and a key turning in the door snaps us out of our fuck-trance. Legs fly in all directions as we struggle to get our trackies pulled up. Rearranging our bodies to look all casual, I smile to myself as I feel Dominic's load starting to ooze out of me. My arsehole knows better than my brain, though, and it clenches tight to avoid leaving a telltale wet patch.

"Daaaad!" Oscar's voice comes sailing through the apartment till he arrives at the living room entrance. He stops short when he sees me. "Ryan?" There's a brief pause as he takes in my presence, then he's flying at me, flinging his little body against mine in a huge hug.

"Hi boys, sorry we took so long." Anna appears in the doorway, arms loaded with presents.

"Don't worry about it," Dominic grins. "We managed to entertain ourselves."

* * *

The true gravity of our brief visit hits home as we prepare to leave. Polite chatter, a comprehensive show-and-tell of Oscar's present haul, and a detailed housekeeping discussion between Dominic and Anna concludes with an awkward pause at the door. This is the final moment for their family unit before it ends forever.

"Hey, monkey," Dominic soothes as he crouches in front of his son. "It's time for me to take off now. I know this is a big change, but you're gonna have a new house and a yard and all your cousins nearby." He reaches up to place his hand on Oscar's cheek. "And you're gonna come and stay with me all the time, OK?"

Oscar's breath starts to hitch. I can see how brave he's trying to be but it's finally too much for the poor little mite. "Dad, please don't go," he says, breaking down into sobs. Dominic pulls the boy into his arms, but it only causes the sobs to morph into gut-wrenching howls. I can hardly bear to see the pain this kid is in. I've been there with my own dad, and the wounds are still raw to this day.

Dominic picks up his little boy and carries him down the hall, murmuring quietly to him.

"Um… this seems like a private family thing," I say to Anna. "I'll just take this stuff down to the car and come back in a little while."

As I gather the mountain of clothes into my arms, I spot the bag I brought with me. I'd forgotten all about it.

I stay down in the car park a good fifteen minutes. My pretext may have been to give them some privacy, but in reality I'm about to lose it. It's like the floodgates were opened on the bay that night, and now anything seems to set me off. I think back to Rani. I try my best to recall the things her silent instruction taught me. With my eyes closed, I breathe long and slow. Eventually, the chaos in my head starts to die down. One by one, the intrusive noises drop out till they're gone altogether and I find my inner peace.

Dominic's standing in the kitchen when I arrive back up at the apartment. He looks tired and drained. "He asked to see you," he says.

Nodding slightly, I make my way to Oscar's bedroom, taking a small detour to grab my bag along the way. I don't knock on the door or say anything. I'm not gonna hassle the little bloke, I'm just gonna be there for him. I quietly take a seat on the edge of his bed.

CHAPTER TWENTY-TWO

"Why did you leave?" His normally-impertinent voice is a broken whisper.

"I'm sorry, Oscar. I just had to go away for a while." I really don't know what to say. I sit there, fumbling with my bag. "Nothing I tell you will make any of this stuff hurt any less, mate. But I want you to know that I'm here for you anytime." I reach into my bag, pulling out my first gift. "This isn't new. It's just my old iPhone, but I've paid for the phone bill for a whole year. So, if you ever get sad, I want you to call me, no matter what."

Oscar takes the gift, his tear-stained face looking up at me. "You mean I can keep it?"

"Of course you can, buddy. That's the best thing about birthday presents, eh?" I pull the other gift out of the bag. Being a typical slovenly male, it's no surprise I haven't wrapped it. "I also got you this."

Oscar's face brightens as soon as he sees the ALF figurine. "Wow!" He turns the box over and over. "He even talks!" Peeling his eyes away from his present for a moment, he gives me a pleading look. "Can we watch ALF lots and lots when I stay with Dad next week?"

"Mate, it's your school holidays and we'll do anything you want." I glance back towards the door. "Hey, I think your dad needs to go now. But I'll see you next week, yeah?" I reach up and ruffle his hair, then haul my body up off the bed and make for the door.

"Ryan?"

"Yes, buddy?"

"Please don't ever go away again."

Chapter Twenty-Three

"What are you doing out here?" I've just stumbled into the lounge room, fresh from bed, to find Dominic lying on his stomach tapping away at his laptop on the couch. Papers are spread all over the coffee table, in amongst actual coffee.

"Oscar's still asleep and I didn't want to disturb him."

I sidle up to him and crouch down, sliding my hand over his pyjama-clad arse. "Well, he could go and sleep in your bed. It's not like we'll need it for a while since I fucked you senseless last night." Creeping my hand underneath his waistband, I run my palm over his furry cheeks and instantly find his hole. I love how it's always *just there*, barely hidden by his little crack.

Dominic purrs quietly. "Go easy in there, I'm still a bit sore. You and your fat fuckin' stump of a dick."

"Point taken." I don't move my hand, though. I just keep gently stroking the puckered little aperture, and Dominic lowers his head into his folded arms with another purr.

"Mmmmmmm… nobody ever worshipped my arse like this."

The sound of the study door opening has me whipping my hand out of Dominic's pyjama bottoms with lightning speed. "Dad? Can I have Frosties for breakfast?"

Dominic turns and gives me a reproachful look. "See what you've created, Ryan? Why can't you just eat Weetbix like a normal person?"

"Hey! I like the tiger on the box, OK?"

"*And* all the sugar." He sits up and calls through the servery window to Oscar, who's already rustling around in the kitchen. "Only a *small* bowl, monkey."

Leaving Dominic to his parental duties, I wander into the study. I've been putting this off for a while, but now that this is Dominic's full-time home, Oscar will inevitably be spending more time here. I duck back down to the main bedroom and rummage through my bag. I know I have a tape measure tucked away somewhere. I wouldn't be a builder if I didn't have one attached to my body at all times.

When I finally locate the fluoro-orange contraption, I return to the little study and get to work. Oscar's bed is obstructing the entire width of the skinny room, so I fold it up and wedge it in its tiny storage space. Pulling a sheet of paper from the printer, I fish around for a pen on the desk and begin to take measurements. Up and down, back and forth I go, leaning precariously over the clutter of furniture, trying my best to get the most accurate picture I can.

"What are you up to?" Dominic's standing at the doorway, hands on his hips with a quizzical look on his face. I see the long line of his penis, creating a distinct impression in the thin silk of his expensive pyjamas.

Walking up to him, I slide my palm over his warm shaft. It's a little firm. At the point where it's beginning to engorge, but not quite at the stage where it's risen much.

"If you keep doing that, you're going to scar my kid for life, you know." Dominic's cheeky grin tells me he's not keen for me to remove my hand, despite his warning. So, instead of letting go, I begin to shuffle his foreskin back and forth through the flimsy fabric.

"You know, *lontra*, I have an idea for the room here. Do you trust me? If I said I could give you your study and Oscar a private sleeping quarters all within this tiny space?"

"I've seen your work before, big bear. Anything you say is…ahhhh…" He shudders as I slide his penis straight into my mouth. Somehow, I've made it onto my knees and Dominic's eight-plus inches of manhood are poking through his fly. Gee, I'm more skilled than I give myself credit for.

Coitus interruptus happens once more as kid-sized footsteps slap along the floorboards into the living room. Standing up, I pull Dominic's waistband out, reposition his penis upwards and clamp it under the elastic. The end of it pokes out over the top, its wrinkly foreskin only half-covering his knob. "There you go, mate. One of the many benefits of having such a long, slender dick."

Dominic arranges his pyjama top over the offending knob, then looks up at me with a grin. "You can finish that later if you like."

"I will, believe you me."

He leans in and places a soft kiss on my lips, then turns to the door. "Oh," he says, looking back over his shoulder. "I couldn't love you any more than I already do, but that limit may change if you can sort out this space."

* * *

I'm glad I took these few days off. I'm in the ute with my little nephew, driving down Parramatta Road to pick up some timber I've sourced. A lot of people owe me favours. It's one of the rewards for me being such a helpful guy and I fully intend to collect.

"What's this song?" pipes up Oscar. The Divinyls are blaring through my tape deck. I think I have every single song they ever released.

"It's called 'Siren.'"

"Why?"

CHAPTER TWENTY-THREE

"Because the guitar sounds like a siren at the start."

"Why is she singing the alphabet?"

"Maybe she ran out of words." I turn and grin at Oscar. "Plus, I think it sounds cool."

Oscar shifts in his seat and nods. "This is my favourite of all of the songs." He stares out the window for a little while. We're passing through Five Dock, coming to the hub of takeaways near Great North Road. "Ooooh KFC! Can we have that for lunch? Can we?"

"What do you reckon, buddy?"

Oscar looks at me, unsure. "Does that mean yes?"

"It means definitely, one hundred percent yes."

"Can we get a twenty-one piece bucket?"

"What do you reckon?"

* * *

"And who's this little fella?" Marisa beams from behind the front desk.

"This is Oscar. Say hello to Marisa, Oscar."

"Hello, Marisa." Oscar's gone all shy.

"Marisa's a rock singer. You know all those songs we play in the car? She does them with her band."

Oscar's eyes go wide. "Really? That's awesome." His face quickly wrinkles into a frown as he scans the office around him. "Then why do you work here?"

Marisa tries to look serious, but I can see her struggling to hold in a giggle. "Well, Oscar, singing in a band doesn't pay very much money. And I have a lot of jewellery to buy." She holds up her wrists and jangles her collection of bracelets. "Now, why have you brought Ryan in to see me this morning? He's meant to be on holidays."

251

"He's making me a special bed. He won't tell me what it looks like."

I ruffle his hair and smile up at Marisa. "I'm gonna back the ute round to the workshop and cut up a bunch of timber for a while." I glance down at Oscar. "You can come and watch, but you have to stay behind the fence, OK?"

"Don't be silly," scoffs Marisa. She swivels off her chair and walks around the desk to join us. "You can stay here with me, Oscar. We'll have fun while Ryan works. We can even go over and get something to eat at the lunch bar."

"I can't. Ryan said he's taking me to KFC when he's finished."

"Aw. Surely you've got room for a milkshake, though?" Marisa's crouched down in front of Oscar, giving him her best puppy-dog eyes.

"Can I have a banana one?"

"What do you reckon?" she says.

Oscar looks from her to me. "Why do you grown-ups always say that?"

* * *

"Hey buddy, can you pass me one of those screws? The big long ones?"

It's the next morning, and Oscar's in the study helping me. That is, if you count swinging around on his dad's desk chair as 'helping.' I've made significant progress yesterday, and the basic structure of the bed is almost finished. Seeing as the existing furniture has been unceremoniously dumped in the lounge room, I need to get this work finished as fast as possible.

"What are we gonna have for lunch today, Ryan?"

"Up to you. But I'll tell you what I feel like. Hungry Jack's."

"Yes! Pleeease? Can I get a whopper with cheese and fries and onion

252

rings and nuggets and a coke and a sundae?"

God, I've taught this kid well. "You can have anything you like, buddy." I lower my voice a bit. "But let's not tell anyone, eh?"

With our menu sorted, Oscar spins around some more as I countersink the screw he handed me. As soon as the drill stops, his voice chirps again. "I really like you Ryan. You're awesome."

He sounds so earnest, I feel my face flushing. "I really like you too, mate."

"Do you think one day you might be my stepdad?"

My jaw drops. The kid's reading my mind. These are hopes and dreams I've never dared voice to anyone, including myself. I crouch down in front of him, nervously scratching my head. "I'd really love to be your stepdad, Oscar. Is that something you'd be OK with?"

Oscar spins around again, doing a complete 360 before stopping. "What do *you* reckon?"

"I'm off to work now, you guys." Dominic's voice startles me, and I turn to spot him in the doorway. "Did you brush your teeth after breakfast, monkey?"

Oscar gasps and hops off the chair, scooting out of the room. Wiping my hands on the legs of my cargos, I rise up to stand in front of Dominic. He studies my face for a moment. "Not *too* much Hungry Jack's today, eh?" With a cryptic raise of his left eyebrow, he leans forward and plants a soft, moist kiss on my lips.

Then he's gone.

* * *

It's Sunday now, and I've just applied the final coat of varnish to my fit-out. I shuffle backwards a bit to admire my handiwork. It's taken me all week, but it's been well and truly worth it. I check my watch. No time to waste. I get cracking right away, shoving everything into my tool bags, then cleaning the room as thoroughly as I can. I make two trips down to my ute, stashing all my gear in the treadplate cabinets, then I haul the new single mattress up to the apartment in the elevator. The varnish I've used is quick-dry but it won't be ready just yet. I take the opportunity to wheel the filing cabinet back into the study on my trolley, then I slide the desk in next to it using a removalist's blanket. It takes some tight negotiation and I really could have used Dominic's help, but I've sent them packing for the morning. I want my surprise reveal, dammit.

Checking my watch again, I decide there's time for a shower now that all the hard yakka's been done. I strip off my gear, wandering naked through the apartment. I've missed doing that the past week. When Oscar's not here, Dominic and I never wear clothes. I adore the sight of his body and I'll never get sick of ogling every inch of it. It's wonderful being able to touch him anywhere, any place, anytime.

Just the thought of this has my dick standing to attention as I step in under the stream of hot water. Pumping some body wash into my palm, my hand finds its way directly to my penis. I groan as I begin to rub the slippery gel into my knob, my hand circling and twisting as I slide it up and down. *Oh, God, it's been ages since I've done this.* It doesn't take long before I'm speeding up at a rate of knots. I couldn't be bothered with edging, I just need to come. Right here is where I need to make a decision. My free hand is stretching my foreskin back and it feels so good I don't want to let go. But my nipples are on fire and I'm *so close.* Moving my hand up, I brush my fingertip over each engorged nub, switching rapidly from one to another. I've made the right choice, because I feel the tension rise immediately. I'm picturing Dominic. I'm imagining his tongue and his lips suckling on these pleasure spots on my chest. I'm imagining his fingers up my arse, twisting and thrusting into my hole, bumping against my prostate as it swells up. I'm imagining his cock, that first sapid taste as I slide it into my mouth. I'm imagining his arse, his hole, the scent of him down there first thing in the morning. An audible groan escapes me as my body begins to shake. My balls scrunch, my arsehole clenches tight and the glorious ache in my cock rises with sharp ferocity. I cry out long and hard as thick jets of come fire out of me, travelling in perfect arcs across the bathtub. My moans are non-stop, I'm not even bothering to temper the intensity that's wracking my body.

Sweet exhaustion grips me as I lower myself into the tub. I lie against the edge, letting the hot water rain down on me. I should feel guilty. Every orgasm belongs to my man these days. But he was here with me in spirit.

When I'm out, towelled-off and dressed, I venture back into the study to check if the varnish has dried. It's definitely good enough. I know how to apply an expertly thin coat, plus the mattress will be against the pine slats, anyway. Going back out to the lounge, I strip the plastic off the plush innerspring, carry it into the study and use every bit of strength in my arms to haul it into place.

Just in the nick of time, too. I can hear Dominic and Oscar chatting away as they amble up the hall. "In here, guys," I call out.

I stand back, bursting with pride as they enter, their mouths falling open with comical synchrony. There, in beautiful matching jarrah, the loft bed soars high above Dominic's desk. Underneath it, bright light illuminates Dominic's workspace. A solid jarrah ladder leads up to the foot of the bed, which is corralled in by an equally solid jarrah railing. At the other end of the room, right next to the head of the bed, is a tall, slim cupboard. Drawers at the bottom, a small wardrobe space above that, and high up at the top, a cubbyhole facing the bed for Oscar to stash his goodies.

"Can I climb up?" says Oscar, bouncing on his toes with excitement.

"Of course, buddy. It's your bed."

He scrambles up the ladder as nimble as a cat, landing with a thud on the mattress. "Wow! My own TV?"

Dominic turns his head, eyes wide, spotting the surprise flatscreen I've fixed to a swivel bracket up near the ceiling. *Well, you did give me free rein to buy whatever I wanted.*

"Jesus Christ, Ryan. How am I ever going to repay you?" His face is awash with emotion. His eyes are shining.

I reach out and squeeze his penis, freeballing low down the leg of his trackpants. "With this."

Chapter Twenty-Four

A couple of weeks later, I'm working on an office reno in the city centre when my phone rings.

"Hey, big bear. Just checking you haven't forgotten our dinner tonight."

"No, *lontra*. You've reminded me every day this week." There are other guys around, so I lower my voice and cup the mouthpiece with my hand. "Plus, it's Friday, I haven't seen you in five days and my balls are full."

"Aaaargh. And now you've given me a stiffy, mate. What time are you finished?"

"Um… I'm probably not gonna be out of here till close to five-thirty."

"Perfect. Come straight over and meet me at my office."

I don't like the sound of this. "Dominic, I'll need to change. I can't show up to dinner in high-vis and King Gees."

"Aw, baby. You know I love you in all that getup. I want everyone to see my hot tradie bear."

As work winds up, I duck into the bathroom and check myself out in the mirror. Making liberal use of wet paper towels, I clean my face, beard and arms of all dust and debris. I also give my clothes a good brushing down, though I'm not too sure it's all that successful. After surveying my hair in the mirror, I decide to just finger-comb it and leave it out. It's thick and glossy after being nuked with an obscenely expensive treatment, and I'm loving the look of my lion's mane.

I trek the few blocks to Dominic's building. I've never been here before. Strolling through the swanky lobby, I feel distinctly out of place. I'm expecting at any moment to be redirected to whatever shamehole tradesmen's entrance they have lurking in the bowels of the building. On the elevator ride, I nervously check myself out in the mirror once more. God, I wish I'd had time to go home and change.

There's a smartly-dressed woman behind the opulent front counter as I enter Dominic's office suite. At the sight of me she fixes a mechanical smile on her face. An impeccably-suited man appears from the room behind and all but scowls at me. "Can I help you?" he snaps.

Arms grab at my back and I'm pulled around to face Dominic, who draws me close and plasters a long, slow kiss on my lips. "God, am I glad to see you, baby." Turning his head to the snooty twosome behind the counter, he says, "Dieter, Sienna, this is my partner, Ryan."

My, doesn't their attitude change instantly. I'm bombarded with warm smiles, firm handshakes and air kisses. My mind flashes to the rowdy blokes, down-to-earth gals and genuine camaraderie I have in my own blue-collar workplace. I'm bloody glad I don't work in the corporate world.

The restaurant is a posh place in The Rocks, about fifteen minutes' walk away. Dominic holds my hand the entire journey, looking at me regularly and beaming with pride. He's positively incandescent. My heart glows with a warmth so potent I'm almost choked up. He doesn't even let go of my hairy paw as we enter the restaurant, leading me right through the maze of crisp, linen-clad tables full of gleaming silverware.

There are several people sitting at our table, none of whom I know. Dominic seems to spend all his time on work, family and me, so I'm not surprised he doesn't have many hours in the day left to socialise.

I scan the faces, pleased to see Dieter and Sienna have not attended. The others here have all greeted me warmly. Sincere or not, at least they haven't muddied my first impression of them.

After Dominic and I have settled in our chairs, a jingle-jangle sound rings in my ears as lithe arms slide over me from behind. They tighten around my neck in a warm hug and I'm surrounded by the familiar scent of essential oils. "Marisa? What are you doing here?" I reach up and squeeze her hand.

"Dominic invited us, sweetie."

I turn around to see her decked out in a stunning, slinky dress. Just behind her is Rani, looking dapper in a sharply-tailored suit. "Wow! You guys look amazing!"

"I see *you* didn't have time to change," says Marisa.

"I wanted everyone to see what a sexy bit of rough I have," chirps Dominic. "I'm even gonna make him keep his workboots on in bed, later."

The table erupts in polite laughter as Rani moves forward and plants a kiss on my cheek. It's a little otherworldly, given our connection has mainly consisted of weekly counselling sessions. But she's a truly incredible person and Marisa loves her, so I'd be honoured if our acquaintance graduated to friendship.

Now our table of eight is full, a general flurry of chatter ensues. I sit back, my usual quiet self, and watch the activity going on around me. It's kind of nice, being included in this circle. The waiter makes his way around the table, ending at Dominic and me. Dominic orders something exotic in French, rattling the words off with precision. *Smart arse.*

The waiter turns to me. "And what would you like, sir?"

Sir? I nearly laugh out loud at the sound of it.

"Steak, medium," chimes in Dominic. "He'll have the biggest one you've got." He turns to me as the waiter flits off. "I know you all too well, baby."

"So, how long have you two been an item?" asks one of Dominic's guests. I'm not even sure I remember her name. *Sheryl?*

"Twenty-six years, Sheree," says Dominic, with a smug grin. "Though we've only spent five of them together."

He leaves his cryptic answer at that. I'm only half-listening to the standard polite responses. I'm too busy taking in the scope of his statement. It's been a lifetime. I loved Owen with every fibre of my being. I would have died for that man, hands down. But a tiny part of my heart always belonged to Dominic, though at the time it was shattered. Guilt washes over me and I stare out the window towards the night sky. *Please understand me, little man.*

"So, are you gonna move in together?" Gosh, Marisa can be damn cheeky sometimes. There's a twinkle in her eye as she looks at me from over the rim of her wine glass.

Dominic is unperturbed. "I haven't got around to asking Ryan yet. But now is as good a time as any." He turns to me and grabs my hand. "Will you?"

"Yes." My reply is immediate, automatic. I don't need to think about this. I fix my own smug smile on Marisa. "I'll move into Dominic's and rent my place out." I've never consciously thought about this, but it's like my psyche has planned it in my absence.

Marisa looks at Rani. They're having a telepathic discussion. I can't see their mouths moving, but for several seconds the communication is palpable. "You know, Rani and I are looking for a place," she says tentatively. "And yours is so close to King Street." She looks back at Rani. "*And* it has off-street parking."

"Well, it's small and daggy," I start. My comments are directed at Rani. "Only one bedroom and I haven't renovated the place. But I've fixed everything up so it's solid as a rock."

"You should see it, Rani. It's such a cute little house!" Marisa grabs her hand, looking at her like an adorable puppy.

With a serene smile, Rani turns to face me. "Sold," she says.

I'm thrilled, but I'm not gonna get carried away. "You should bring Marisa over and come see it, at least. I'll even tidy up."

A wry smile spreads over Marisa's face. "Well, so long as you pick up all your dirty undies, I'm sure we'll survive."

"He never wears any," chirps Dominic.

I'm too hyped up with the energy pinging around the table to even bother blushing. "Guilty as charged."

My steak is huge, just the way I like it. I look at Dominic's plate, full of crisp salad and… *weird little chickeny things?* "What's that?" I ask.

"Frog's legs. Want to try some?" He shoots me a toothy grin. He knows my answer to that would be a big fat *no.*

With our mains finished and cleared away, I excuse myself to go and have a cigarette. Outside, I lean on the railing of the small terrace as I smoke, gazing across at the harbour. The view is spectacular and I'm sure it contributes greatly to the menu prices at this joint.

"I see it, Ryan. The resemblance." Marisa's standing next to me, having seemingly appeared from nowhere.

I don't need to bullshit her. She'd be onto me in a flash.

"I'm not gonna pry," she says. "Beauty comes in all forms. You've found it with him, and it's nobody's business but your own." She reaches up and puts her hand against the side of my beard, gently turning my head to look at her. *"Nobody's."*

I search her face, finding only sincerity there. I know I'm safe with her. Retrieving my wallet from my pocket, I hand her a small photo from it. I had it laminated decades ago when Dominic left, but it's still weathered over time.

Marisa examines the picture with a wide smile. "Oh, my God, the two of you are so cute! Is that your mum behind you guys, Ryan?"

"It's *our* mum."

***

"Wait till you try the special dessert I ordered," says Dominic, when Marisa and I return. "You'll love it."

After the frog's legs, I'm not so sure. The waiter appears with a silver tray. Perched atop it is an elaborate crystal goblet, and he lays it on the table in front of Dominic with great reverence. "It's kind of like a pannacotta, with almond essence, amaretto and toasted marzipan flakes."

I blanche. Three of the things I hate the most. Triple almond essence, enough to make me throw up. Mum used to have a bottle of almond essence in the cupboard when Nathan and I were little kids. We used to make each other sniff it to gross us out. It smelt like ants.

I look at Dominic, his cream-laden spoon hovering towards me. He seems so excited for me to try it and I don't have the heart to disappoint him. Doing my best not to grimace, I squeeze my eyes shut as the spoon slides into my mouth. It's disgusting. I swallow it down with one huge gulp. Nasty, hard lumps of marzipan graze my throat as the vile stuff descends towards my stomach. I open my eyes to see Dominic down on the floor, an expression of horror on his face. "Fuck… um… will you marry me?" he gasps.

I'm not entirely sure what's going on, but Marisa fills me in. "That's one *really* expensive crap you're gonna be doing later, Ryan."

***

Slowly waking up in Dominic's—*our*—plush bed the next morning, I discover that I'm alone. I have no intention of getting up yet, so I snuggle back down for a little lie-in. Soon after, a box lands with a thud on my chest. "Laxettes," announces Dominic. My eyes snap open to see him there with a smirk on his face. "You're taking the maximum dose. And by the time they work tonight, I'm gonna pop the question again."

Dominic dives onto the bed as I open the box and swallow three of the bitter chocolate squares, with one extra thrown in for good measure. Slipping under the covers fully clothed, he cuddles up to me and runs his palm over the curve of my belly, landing with his hand cupping my cock and balls. "Gee, *lontra*. I rimmed and fingered you and sucked you dry last night. Aren't you sick of me by now?"

"Never, big bear. You make me so fuckin' horny I don't think an hour ever goes by without me cracking a fat." He grips my hardening penis and pumps my foreskin up and down a few times. "Maybe it's time for *me* to suck *you* dry."

"Well, unless you want a stomachful of morning piss, you're gonna have to wait a while." Pecking him on the nose, I heave my sleep-weary body out of bed and pad to the bathroom. Dominic follows me in and leans against the wall as I brace myself over the toilet, dick in hand. "Are you right there?" I chuckle.

"I like watching you," he states plainly, as my wild torrent hits the water.

While I'm revelling in the relief provided by my rapidly-emptying bladder, I have a sudden thought. "It's not gonna be legal, is it."

He knows what I'm on about. "Baby, us poofs couldn't get married till December 2017. Let's just pretend we're in a time warp." He sidles up behind me as I finish my piss, sliding his hands over my naked buttocks and kissing me behind the ear. "I'll get a domestic partnership contract drawn up. Nobody ever needs to know the details," he murmurs.

Nobody. I have a call to make.

* * *

"Hey, Nathan, maaaaate. Sorry it's been a while." I'm out on the balcony in my down jacket and the late winter wind is freezing. But I really need the privacy. On top of this, I'm nervously smoking as I psych myself up for what's to come.

"Hey, Ryan. No dramas. Things have been hectic as hell here. Summer's been doing more hours at work and we're flat out getting Aura and Poetry to all their bloody extracurricular activities."

I smile to myself. Nathan's hippy-dippy wife is a total earth mother and those girls' names are as hilarious as they are cute. "Good to hear, mate. I gotta make my way over there and see you all again sometime."

"Geez, Ryan, just take a few days off and hop on a plane. The girls'd love to see you."

"Nah, mate. I'm staying firmly on the ground. Never gettin' on one of those fuckers again."

Nathan sighs, going quiet for a minute. "You know, I hardly remember dad."

"I do."

Neither of us are sure where to go with this. I was a daddy's boy and he was a mummy's boy. Both our parents are gone. It's the end of an era and we've never talked about it. I hear Nathan sigh down the phone line. "Mate, are you happy? Are you seeing anyone?"

Here we go. "Um, yeah. Engaged now, actually."

"Oh, fuck, man, why didn't you say? Congrats!"

I light a fresh cigarette and take a huge drag, slowly blowing out the smoke to calm myself. "It's Dominic."

I'm expecting outrage. Confusion, disgust, a barrage of vitriolic questions. But Nathan just goes quiet again for a while. "You know, I knew you guys were rooting back then. I heard you." I have no idea what to say. He waits a beat, then continues. "I didn't understand at first. Then later on it fuckin' grossed me out. But you were with Owen by then, so it was all way in the past."

I clear my throat. "Um, yeah. We ran into each other by pure chance. I hadn't heard from him in twenty years and as far as I was concerned, I never would."

"What about his wife and kid?"

"Separated just after mum died. Getting divorced now. I fuckin' love that little boy of his."

"And you love him? Dominic?"

"I never stopped."

Nathan considers this. My guts are churning. A full ten seconds goes by before he speaks again. "Well, after all the shit you've been through, it's about fuckin' time something good happened for you, Ryan."

* * *

Late that night, I finally feel an urge. "OK, it's time," I announce to Dominic, who's slumped beside me on the couch.

He jumps straight up. "I've got it all ready for you in there. Everything you need."

"Yeah, thanks. I can handle this."

I make my way down to the bathroom. On the counter, he's laid it all out: gloves, containers, a clear jar full of some kind of solution. I give it a sniff. Sort of vinegary. I've just dropped my daks and sat on the dunny when the door bursts open. "Any luck?"

"No! I haven't even started yet!"

Dominic gives me his best basset hound expression. "Aw, you look so cute sitting there." He waltzes into the bathroom towards me.

"No! You can't come in here! You'll never wanna have sex with me again!"

He chuckles, his eyes crinkling up at the sides, highlighting his gorgeous little crow's feet. Lifting his leg over mine, he straddles my lap, loops his arms around my neck and kisses me on the lips. "Big bear, you're gonna be my husband. We can share everything, now."

I can't even stifle a snort. "*Lontra*, it's extremely hot when you watch me having a piss. But this is something I have to do on my own. Now, fuck off. I can't hold it in any longer."

Giving me a final peck on the forehead and a twisted grin, Dominic hops to his feet again and disappears, shutting the door behind him.

A good while later, I emerge from the bathroom to find him perched on the couch, an eager look on his face. "It's done," I tell him flatly.

"Is it? Do you like it?"

"A chunky, masculine gold band with black titanium angled pattern around it? Fuck, Dominic, I fuckin' love the fuck out of it." I'm feeling teary. "And yes. Fuckin' *yes*."

"Yes what?"

"I'm saving you the trouble of asking me again."

"Oh, God, big bear." He rises up and pulls me into his arms. "I'm gonna make you so happy."

I tighten my grip around his slender shoulders, squeezing him with all my might. "You already do, *lontra*."

"Where's the ring?" he says.

"Soaking in that concoction of yours. For a fuckin' *long* time."

"It's a beautiful night. Put your jacket on, grab a couple of beers and we'll have 'em outside while we wait, eh?"

After fetching two Coronas and rugging myself up, I wander outside to see Dominic sitting on the ground, propped up against the wall with a chair cushion underneath his sexy little butt. He pats the other cushion he's laid beside him.

I slide down next to my man and he cuddles up close. As his lithe body presses into mine, a feeling of complete security fills every cell of my being. We sit there, casually chugging at our stubbies till they're drained.

"What about Oscar?" I say.

Dominic looks at me. His dark eyes tell me so much, things I could never put into words. I don't need to explain myself.

"We'll cross that bridge when we come to it," he says. "He can learn about Uncle Ryan when he's much, much older."

As if on cue, a nine-year-old appears at the door wrapped in a quilt.

"What are you doing out of bed, monkey?"

"Couldn't sleep, dad. Can I sit here with you guys?"

Dominic holds his arm out to Oscar, but he slides over his dad and settles against the both of us, lying his head over my stomach and his backside on Dominic's lap. "Dad?" he says.

"Yeah?"

"I love you."

"Aw. I love you too, Oscar."

"Ryan?"

"Yeah, buddy?"

"I love your fat belly."

"Oh, you *cheeky* monkey!" Dominic laughs, tickling Oscar's ribs, making him squirm and squeal.

I look down at the both of them. My *lontra*. My cheeky little monkey. With a deep, contented sigh, I raise my head to gaze up at the night sky. The dark expanse stretches as far as the eye can see, and over to my right is one bright, shining star. As I stare at it, it glimmers ever so slightly.

"Hey, little man," I whisper. "Everything's gonna be alright."

Hello there, beautiful people!

I'm so glad you've come along on Ryan and Dominic's journey with me. If you enjoyed their story, I'd be thrilled if you would drop a little note somewhere—Goodreads, Bookbub—wherever takes your fancy. These reviews make all the difference for us little ol' authors and I'll be forever grateful.

Big bear hugs!

About the Author

Having started with a clear mission to create a hybrid of grunge lit and gay erotic romance, Colin's books are gritty and realistic depictions of same-gender-loving life in the Australian urban landscape.

Colin's other books include the novels *Hound* and *The Lookout*, both published by Pink Flamingo Media, and a collection of short stories called *One Night Stand.*

He lives in Sydney with two great blokes, two rowdy Italian Greyhounds and a non-binary talking budgie.

You can connect with me on:

 https://linktr.ee/colindereham

Also by Colin Dereham

Find the other books in the Bondi Bears series here: https://linktr.ee/
colindereham

The Lookout

When he advertises the vacant bedroom in his apartment on a gay houseshare site, sexy teddy bear Angus ends up with more than he bargained for. Tall, dark and handsome otter Tom and blond muscle-bear Patrick couldn't be more different in personality, but Angus is so taken with them that he asks both men to move in. After a boozy first night together culminates in a skinny dip in the complex's swimming pool, Angus, Tom and Patrick fall into bed with each other. The explosive chemistry between them continues throughout a hot spring and summer. Days spent on the beach blend into nights of wild passion in Angus's huge bed, which all three inevitably end up sharing.

Fun, upbeat Patrick and quiet, affectionate Tom are everything Angus could have wished for. His nurturing side kicks in, creating a happy home for all three.

With Patrick working over the Christmas period, Tom and Angus go to visit Angus's family in the country. When they return, Patrick has changed. He's distant and sullen; there's no sign of the vibrant, happy man they've known for the past few months. At first, Angus thinks Patrick may be jealous of the close bond he's developing with Tom. He and Tom pull out all the stops to make Patrick feel as loved as possible, but their efforts go unnoticed. Then a chance discovery in the kitchen bin leads Angus to think there may be darker reasons for the change in Patrick's personality.

Tensions brew until late one night, when a disastrous phone call brings Angus's world crashing down around him. Desperately trying to make sense of what happened, Angus must rely on the love and support of others around him to slowly pick up the pieces and rebuild their happy home.

Hound

Gary's lived with bipolar disorder since he was eighteen. He's stable and has a great career, family and friends, but at forty he's never had a relationship. Casual sex has always been the easy option—fun, plentiful and no risk of upsetting the unruly emotions that simmer below his calm exterior.

This all changes the moment he meets Jeff. There's no doubt in Gary's mind that Jeff's The One. But even though Jeff seems to be equally smitten, he only wants a part-time arrangement. Jeff works long hours, travelling constantly, and his last relationship was so abusive he's seemingly ruled them out for good.

Gary does his best to settle for things the way Jeff wants. He's not going to give him an ultimatum. Losing Jeff would be unthinkable. In any case, Jeff will come around. But each time Gary feels they are making progress, Jeff restates his position. Gary struggles with the way Jeff can be so loving, yet still maintain that he doesn't want a relationship. Gary's confidence begins to erode. Maybe he doesn't deserve more. After all, he's flawed. Damaged goods. Bipolar.

Time is running out for Gary—he knows these arrangements have a limited shelf-life and he can see Jeff is slipping away. Things reach crisis point when Jeff makes a devastating announcement, plunging Gary into a pit of despair. Gary is forced to resort to drastic measures to find a way through his quagmire of self-doubt and fight for the relationship before it's too late.

One Night Stand

Gritty, realistic and finely detailed, "One Night Stand" examines the intense and explicit bonds formed between men when they are drawn together in the heat of physical attraction. Whether it's a weekend fling that can sadly go nowhere, a marathon of passion that sparks a potential relationship, or former bedroom buddies now on the brink of finding their happily-ever-after, this collection probes deep into the grey intersection where sex and love combine.

BEAR AFFAIR When they meet at a Sydney bar, good-time bear Gary and sweet ginger teddy Angus experience an electrifying connection that leads to a night of unbridled, intense passion; a loving, sensual aftermath; and a painful, bittersweet decision.

BLINDER Isolated and struggling with his recent descent into legal blindness, Ben accompanies his friend Damo to a gay wedding, where they meet Ric and Tony. After a sizzling evening of intimacy between the four, Ben is floored by the intense chemistry he shares with Tony, and desperately hopes this spark will ignite into something more than a one-night-stand.

BOURBON AND CIGARETTES Plagued by the rocky start to his now-idyllic relationship, Jeff consults an unorthodox psychoanalyst to examine his fear of commitment. Working through his past history as a victim of domestic violence, Jeff begins to see a clear path ahead of him, and a scorching evening with the man he loves seals their happy future together.